PRISM OF HER SOUL

ROB DIXON

CONSILIO

First published in Great Britain in 2024 by Consilio Publishing.

ISBN 978-1-7385-0280-6

Cover design and interior layout: Consilio Publishing

Cover Illustration: Elizabeth Trinity

Editor: Lisa Williams

Published by Consilio Publishing

Printed in Great Britain by CPI Antony Rowe

First Edition: March 2024

Limited print run of 300 copies

For permission requests, write to the publisher at info@consiliointernational.co.uk.

Printed on acid-free paper.

Dedicated to my children.

The virginal sheets of paper that make up this bound volume were innocent until they were forcibly impregnated with ink. They have been left forever stained.

This novel is a dark, unsettling, mysterious work of fiction, so please beware, keep calm and read on.

Prologue

'**G**o ahead caller, what's your emergency?'

'Yeah, listen, I need help. I just saw summut really fucked up. There's this bird, she's naked, covered in blood, and there's, uh, a...a...a... ' His breathing was erratic, and his vocal cords pinched as he strained to get his words out.

'I appreciate you're upset but I need you to stay calm. Can you provide your name and your location?' Maybe she was stereotyping, but she was sure her mental image of a man in his late teens or early twenties with limited education, a dark hoodie and his ass hanging out the waist of his joggers was pretty damned close.

'Nah.' His response was immediate. There was no misunderstanding with his answer. He already felt too involved. 'No names. I can't... but someone needs to get 'ere now.'

'I understand, but we need your details to assist you properly. Can you tell me where you are?'

'Look, lady, I'm on Lakeside by the Lawns. I don't know the number, but you can't miss the house. It's a bloodbath. The front window looks like it's been covered in ketchup. I saw the woman... in the window... blood all over 'er... '

'Help is on the way. Can you confirm if the woman is still there? Is she a threat?'

'I dunno,' his voice pitched, 'when I first saw her 'bout twenty minutes ago, she was just stood there looking out the window, like in a trance. She looked proper messed up, I mean mental. I don't know how long she'd been there, she didn't notice me at first, but when she clocked me, I bounced.'

'I appreciate your concern for your safety. Try to describe the scene as best as you can. Did you see anyone else around?'

'Nah, just her. Honestly, mate, it looks like a slaughterhouse.'

'I need you to stay on the line. Officers...'

The call ends. He'd said his piece. Stealing was one thing. He'd only wanted an easy rob to get his next fix. Seeing the deranged woman covered in blood when he'd peered in the window... no way. Stuff that. This, this was next level.

Chapter 1

Kate is driven and wants to win in life. Fortune has bestowed the confident thirty-three-year-old beauty with a silver spoon upbringing.

In Kate's structured life, everything has a place; neat and tidy is the mantra her mother had drilled into her as a child. She lives alone in Courtfield Mews, an old Victorian terrace house in the Borough of Kensington and Chelsea, London. Constructed in the early 1870s by the builder William Radford, the house had once welcomed her father as he carried his child-like new bride over the threshold a century on. Kate has lived there for almost all her life except for the three months she spent in Toulouse, living with her one true love, her father.

Wanting to put her stamp on the property to make it her home, and with her mother Sarah's blessing, she'd recently overseen the renovation of the property, nothing structural, just cosmetic, to give the 'old lady' a new set of clothes. The minimal furniture and the sterility of the modern decor made the house look more like a showhouse than a home. The only displayed items were photographs of her most memorable occasions and the few people she would let into her life. Even though she was outgoing and photogenic, Kate disliked her image being captured.

Kate loves watching people. Her neighbours had come and gone over the years, trying to climb the property ladder and keep up with the Joneses. With each new occupant came another set of lives to study and stories to hear whenever she'd have the pleasure of meeting the residents living on the other side of her living room wall. Her old-fashioned father, the son of a Second World War hero, had always taught her that: 'Good neighbours are like a safety blanket. You look after them, and they'll look after you. In an emergency, you never know when you may need to call on someone.'

While hardly ever at home for more than a few days at a time, Kate lives by her old man's mantra. The state-of-the-art audio-visual equipment was rarely used, and when it was, the music would be carefully chosen to reflect her mood, listening to classical music while researching for work and indie music when she wanted something to numb her mind. Her car, like her house, is kept in immaculate condition. She drives a Mini; she loves Minis. It was her first car after she'd passed her driving test in her late teens, and she was more than comfortable with her latest model.

As an only child, she was showered with affection from her father but never spoilt. Her mother was always more of a matronly figure than a typical mum, which made Kate feel tutored more than loved. Kate was never meant to be an only child, but complications during her delivery had put a stop to any future plans her parents may have had to extend the family, and she'd always felt somehow blamed for this by her mother. Kate was never one to hoard souvenirs or mementoes of her life but she had a sole possession that had been with her from an early age.

The elegantly dressed porcelain doll, a sixth birthday gift from her Uncle Tom, had a face made from the finest white clay modelled into the most beautiful visage along with the daintiest of hands. Auburn hair and bright blue eyes enhanced the handmade golden frilly dress made of the softest silk, and its name was embroidered in a fine braid on the hem. Her uncle was interested in antiquities and found the doll in a side-street antique shop off the Champs-Élysées in Paris. He, too, had fallen in love with the doll. As a child,

Kate spent many hours talking to the doll, expressing her dreams, hopes, and fears. Treating the doll as a real sister, it became the sibling she would never know. Kate derived great comfort from its mute presence, and it had been her angel. The china toy had always been there for her unconditionally whenever she needed someone to talk to. Kate felt that her mother hated the doll. It seemed that Sarah was jealous of her relationship with the porcelain beauty.

Just after her sixth birthday, Kate started blacking out and losing time. For most of her pre-adolescent years, what appeared to Kate to be persistent dreams were actually her cataleptic reality; an illusory Kate would stand transfixed, staring into any available mirror until something would snap in her head, causing her to hit out at her offending reflection, often leading to severe cuts to her hands and resulting in a visit to the local surgery. Unaware of what had gone on, Kate would wake up in her bedroom wondering how she'd even made it to bed. For the two years between her seventh and ninth birthdays, her concerned father had taken her to see various physicians and neurological specialists for evaluation. There was no apparent medical reason for the seizures. After all medical tests had been exhausted, and with no exact diagnosis, they put Kate's 'dizzy spells' – as her mother preferred to call them – down to heat exhaustion. The attacks stopped around the time of her first period, and 'the chemical re-balancing of her adolescent body' was now the diagnosed cure. After the seizure years abated, Kate's outlook and upbringing were relatively normal for a daughter of two professionals.

Situated in a grand old Georgian building along one of the most famous streets in London, Harley Street W1, Kate was educated at Queen's College, London, for her secondary years. The college was founded in 1848 and was granted a royal charter by Queen Victoria in 1853 to further women's education, the first such decree by a reigning English Monarch. It carried the torch as one of England's oldest and finest all-girls public schools. Kate had excelled in her studies, particularly in the arts and literature, and both her parents knew that whichever road she took, the college would give her a solid foundation on which to build a career.

Kate's parents had raised their daughter to respect the world around her. Though her impassive mother had strong moral values, she'd taught Kate not to be ashamed of her body or her femininity. The three would spend the occasional long weekend away at a naturist camp, which felt like a spiritual retreat. For Kate, being naked was as natural as breathing, and her God-given body was neither 'rude' nor 'dirty,' which was the Victorian attitude that still permeated British society. Her parents believed that naturism, as an unpretentious display of physical imperfections, encouraged respect for oneself and others. Like all young children brought up in an overtly nudist environment, Kate was never fussed about the 'private parts' of the human body; she was too busy playing bat 'n' ball with her peers. As she edged towards her double-digit years, her mother always gave a matter-of-fact answer, ensuring no misunderstanding existed. Kate had no prurient curiosity; she understood that sex, nudity, and sexual nudity were each completely different. Fascinated by the human natural condition, the youngster would intently study the shapes and sizes of the bare bodies around her, enthralled by the scars of life and the tribal markings of tattooists' ink.

One observation that really hit home for Kate was how the flesh would lose its essence and droop over time as if the years weighed heavy on human skin. In Kate's juvenile mind, every crease and every line was an additional piece of baggage collected along the highway of life. She accepted how the body would deteriorate and wither, comparing how the physical form changed like the four seasons over an eighty-year lifespan. Most importantly to Kate, after hours of unwritten visual research, she concluded that no one was perfect and that the body was ultimately just a medium to carry the mind and soul.

As Kate reached puberty, the sexual changes became apparent. She knew how her body would visually alter but she was never prepared for the oestrogen-fuelled feelings that seemed to bombard her every thought.

The inquisitive youngster started to discover her sexuality just before her teen years. Her first experience was fooling around in a homemade tent in the garden of one of her friends, playing 'You show me yours, and I'll show you mine'. For years, having seen the naked form from afar, and while she had tentatively probed and examined her own body, she'd never explored another human body up close and personal. Slowly and methodically, she tested her senses on the bodies of two friends, an eleven-year-old girl from school and a twelve-year-old boy who lived down the road. Tingling sensations accompanied the new and uncertain feelings as the three were fascinated with each other. From the tactile moment that her trembling fingers touched the others intimately, Kate's innocence was gone.

This was an awakening for a dormant personality that lay deep within her.

Entering her teen years with an appreciation of her adolescent body, the teenager enjoyed listening to the many older women who constantly reiterated that she would 'only be young once' and that she should enjoy every aspect of her youthful body, otherwise, she would rue letting life drift by. Taking on board all of the advice from her peers and remembering an early lesson from her mother, she was always safe and in control. Kate became a lascivious exhibitionist and never missed an opportunity for gratification. The sensuous vamp with silky long brunette hair was now in the mid-summer season of her life. Mesmerising hazel eyes accentuated with naturally long lashes harmonised with her attractive and healthy complexion. Fulsome cheeks balanced her visage, set with high cheekbones and a petite nose. Behind her striking smile and gleaming white teeth hid a hypnotic voice. With all the necessary qualities, blemish-free and slightly tinted, the smooth skin that completed her facial features perfectly emphasised her toned face.

Kate's stunning physique was also impressive, and her voluptuous curves appeared as if modelled on that of Eve's.

From an early age, it became crystal clear to Kate that her gorgeous looks, femininity, and blossoming sexuality could be used to cajole and tempt even the most unyielding and belligerent male into accepting her point of view.

After twenty-odd years of mastering the art of flirtation, the enchantress had honed it to perfection. She innately understood that her beauty could be her best friend or worst enemy, especially in business. Everything was worn for a reason: her make-up, perfume, clothes, and price was not an issue. Kate understood that in business, image was everything; that a figure-hugging smart D&G suit and a pair of Jimmy Choos would project a strong sense of style but was still formal enough to keep her intended message of a professional, no-nonsense business partner at the fore. In Kate's life, there were times when something a little less sophisticated and more 'eye candy for chavs' would do, and her wardrobe accommodated clothes that fitted the bill for those occasions perfectly. Tonight's event, however, was a completely different ballgame. For a gilt-edged date with knighted gentry, a black cocktail dress would be the order of the day.

Chapter 2

Kate gently rested her hand on David's left arm as they strolled through Bloomsbury Square, enjoying the last embers of a summer sun. It was a comfortable 18 degrees, and dusk was eating into the remaining daylight. Turning into Great Russell Street, one of Britain's architectural landmarks stood before them. The imposing Montagu House was a monolith from a bygone era and, since 1759, had accommodated the hallowed and historic British Museum, one of the finest collections of cultural art and antiquities 'foraged' from lands across the world.

The People's Republic of China and the historic British Museum
cordially invite you to the private viewing of the grand exhibit
The First Emperor: China's Terracotta Army

The Reading Room, The Queen Elizabeth II Great Court
The British Museum, Great Russell Street
London WC1B 3DG

7.30pm onwards. Monday, 10th September, 2007

The invitation had been sent from the Chinese Ambassador and was addressed to Sir David Appleway and guest. David reached into his left jacket pocket and removed the gilt-edged alabaster-coloured card before passing it to Kate, his guest, as she briefly peered down at the invite, thrilled that he had asked her to accompany him. It was one exhibition she would have visited when it was open to the public, so this was both a unique and unexpected privilege. Researching the Terracotta Army, she had established that the First Qin Emperor was an extraordinary megalomaniac who reunited China after conquering the warring states. Having built the Great Wall and accumulated a great art collection, the Mausoleum of the First Emperor Qin was constructed of three pits containing about 7,000 soldiers and other figures, both man and beast, that the Emperor believed would be required in his afterlife. Never wanting to make the journey to the spirit world alone, he had his 3,000 wives and concubines follow him to the grave after failing in his obsession to find the elixir of life.

Proceeding through The Great Court, their footsteps echoed around the vast space, filling the void. A serpentine tunnel led them to a set of stairs; step by step, they made their way up and into the circular Reading Room. Arching her neck heavenward, the domed roof was doing its damnedest to distract Kate from her reason for being there. Having opened in 1857 and hailed as one of the most remarkable interiors in the Empire, the recently restored Reading Room had all of the 19th-century grandeur envisaged initially by its architect, Sydney Smirke. The unconventional gilded papier-mâché dome interior, complete with blue and cream paintwork, had looked down in glory on many illustrious historical figures. Karl Marx, Lenin, Thomas Hardy, Gandhi, and Rudyard Kipling were all regulars at the British Museum, and now the Terracotta Army had joined its growing list.

A large audiovisual presentation greeted them, outlining the history of the Emperor, as they followed the winding exhibition to its heart in the main room. The temporary residence for the selected few terracotta emissaries was a far cry from the dusty pit where they had spent an eternity. The washes of creams and browns contrasted with the white sheeting that covered the walls. There was a distinct lack of atmospheric sound, and the seemingly unimaginative lighting – the darkness was to preserve the precious artefacts – almost disappointed Kate. This was not the visual spectacle Kate had pictured in her mind, but on reflection, no venue would ever be able to do justice to the battalions of stone soldiers.

Kate stared intently at the decaying, broken bodies on display. A small group of partially dismembered warriors shared the stage with two clay musicians, an acrobat, a strongman, and a couple of civil officials. Four half-sized terracotta horses pulled a half-scale bronze carriage embellished with gleaming gold and silver. In an extraordinary feat of mass production, each figure was given an individual personality. The ornate clay body parts used to construct each figure – the head, arms, legs, and torso – were created separately and assembled. Intricate features on every head gave each statue an identity, a soul. The determined faces would have reassured the Emperor as he finalised his battle plan to conquer the ramparts of the afterlife. Kate gazed at the hanging white sheets, which temporarily turned into a canvas, to envisage how inspiring the army must have been when the newly created torsos lined up, awaiting their calling for a life yet unknown.

Kate was not oblivious to the conversation that had just taken place beside her; she had decided that discretion and ignorance would be the polite response in this situation. She knew David almost inside out, and he would introduce her to the gentleman if and when appropriate.

'Kate, may I introduce the Chinese Ambassador?' David directed.

Her attention was refocused and seamlessly transferred from the white sheeting to the well-turned-out Chinese gentleman standing before her.

'It's a pleasure to meet you, Mr. Ambassador. I'm Kate Summertown, David's understudy,' she said as she presented him with her soft hand adorned with a solitaire ring.

'The pleasure is all mine,' he replied, taking her hand. He gradually and deliberately nodded his head, looking her down and up. Admiring the knee-length black cocktail dress that contrasted with her soft, tanned skin, he smiled at her favourably.

'Understudy, I think not,' the Ambassador paused briefly and continued. 'Sir David talks highly of you. He informs me that you are turning out to be a real asset to the business, dedicated and honest. Fine attributes indeed.'

'Why thank you, Mr. Ambassador,' Kate responded confidently.

They both looked intently at each other, checking to see if they had the respect of the person staring back. A stocky man, with a clean and well-maintained appearance, the Ambassador was relatively tall compared to his comrades. His short-cropped, jet-black hair enhanced his facial features. The only visible blemishes were the pocked scars of illness resulting from a childhood infection that followed the jowl of his left cheek. Powerful-looking hands with manicured nails exposed themselves from the cuff of his starched white shirt, almost entirely hidden by the dark blue suit that covered his frame.

His demeanour was one of quiet respectability, and his voice perfectly matched it. David and the Ambassador shared a mutual respect for each other and a solid friendship. Kate knew that away from the officialdom that ruled the Ambassador's life, the two gents would often meet privately on a more personal basis, usually sharing a few bottles of claret and the odd gin and tonic.

Simultaneously, and without any prompt, their eyes moved to the headless statue of a pot-bellied strongman that towered over them just yards away. The near-naked colossus, broad and fleshy in girth with conspicuous nipples, bulging biceps and powerful legs, would have been unemployable within the massed ranks of the military. This individual was an entertainer. At this moment, Kate realised how vital a face was, especially the eyes, a window into the essence of the being. The faceless strongman was missing his identity, his uniqueness, his individuality.

The brief silence in the room was broken by the Ambassador's voice as he continued speaking, ensuring he was on message with the spin he was due to relay to anybody who cared to listen.

'The First Emperor: China's Terracotta Army explores one of the greatest archaeological discoveries of the twentieth century, giving an insight into China's First Emperor, Qin Shi Huang, and his legacy. As you can see, this exhibition includes some of our world-famous terracotta warriors from Xi'an, China, who were buried alongside the First Emperor in readiness for the afterlife, as well as some of the most striking recent discoveries made on the site. In introducing his idea of a unified state and effectively creating China in 221 BC, the First Emperor of Qin created the world's oldest surviving political entity.'

An oriental lady in her early twenties, wearing a knee-length crimson Cheongsam, approached the trio. The short-sleeved silk dress was delicately embroidered and accentuated her petite feminine figure. She waited patiently for the Ambassador to finish his spiel before summoning him with a discrete bow of her head. The Ambassador acknowledged the gesture and made his apologies.

'Please excuse me for one second,' he said, addressing Kate.

The Chinese messenger briefed the Ambassador in a whisper and waited at his side patiently as he acted on the message.

'I'm sorry our meeting has to be this brief, but I'm sure we'll meet again,' he directed to Kate.

'It's been a pleasure, and thank you for taking the time to speak with me, Mr. Ambassador,' Kate replied.

The Ambassador turned his attention to David and continued: 'Goodnight, David, next time we meet, we'll have a proper talk. I want to…how do you say… that's it,' he paused, 'pick your brains,' he said with a wry smile.

David winked at the Ambassador to signify that he understood tonight was not the time or the place for any meaningful discussion.

'Sir David, Miss Summertown, please enjoy the exhibition.'

Looking into their eyes, he took two steps backwards, and with a less controlled nod, he turned and hurriedly walked away. The attractive messenger gently bowed in the couple's direction and immediately followed her superior a few paces behind.

Viewing the artefacts on show, David and Kate leisurely perused the exhibition for a further couple of hours before they decided to call it a day and headed towards the exit, only to be met by the Chinese Ambassador with a red box held in his arms.

'Please, Miss Summertown, accept this gift on behalf of the People's Republic of China,' he smiled, handing the box to Kate.

She was startled that the Ambassador himself had taken the time to present the package; at most 'jollies', some dizzy PR girl would be at the exit handing out a bag full of corporate gifts complete with fluttering eyelashes and a flirty smile.

'Thank you,' she stuttered as she accepted the gift. 'May I open it?'

'Of course. It's yours,' replied the Ambassador as a slight frown of uncertainty appeared across his face, forcing his forehead to wrinkle.

Kate lifted the lid as the two men looked on in anticipation. A weighty fifteen-inch clay replica of a terracotta warrior lay in the box, surrounded by the ruffles of white silk that lined the package. Before Kate could comment, the Ambassador chipped in.

'I hope you like it. I understand that a china doll holds a special place in your heart,' he smiled as he spoke.

Kate felt slightly uneasy as she checked out the figurine, ruminating over the probable throwaway comment just made to her. She pushed any misinterpretation to the back of her mind and graciously accepted the gift.

'It's beautiful, what can I say? Thank you,' she replied gratefully.

'No, thank you for coming.'

The Ambassador's frown disappeared, replaced by a heartfelt smile. Without further ado, the diplomat nodded and left them at the exit.

Walking out into the cool night air, David asked Kate: 'I know it's going to be a hard one to crack and that it will tie you up for a few months, but, off the record, how do you feel about the forthcoming Provethan pitch? You know that it's a massive opportunity. I just don't want you getting your fingers burnt.'

'Tut, David, of course I want it, and that's why you gave me the project. Don't you worry about Provethan; I know what they need, and I know how to win this one. Oh... and on the record, I don't get burnt,' a cocksure Kate replied.

Not wanting to talk shop any further, David ceased. He had made his point, a gentle reminder of concern for his prodigy. 'I know you won't, my girl, and I know you won't let anyone down. Now, let's go and grab a bite to eat.'

Chapter 3

Kate's parents met in a field at the height of Flower Power during the summer of love.

The only child of church-going parents, the demure and quietly spoken Sarah Denise Tindle was an attractive slip of a lass, born in the small Wiltshire town of Swindon. Her middle-class father was a respected civil servant. At the same time, her mother found meaning and identity in her mundane life through the traditional role of a domestic goddess by tending to her husband's needs and raising their daughter.

After passing her eleven-plus, the ever-popular Sarah was grammar school educated to a high standard. From her early teens, as the second wave of feminism began to germinate, she became obsessed with women's rights and the struggle for equality that her mother could never empathise with. Her dream-filled head of youthful innocence, Sarah was a free spirit confined in a cocoon. Passionate about the future, Sarah's feminist tendencies had periodically caused problems in the household. Her mother had a fundamental problem with her virgin daughter's belief in sexual freedom and an urge to give her own life real meaning. Her father, however, could see a fundamental change in the post-war society and was quite happy that his expressive daughter could and would be herself, just to get it out of her system before conforming to the set rules of an established and civilised society.

After carefully arranging the trip, she and her best friend Linda travelled to Woburn in the summer of '67 for the 'Festival of the Flower People'. The two young ladies – Sarah approaching her eighteenth birthday and Linda just turned eighteen – were inexperienced and naïve. They had been enthusiastically awaiting the psychedelic musical feast, which was due to be headlined by The Small Faces, for weeks. Travelling through the winding lanes of the English countryside from Swindon, a beaten-up light blue VW Beetle carried them to the grounds of Woburn Abbey in good time to meet their chaperone for the weekend.

Linda's cousin, Paul, was a few years older than the girls. Sarah had known Paul for most of her life and knew he would be a safe and entertaining host. Their canvas palace for the weekend was a functional but tattered ex-military tent that bizarrely sheltered a sapling as the centrepiece. Paul had two mates with him.

Tom, who stood in the tent vestibule, introduced himself to the two fresh-faced ladies by thrusting a joint in their direction as he coughed and spluttered a heavy, green-tinged puff of smoke from his choked lungs.

His lengthy brown hair was tied back in a ponytail, and his flared denims and shabby T-shirt were partially hidden beneath an unbuttoned suede waistcoat. A scruffy, youthful beard sparsely covered his chiselled features, but Sarah still thought he looked incredibly handsome.

Tom's identical twin, Anthony, was much more reserved as he rose to his feet from the knoll he occupied and greeted Sarah and Linda differently with a loose grasp and a tender kiss to the back of each of their right hands. Clean-shaven, short back and sides, and a tidier appearance – although still wearing denim – differentiated the two Wantage-born brothers.

It soon became apparent that the twins were as thick as thieves, best mates in every sense. The event kicked off when a balloon floated over the site, dropping hundreds of red carnations on the Flower People below. The girls were in heaven.

The weekend progressed like a slow-emptying hourglass, and as a web of friendships blossomed through a marijuana haze, it came to light that Sarah and the twins shared one thing in common. All three were born on the 1st October, 1949. Tom was 27 minutes older than Anthony, and this tiny detail was enough for the firstborn to refer to himself as 'the older brother'.

The tent was filled with the distinctive sounds of narco-enhanced giggles and the crunching of various munchies' attacks. Drug-induced conversations drifted around the space as the five friends bonded, and if they ever ran out of conversation or an awkward silence pervaded the tent, the tree at the centre became a humorous focal point.

As the testosterone-fuelled twins vied like a couple of horny stags for the two innocent girls' attention, Paul watched on with amusement and a stupid grin that was plastered on his face all weekend.

Their decorated father had raised the twins after his wife died of heart disease when the boys were just two years old. Tom was a renegade with a penchant for antiquities, especially fencing them around London. He had been clouted around the head by more than one police constable in his time, having rebelled against his commissioned father's strict disciplinarian code. On the other hand, Anthony looked up to his father with pride and he unquestionably accepted his upbringing. He understood that it could not have been an easy feat rearing twin boys single-handedly while commanding a battalion of soldiers.

Much to his father's dismay, Anthony had refused a career in the military as he had his heart set on joining the police force. However, between them, they settled on a career in law that he knew was an acceptable compromise in his father's eyes; at least his education wouldn't be wasted, and it would certainly please his twin and avoid any friction with Tom's activities.

Sarah's transformation began at the end of her most exciting and liberating weekend; she emerged from her oppressive cocoon as a butterfly, an untamed spirit. Spending her time concentrating on her studies, free-loving, and exploring her sexuality. Her mother was horrified when she discovered that her only child had become a member of the 'burn your bra brigade' and that any form of underwear, even while wearing the shortest of miniskirts, was just a faux pas.

Sarah lost her virginity in the confines of a darkened bathroom at a friend's house party with a fumbling, spotty student called Graham just after her eighteenth birthday. A genuinely enlightened exhibitionist with a voracious appetite for sexual thrills, almost anything went as the temptress shagged her way through the nineteenth year of her life. Multiple partners, including women and group sex, had become the norm for her at the weekend. While any type of hard drug was a definite no-no, Sarah was not averse to the very occasional use of light narcotics.

She'd had no contact with either of the twins for almost a year after the festival. Sarah was eagerly looking forward to Linda's nineteenth birthday bash, knowing only too well that the brothers would be there as Paul had let slip this detail to his cousin.

Sarah spent most of her day pampering and preparing herself for the highly anticipated reunion. The twins were taken aback as they looked across the crowded dance hall at the young woman standing at the end of the bar. Stunningly attractive, Sarah had changed. Anthony was amazed at how alive she was, her confidence and aura left him agape. Dressed in a purple crushed velvet mini dress, she mockingly teased the twins with a beckoning wave and a 'hello boys' flash of her nakedness as she fleetingly lifted her skirt. The two men almost fell over themselves as they rushed headlong towards her. After carefully assessing and scrutinising the two potential partners, Sarah subconsciously decided. If she had not known the twins, she would have suggested having them both – and at the same time – but, unfortunately, she had to be on her best behaviour on this occasion as family and friends were present.

Enjoying each other's company, Sarah and Anthony had fallen for each other. They shared a passion for justice, both studying to become lawyers and, after a steady courtship, had become engaged. They married at Christ Church, Swindon, just before their twenty-first birthdays. Tom was honoured to be his 'little brother's' Best Man, although he had always rued the missed opportunities in the fields of Woburn and at Linda's bash when he'd had an equal shot at Sarah's affection. A wedding gift of a sizeable down payment for a house in South London from Anthony's father was the foundation for their strengthening marriage and a base for their further education. Both studied law at the London School of Economics, and both attained first-class degrees driven by each other.

Anthony knew Sarah had a passion for sex, both heterosexual and bi, and he was pretty happy when they attended the occasional 'free-love' party in the early '70s. She was the girl he had fallen for, and he did not want her to change. Secure in their trust and understanding of each other, they agreed on an unwritten set of rules: if they always, and without fail, took suitable precautions; neither of them knew the other party (or parties) involved; and they never used the other party (or parties) more than once, then no harm would be done. The openness was reciprocal, and Anthony had also enjoyed the company of other women on infrequent occasions. While both Anthony and Sarah might engage with others, they only made love with each other, and as each of them relived their own sexual encounters with their eager partner, it enhanced the act of lovemaking they shared together. The freedom of sexual expression, which had always been paramount to Sarah since her teens, allowed their unbreakable relationship to flourish based on an honest openness that most traditional couples of the day could not contemplate.

Both Sarah and Anthony became successful lawyers. He had worked legislating for the Thatcher government in the 1980s. Margaret Thatcher was the nemesis of the trade union movement. With a helping hand from the then miners' leader, Arthur Scargill, she destroyed the union's power base for more than a generation. Ironically, Anthony had spent the last five years of his life working to repeal some of the laws he helped draft.

Sarah was twenty-five when she became a devout Christian, having found God just after giving birth. She temporarily put her career on hold until Kate was old enough to attend school full time and then returned to her established career, specialising in human rights. With her newfound religious beliefs as a guiding star, she won groundbreaking cases in family law and women's rights, juxtaposing her pro-life ideology. Kate never quite understood her mother's faith, and, neither did Anthony. Sarah was strict but fair and had emotionally detached herself from her daughter in a cold-hearted caretaker way. Through all of Kate's childhood and teen years, she received emotional stability from her adoring father. Anthony worked away for weeks, and the bell ring was always his sign he was home. He never used his key, he liked to surprise Kate as she answered the door.

As Kate matured, it was apparent from the photographs and stories of her mother's rebellious years – which lasted from her teens to her mid-twenties – that something deep within her had changed. From just before Kate's birth, it seemed to all who knew Sarah that, as her wardrobe changed, her joie de vivre disappeared. Out went the vibrant colours, the frilly blouses, and the miniskirts to be replaced by baggy and frumpy clothing. Sarah was still comfortable with her nakedness, in a natural way, but ostentatious and flirtatious displays of overt sexuality, which had once been her style, had ceased. Their once-open marriage was now closed.

During Anthony's occasional melancholy moments, he would affectionately reminisce with Kate about his early relationship with the one true love of his life, implying that post-natal depression combined with Sarah's infertility was the turning point in their relationship, especially the reversal of her feminist views on a women's right to choose termination as a means of contraception. She now considered abortion a sin, an affront to God's will.

Around the time of Kate's sixth birthday, the death of Anthony's father hit him hard. Although Tom was hurting, his 'c'est la vie' attitude rattled his younger brother. For some unknown reason, the older twin became belligerent and insisted on selling the family home in Wantage to increase his stake from the inheritance. He couldn't comprehend why Tom needed so much capital and that, after all they had been through together, he wouldn't open up and confide in him. Maybe it was gambling debts, maybe it was women. Either way, Anthony never really knew. The acrimonious aftermath drove a wedge between the two soulmates, and as the sorry situation reached a point of no return, the brothers hardly ever spoke. Though Anthony tried to rekindle their relationship, Tom showed no willingness until the drift became irreversible. Tom disappeared from Anthony's life and eventually moved to Paris. Only ever meeting up at the odd reunion, the twins exchanged formalities and the occasional Christmas card but nothing more. Anthony, the 'responsible' of the two, never truly understood where they had gone wrong; he was filled with regret and the pain of failure that he knew would have their father turning in his grave. Anthony lived his life hoping they could finally bury the hatchet and again become the good friends they had once been.

Her parents' relationship noticeably deteriorated as Kate became more independent. Sarah had become a workaholic, her head buried in case files and dusty old legal books. However much he still cared for her, Anthony had decided that he had spent long enough with Sarah; the carefree teenager he'd fallen head over heels in love with had changed beyond recognition. She had almost turned into his mother-in-law, which they had often light-heartedly joked about. He was leaving the woman he loved because he loved her, parting when he did to avoid any hatred and bitterness that would destroy any chance of a future friendship. Kate had seen it coming for years; the cold and distant nature of Sarah towards everything and everyone in her life had slowly sapped the love she had once shared with her husband. The two were divorced just after Kate's 18th birthday.

Anthony bought a gîte on the outskirts of Toulouse, which gave him time to write articles for legal publications and review referred cases on an ad hoc basis. Kate had lived with him for three months during the hot summer months in '95. Anthony settled down, getting on with his life with the help of a thirty-something French girlfriend named Natalie, while Kate and Sarah lived in Courtfield Mews.

Just after Kate's twenty-first birthday, Sarah received a fateful call from France. After a busy day studying, Kate returned to the house around 8pm and cheerfully walked straight into the sombre atmosphere awaiting her in the lounge. Sarah was sitting on the sofa, visibly pale and distressed.

'I'm sorry, Kate, I think you had better take a seat, darling; I have some bad news,' her mother said in a serious tone.

Still wearing her jacket, Kate put down her portfolio and sat. This was the first time she could remember her mother sounding even slightly compassionate, and her gut feeling told her this was grave. Her mother had always informed Kate of any tragedies, and even when her own parents passed away, Sarah had never been this emotional. With trepidation in her fracturing voice, the divorcee factually relayed all of the details as she understood them.

'I had a call from your father this morning, and he informed me that he's been diagnosed with testicular cancer,' she said sobbing.

Kate felt the blood instantly drain from her body as the dreaded C-word was mumbled through her mother's flowing tears. Sarah wiped her eyes with a crumpled and sodden white handkerchief.

'He wanted to see Tom and me to sort out a few things. He told me he was leaving Toulouse as soon as he put the phone down,' Sarah continued.

Kate could hear the words but was struggling to comprehend the cancer eating away at her father.

'Anyway... ' Sarah cupped her mouth with her left hand as she looked at her distraught daughter, the maternal feelings she had suppressed for most of Kate's life flowed to the surface. Unsure how to approach her disbelieving daughter, she hesitantly got to her feet and sat on the arm of the chair where Kate was seated.

Sarah was battling to contain her own emotions. As she held Kate for the first time in years, she reluctantly finished relaying the news.

'I had a call from Natalie about an hour ago,' Sarah held back. She inhaled heavily, reluctant to add to her daughter's torment, but knew there was no other option than to continue. 'Whilst driving back to England from Toulouse, your father lost control of the Porsche and careered off a mountain road near Cahors,' her voice trembled, almost unable to force the painful words out. 'I really am so sorry, Kate, your father is dead. He was pronounced dead at the scene.'

Sarah could feel Kate's spirit being crushed under the weight of the heartbreaking news, as utter shock and anger gave way to uncontrollable sobbing. Sarah was grieving; she'd almost forgotten how much she loved Anthony and wished things could have been altogether different. The anguish of that fateful day could never be understated for either of the two women. Mother and daughter had connected for the first time since Kate's birth.

Anthony's well-attended funeral service was held at a small crematorium in Toulouse, and his will stated that he wished for his ashes to be scattered in England.

As requested, the three loves in his life carried out his testament precisely as he'd specified. Kate and Tom stood silently by as Sarah carefully opened the sealed urn and emptied its contents at the base of a maturing tree in the field at Woburn, where he had met his bride. Picked up on a gentle breeze, the ashes formed swirling grey clouds of charcoal, and as his physical remains disappeared before their eyes, Anthony's presence on Earth was gone. Kate hadn't seen her uncle for years, and although he looked well enough, he had aged considerably from the man she remembered, and he certainly looked a lot older than his recently deceased twin. She had the distinct impression that Tom and Sarah were only together in the field to please Anthony. Tom fought back the tears welling in his eyes, and he looked as if the pain of a thousand cuts, or missed opportunities to make amends with his twin, tore through his shattered heart. No sooner had Sarah finished reading a poem and reciting a small prayer than he ruefully kissed and held Kate briefly before he shared a regretful farewell smile with Sarah and promptly left.

The death of her father was a turning point in Kate's life. She had lost the rock she had always relied on, the one who always had a bag of magic kisses to fix her bumps and bruises as a child, whilst telling his hardy offspring that all would be fine. Anthony was her crutch, her best friend. Whether Sarah realised that her only child was now missing the most important person in her life or that she had neglected her daughter for most of the twenty-odd years of her life, Kate was never sure, but her mother had changed. Initially, it was difficult for both women to adjust to the new situation. While they would never be bosom buddies, they felt more relaxed and familiar. They started to smile in each other's company, which was groundbreaking for Kate. Once fiercely independent, Kate was now withdrawing to the security of her mother's arms, a comfort blanket she had never been swathed in before. Happy that her only living relative was steady and stable, Sarah moved to her parent's old house in Swindon. Kate was twenty-six and looking forward to finally living independently, free to do the things that truly excited her.

Chapter 4

S ir David Appleway was the senior creative director and founder
of APGH Media Relations. The acronym APGH meant nothing
in particular, and on the odd occasions when people asked him the
importance of the initials, he added fictional names as a marketing
ploy to make the agency seem more grandiose. But since it was
firmly established, for more than thirty years, he was more than
happy to elucidate the 'pretentious little white lie'.

A supremely talented designer with a thorough understanding of
his trade, David was a guru who had been there through the heady
days of the 60s and the explosion of creativity that came with it. He
had it all: good looks, even though he was fast approaching 65, an
athletic frame, and mannerisms that fitted his status as a leading
contributor to the changes in the design and marketing arena over
the preceding three decades. For 30 years, Sir David's vision and
foresight had set trends. The only blemishes on his character were a
liking for the odd Jack Daniel's and the occasional toke.

He had given Kate her first opening when she had finished her
design and marketing degree at the prestigious London College of
Printing. As well as being a significant benefactor to the college,
David often gave lectures to the students. This was more of a selfish
interest to keep his hand in and to spot the up-and-coming talents
that would keep his agency amongst the world's best. As a student
in her late teens, he had observed that Kate had the all-important
X-Factor from the first day he met her. He soon became her mentor,
and she'd been groomed to be his long-term replacement. David

became a surrogate father figure to Kate after the death of Anthony, and whilst her studies suffered in the immediate aftermath of the heartbreaking news, David continually pushed Kate. He wanted her to fulfil her potential by squeezing out every last drop of untapped ability and, to ensure she never lost her pizzazz. After that episode, he was now her go-to whenever she needed guidance or a shoulder to cry on. She trusted his opinion and respected his judgement.

After more than ten years of climbing the ladder, Kate was part of the furniture and the Director of Communications at APGH. Her challenging job entailed securing new marketing accounts. Power crazy she wasn't, but a control freak she was. Kate knew what she wanted, and she almost always got it. Primarily, it was down to her knowledge of the industry, the time she spent researching her clients before a pitch, an eye for design, and, just every now and then, her knack for being in the right place at the right time. Her photographic memory was legendary, and it seemed, to everyone who knew her, that she never forgot a thing. Even the most minuscule detail could instantly be recalled from her encyclopaedic catalogue of lived events, times, and places. Having learnt the art of debate from listening endlessly to her parents discussing cases, her inherent ability to fight her corner was remarkable. Prospective clients and work associates would listen with reverence to her every word, with the men wanting her and the women wanting to be her. Being so 'talented' and more than content keeping her very private life away from her very public day-to-day life had left Kate open to sinister and salacious accusations about her sexuality. Behind her back, almost all of the men, who'd had their offers of affection rejected, would spitefully label her a 'lesbian', while most of the women, who were simply envious of the whole package, would viciously brand her a 'prick-teaser'. Kate knew this, it didn't bother her and certainly would not sidetrack her from her goal, whatever that may be. She was outwardly thick-skinned and not in the slightest bit interested in office gossip and innuendo, and as far as she was concerned, tittle-tattle was, in the main, for the bored masses.

The APGH office was situated on King's Road, about a 20-minute walk from Courtfield Mews. Kate tended to make the short walk to work daily, weather permitting and knowing that she would be office-based for the entire day. The walk was always a good time to gather her thoughts, and a slight detour to a local Deli would ensure that she'd have freshly prepared salad or pasta for lunch.

Spread over three floors of the towering building, APGH was home to the brightest talents in London. The plaster had been stripped from the internal walls to reveal the original salmony-pink brickwork, ensuring a rustic heritage feel. Large canvas prints adorned the walls adding splashes of rich colour. Around the outside of the open-plan areas on each of the three levels were various rooms, glazed windows with frosted vinyl decals, a health and safety prerequisite to stop employees from walking into the polished glass. The upper echelon was home to the company's senior management, and Kate's office was across the open-plan area from Sir David's. His was hardly ever used because he was rarely ever in the office.

As some had initially mooted, career-minded Kate was not just David's plaything, and her portfolio of multinational clients vindicated her position within the company. She was a precocious talent with a wise head on young shoulders, and her industry peers respected her work ethic. Getting under the skin of a potential new business, her remit was boundless, and no stone was ever left unturned. Kate understood wholeheartedly that just reading pages and pages of information, meeting prospective clients, and doing site visits to gain an insight into their market would not make her an expert; that was somebody else's job.

Her reason for wanting a senior position at the firm was to sell the already established and globally recognised talent of the agency that employed her. Her formula for this was relatively simple and thoroughly tested: getting to know a would-be client's market intimately, combining energy and innovation, a creative mix second-to-none, and an unrivalled level of service expertise. After any successful pitch, Kate would prepare a Handover Report that she knew would take two weeks to complete.

The detailed report was for the new client, although APGH employees and specialist freelancers would be required to supply content and sign Non-Disclosure Agreements. Once complete, the report would summarise the account's handover procedure, give biographies of the leading players, and provide a precise rundown of the winning three-year strategy.

With the Handover Report put to bed, the well-travelled Kate would always take two or three weeks of rest and recuperation. Returning from her holiday refreshed and revitalised, she would always look forward to commencing research on a new tender, a new challenge.

Her success rate at turning prospects into clients was close to 90%. On the odd occasion that Kate lost a pitch, she knew that she was flogging a dead horse as soon as she entered the room, more often than not, being met by the lack of interest of the decision makers as their minds were lost under the influence of a few lunchtime beverages, making her reason for being there a sham.

Provethan Pharmaceutical Inc. was Kate's latest pitch in the United States and the United Kingdom. Provethan was one of the world's leading pharmaceutical companies, with world-class research centres and offices across the globe. A leader in healthcare, the organisation is committed to providing effective and affordable treatments and remedies to cure innumerable diseases across a broad spectrum of therapeutic areas. It promised and delivered a successful range of existing and newly-developed products enhancing and changing the lives of millions of people. Kate would be heading up a small team of four, and she had almost six months to research and meet Provethan; during that time, she would expect to spend six to eight weeks stateside, reviewing their existing marketing strategy, with the ultimate goal of winning the multi-million dollar corporate marketing account.

Chapter 5

Following the dark years of Hitler's war – a campaign that spread hatred, distrust, mass murder, and mayhem across continental Europe and Africa, eventually engulfing Asia and the United States of America bringing the world to the edge of the abyss – the tiny shoots of prosperity had begun to take root. The world was looking forward to a more peaceful and democratic future.

From birth, Zhou Dingbang was destined for great things. Now in his late fifties, he entered the world on a historic day that would forever change the political make-up of the world and mean the dawning of a new superpower.

Zhou's childhood was filled with images of death and destruction while being educated in the ways of the new Republic through communist party doctrines. Intelligent and forward-thinking, the only option available to him was to conform. After studying public administration and politics at Beijing's foremost University, he steadily progressed through the ranks of the Communist Party, reaching the upper echelons of the establishment.

The phone rang.

'Hello, David.'

'Hello Ding, I've been expecting your call.'

'I hope you are well. How are things?' asked Zhou. 'Not so bad, you know how it is. What can I do for you, my friend?' replied David, pleased to once again speak with his intellectual buddy, whom he considered an open-minded equal.

Ding was Zhou's nickname. It had been since his school days, and very few people outside of China were privileged enough to refer to him by it. 'Ding' was a term of endearment, and David understood very well that this permission was a bond of considerable trust and respect.

'I'm confirming I'll see you at the New Year celebrations tomorrow,' Zhou inquired.

'Of course you will, I wouldn't miss it for the world. I'm really looking forward to it. Why's that?' David understood from the tone of Ding's voice that more was to come.

'Well, I've been thinking. After my initial meeting with Miss Summertown at the Terracotta Exhibition and following our further discussions, I have made some extensive inroads into the commission I've outlined. In anticipation of the near completion of the brief, could you extend the invitation to her? I wish to meet her again, somewhere more spirited than the first time we met. Tomorrow would be the perfect opportunity for me to get to know what makes her tick. Is that possible?' Zhou asked.

'That's fine; I'm sure Kate could do with a night out now that she's finished tying up loose ends on the Provethan tender. She's been a busy girl for the last six months,' replied David.

Having got the pressing part of the conversation out of the way, he changed his tone, hoping to relieve the tension of the conversation and continued light-heartedly.

'Anyway, she'll make me look better as I walk in! I mean, I'd look!' David chuckled at his own quip, which prompted Ding to join him. With the formality of the conversation broken with some mildly sexist humour, David could hear Ding relax. He understood damn well the significance of the briefing and the personal danger Ding was about to expose himself to.

'Excellent, thank you, David. I really appreciate your assistance. Please don't say a word.'

'Ding, that goes without saying. I'll see you tomorrow.'

'Enjoy the rest of your day, and I'll see you both tomorrow,' Zhou ended the call.

Satisfied with the call's outcome, a relieved Ambassador smiled as he reclined in his highly polished Chesterfield. Zhou was looking forward to Kate commencing the project. This was the ideal backdrop for an initial discussion that would transcend cultural boundaries and hopefully set the stage for a collaborative journey. He expected the proposal to help further his vision for the gradual release of his kin.

Elsewhere, in a windowless bunker, sparse of furniture and unknown to either Zhou or David, a third party listening in to the conversation took off his headphones, stopped the recorder, and noted down the conversation. He whispered to himself in perfect Cockney English: 'Oh yes… how fate dictates. Let's all celebrate the Chinese Year of the Rat.'

The man, who was in his late twenties and of Chinese descent, scrolled down his contact list on his mobile and dialled. Changing his tone, he forcefully reported in perfect Chinese. "The meeting is on. Tomorrow. She is the one.'

His superior's hawkish tones relayed a new set of instructions in Chinese. Having received his mission, he confirmed his position: 'I understand. All three. It will be done.'

The black cab swept into the drop-off zone at one of London's plushest hotels. Though it had been short notice, Kate was excited to be out once more with David. The extended invite to the Chinese New Year extravaganza was most welcome after her doggedness to the Provethan bid. It had been months of hard graft, but the end was in sight.

Stepping onto the red carpet, Kate was captivated by the beautiful people entering the grand ballroom. Observing the room,

Kate's eyes dazzled at the glitz of the elegant attire, the sparkle of those adorned in jewellery, and the cut of the suits, which confirmed to her that these were wealthy people. The guiding lights of the Chinese community in Britain and beyond were engaged in lively conversations amid the festive ambience.

The ballroom was aglow with vibrant red and gold decorations, enveloped in the rhythmic beats of drums accompanying a captivating dragon dance, all scored by the random explosions of firecrackers.

The Lunar New Year is the most important annual festival to billions in China. It is a time to spend with loved ones, eat, and drink. Outside of China, the Lunar New Year is also about spreading Chinese culture and political influence across the globe.

An animated dragon crafted from vibrant coloured paper and wood danced and weaved through the festive crowd. For Zhou, this was the ideal backdrop for a probing exercise that transcends cultural boundaries and would set the stage for a collaborative journey into the future of his homeland.

David and Kate were excitedly greeted by the Ambassador within minutes of their arrival.

'David, welcome.'

The men briefly hugged in a show of mutual friendship, displaying to all who cared that their relationship was built on the solid foundation of a trusted past. The Ambassador stepped back and courteously greeted Kate.

'It's my pleasure to meet you again, Miss Summertown.'

Dressed in a simple but stunning red silk dress with matching shoes, she felt accepted. The diplomat's warmth was noticeable as he took her offered hand with both of his.

'Mr Ambassador, the pleasure is all mine,' Kate replied warmly.

Kate noticed that, to the crease, he seemed to be wearing the same garments that clothed his frame at the Terracotta Army exhibit.

David and Zhou were animated with each other as Kate took in all the excitement that surrounded her. Compared to the anticlimax she had witnessed at the museum, she was now in a state of rhapsody as the colours, scents, sounds, and lights aroused her senses. Jugglers performed all around the guests as a dance of light and fireworks entertained in the corner of the room.

'David, may I steal your guest for ten minutes? I want to enlighten her about the wonders and rituals of a Chinese New Year celebration,' raising his eyebrows, Zhou smiled.

'Please do,' said David, acknowledging the importance of the request, and walked away, pointing toward a hospitality area next to the dancers to indicate they could find him there when they had concluded their confidential chat.

Having slowly strolled a few paces from where they left David, they were met with a framed dragon, which caused them to stop. Zhou smiled warmly.

'Miss Summertown, I'm delighted you could join me for this auspicious occasion.'

Kate was genuinely grateful. 'Thank you, Ambassador. It's an honour to be part of this magnificent celebration.'

Zhou was heartened by her gratitude.

As the dragon captivated its audience, Kate was unaware of his hidden agenda.

'The Dragon Dance marks the new year's beginning. For the Chinese, it's a time of renewal and hope - for you and your dreams for the future, and for me and the things I need to do.'

She nodded: 'I appreciate the symbolism. Ambassador, please call me Kate. Only my mother calls me Miss Summertown,' she joked.

'Well, please call me Zhou.' They laughed as they mutually acknowledged this new bridge of respect and trust.

Kate stood head and shoulders above the other beautiful women in attendance, and this did not go unnoticed. Zhou was enchanted by her and keen to talk with the beguiling professional.

Dancers draped in gold from head to toe were wearing exquisitely designed ornate headdresses and gracefully entertained attendees as the two looked on. The gold was dazzling, and the intricacy of the garments was a spectacle in its own right. Long golden fingernails gave the hands a haunting yet beautiful extension. Kate thought to herself that the Ambassador looked lost in the movements of the dozen women.

'This delightful dance troupe is affiliated with the Renmin University of China - my old University, ' he noted as he turned to Kate. This was her first personal detail straight from the horse's mouth.

Chapter 6

After ten minutes of discretely observing each other whilst watching the entertainment, they sauntered into a small and very private hospitality area decked in crimson. Kate and Zhou each gratefully accepted a flute of Champagne a delicate-looking and timid Chinese hostess offered. The handful of guests quietly conversing in the room with soft piped background music proved a perfect place for the Ambassador to speak with his chosen one.

'Please sit,' he hinted, guiding Kate to the privacy of a discreet leather booth upholstered in bright vermillion leather and edged with gold studs. Taking their seats, Kate gazed at the Chinese lanterns lighting the area.

'As I briefly mentioned when we first met, your professional acumen and sterling reputation precede you, Kate. David has always been highly impressed with your meticulous research, capacity to grasp intricate briefs, and, perhaps most importantly, your ability to maintain impartiality,' he said looking into her eyes,

'These are qualities I deem essential in an equal. David informs me that you have prepared an exceptional response for Provethan. I'm curious to know more about how you found the process?'

Kate was both humbled by his complimentary words and taken aback at how the Ambassador seemed so relaxed and at ease in her company. '

The bid work was demanding,' Kate replied. 'The travel to the US for meetings was both taxing and relaxing, but our proposal was submitted on schedule and, fingers crossed, we will know within the next two weeks. I know one thing, our team has prepared a solid business proposition, and we are well positioned to be awarded the contract.'

Zhou subtly observed as she adjusted her body towards him. Unbeknownst to her, now was his opportunity to gauge her reactions and suitability for a 'work' commission.

Considering the breadth of his last question, Kate felt compelled to ask one of her own and wanted a glimpse into his background.

'So, Zhou,' she sheepishly quizzed, still uncomfortable using his birth name. 'How is it that you ended up the Chinese Ambassador to the Court of Saint James?'

Zhou smiled coquettishly as he looked down at his lap and back up to Kate's softly lit face.

'That's an intriguing question, young lady. One which I often ask myself. I'll start at the beginning for you to truly understand me.'

Zhou began to share his life story. 'Kate, I hail from a time of turmoil, where the seeds of prosperity were sown amidst the chaos of a world war. By fate, I was born the day Mao Zedong declared the birth of the People's Republic of China, my destiny intertwined with the historic birth of what is now the new superpower.'

It struck Kate as she sipped the glass of bubbly the Ambassador was not drinking. Believing he was uncomfortable and only holding the glass as a European courtesy, she gently placed down the flute to put him at ease. This allowed Zhou to follow suit and put his untouched drink on the table beside hers.

Zhou, now more at ease, continued talking and Kate listened intently, transfixed by his words.

'Mao's vision shadowed my formative years. Educated in the tenets of the Communist Party, I saw the birth of the new Republic through the lens of political doctrines. Despite the darkness, I pursued an education in public administration and politics, paving my way through the ranks of the Communist Party. My political career and life took a giant leap forward in 1980 when I was assigned to the Chinese embassy in France.'

Zhou stopped talking as he carefully observed Kate's reactions, noting her attentiveness and gauging her ability to absorb the complexities of his experiences.

'My earliest memories of China on the news were of the demonstrations in Tiananmen Square and the Tank Man,' Kate responded as the remark slipped through her glossed red lips.'

It was just before Kate's teen years when news of a massacre in Tiananmen Square and the famous image captured by a solitary photographer shocked the world. Facing back down a multilane highway, ironically known as the 'Avenue of Eternal Peace', stood a man, wearing a white shirt, black trousers and carrying a bag in each hand. Looking lost and pathetic, drowning in acres of barren concrete, the belligerent young male was prepared to pay with his life. This was his city. A hundred tonnes of tracked armoured steel painted green and beige, moved closer. The four red army tanks' turrets raised and pointed forward, in line one behind the other. Smoke bellowed from their steel bulks, reinforcing the message to all watching that nothing would stop the might of the wielded fist. The man made of flesh and blood, a speck of sand in the eye of the oppressor, encompassed the dreams and aspirations of a billion people.

Zhou paused. 'Ah, yes. You call him the Tank Man, and we, though it's very rarely mentioned, call him the Unknown Rebel.' His demeanour changed slightly as a rueful sadness enveloped him.

Briefly considering his next words, he continued with his story. 'Times were very different then, and dates hold importance. Beginning in the mid-eighties, Communist states were collapsing like a row of dominoes all over the Eastern Bloc as the Warsaw Pact crumbled. In the spring of 1989, students, labour activists, and intellectuals held a series of demonstrations to protest the perceived authoritarian and socio-economic policies of the Chinese Communist Party. They called for democratic reform of the corrupt government that had been in place since the birth of Mao's nation. In May 1989, the world's media were in China covering the visit of our Soviet ally, Mikhail Gorbachev.

In early June 1989, I worked as an attaché at the embassy in Spain, as the most potent anti-China images ever beamed across the globe. And it wasn't propaganda, it was our new reality.'

Kate could feel his pain.

'I was a forty-year-old diplomat, and those images hit me hard. They almost broke my spirit.'

Kate was thunderstruck at the honesty of the Ambassador's testimony.

'That night, I witnessed the brutal suppression of democratic aspirations in Tiananmen Square. The crushing of my countrymen, by my countrymen. The iron fist, once rusting, was polished with renewed brutality. Though it's never been openly reported, thousands perished in a mindless act, staining the ideals of Mao's revolution.'

He gently bit his top lip with his teeth, staring vacantly at the redness of the walls.

He continued. 'Then, the next day, the image of the Unknown Rebel shook the world, leading to a media blackout and shaping global views for a generation.'

'Wow, that's a profound and life-changing experience, Mr Ambassador,' Kate chose her words carefully, believing that on this occasion, with the honesty she had just witnessed, using 'Zhou' was simply not sufficient.

Zhou continued subtly probing Kate's reactions, evaluating her emotional intelligence and resilience in the face of the challenging narrative.

'Indeed. In 2004, after working in some of the less salubrious embassies worldwide, I became the Chinese Ambassador to the United Kingdom, a position I hold with mixed emotions. While my love for China endures, I am conscious of the struggles faced by my fellow countrymen. I believe in One China. However, my eyes are open after nearly thirty years of living in continental Europe. I aspire to a future where lessons from history coexist with a more democratic society.'

'Your perspective is enlightening,' replied Kate, in awe that this hardened diplomat had both a heart and a conscience.

'So, why am I telling you this? I'm telling you because I believe my people could live peacefully as a 'democratic' society. They should never ignore the lessons learnt from the historical turmoil that was effectively and brutally dealt with under Mao while never forgetting the brainwashed and coerced existence that I lived under. I owe it to my fellow countrymen to further the cause of a free China with the help of my comrades within the Politburo,' Zhou observed with a renewed sense of optimism.

'I may call on you in the future. I think you could help me crystalise my thinking.'

'Zhou, working with you would be an absolute honour,' declared Kate.

'Your reputation precedes you, Kate. Fate has led us to this juncture,' Zhou proclaimed, with a fatherly smile.

'I imagine you already have my number, but please keep all work-related communications through David to ensure everything is clear. I love and respect him too much to do anything that would jeopardise my relationship with him, and I know you feel the same,' Kate nodded her head to emphasise her point.

Zhou rose to his feet. 'Shall we go and save David from himself?' he winked.

Chapter 7

After a solid presentation to the senior board members a month before at Provethan's worldwide headquarters in Illinois, Kate was still waiting. APGH had pitched against two other full-service marketing giants. She knew there could be only one winner, and her instinct told her this would be a close call. Today was decision day, the 22nd of February, and Kate looked forward to a weekend off. Friday was a good day to receive news. If it was terrible news, it allowed for a whole weekend to lick your wounds, pick yourself up, dust yourself down, and get ready for an exciting new challenge. Just after lunch, a communiqué arrived from Provethan, addressed to Sir David. Kate's phone rang.

'Kate, can you pop in and see me? I have some news for you,' came David's instruction in a disheartening tone.

'Well, yes, of course, I can. I'm on my way.' Kate was perplexed. She was convinced that the pitch had gone according to plan and that every base was covered. However, David's tone had left her feeling that they had lost the pitch and something had gone awry. The short walk from her glazed workstation, across the open-plan desk area, to David's office took only half a minute. Kate's hands had started to moisten as her heart began to beat at a slightly quicker tempo. Knocking twice as she entered his office, she watched David as she pushed the door. He was looking leaden, staring down at the communiqué.

'Well, Kate, I won't beat around the bush…we've had confirmation from Provethan,' he paused as if he was choosing his words carefully.

Kate's heart sank. She had slogged her guts out for six months and was just about to hear a 'thanks, but no thanks'.

David exited his chair, paced around his desk to the sullen Kate, and squeezed her fatherly. Kate was now resigned to hearing the bad news. The hug provided Kate with solace, knowing that at least he couldn't see failure written all over her face as he spoke into her ear.

David took a deep breath. "It's been sewn up. We take over the Provethan account in three months! Congratulations, Kate, you've done it again."

Kate was ecstatic. 'Yeeeeesssssssssss!' she exclaimed, ensuring everyone in the company could hear.

'Bastard! You bloody had me then. You bugger!' She jabbed him in the chest as the unpleasant tension she had felt instantaneously washed away. David chuckled like a schoolboy as the colour returned to his associate's face.

'Kate, you never fail to amaze me. I've cast an eye over the tender, your proposals, and the pitch. All top class, sorry, I'll rephrase that, world class. You have allowed Provethan to move forward and completely dominate its marketplace. It's sublime.'

David let go of Kate, walked over to his fridge, hidden behind the façade of an office cabinet, and pulled out a bottle of Louis Roederer Champagne and two chilled flutes. Popping the cork, the fizz gushed as it launched the projectile upwards. The bung hit the ceiling, leaving a slight indentation next to a couple of similar marks, the result of previous bubbly bottles being opened in celebration. David expertly poured the first flute before passing it to Kate.

'To you!' he said, as their glasses clinked. The Champagne tasted exquisite and even sweeter to Kate as her accomplishment sank in. The two companions discussed the best way to move forward, the potential specialists lined up by the headhunters, and the handover report.

'Complete the report and come and see me in two weeks, I'll have a new brief for you. It's unlike anything you've done before, but it should give you something to get your teeth into. You'll primarily be working on your own on this one, as it is of a delicate nature,' David explained.

'Oh! How intriguing. Do you want to brief me today?'

'I can't, Kate, not just yet. The briefing hasn't been finalised yet, but it will be shortly.'

'Don't worry about your leave. You don't need a break before I brief you. You'll be able to work on this new project around a holiday.'

His finger trawled down the page in his open diary. 'I'm away in the States for ten days, so… shall we say the 7th of March, one-ish at the Old Grain House?'

'That's fine. I look forward to it,' Kate raised her eyebrows and smiled at David. She turned and floated out of the office. All that was left for Kate to do was pass on the exciting news to the three associates who'd worked closely with her on the brief, arrange a few drinks, and party. What a perfect day!

Set in a small village on the outskirts of London, the charming Old Grain House was a typical olde-worlde English country pub. Originally a grain store part of a more significant mill site, the building's usage had been changed years before. Entering through a tree-lined gateway set in a white picket fence, Kate's Mini crunched across the gravel car park before coming to a halt next to David's metallic blue Aston Martin DB9. Kate could hear the rushing water of the River Thames that snaked through the grounds of the pub, which was adjacent to a disused water mill. Dark green ivy was intricately woven into the crumbling mortar, gripping the 250-year-old brickwork structure and covering the exterior. White beading broke up the large windows oddly positioned in the walls.

Making the short walk to the pub entrance, Kate shuddered as the north-westerly wind sent a chill down her spine. The grooved oak entrance door was small enough to cause her to duck as she walked into the fire-lit bar area. The cobbles on the floor had been ground and polished over the years and made for a treacherous venture if you missed the opportunity to wipe your feet on the mat as you walked in. David was seated at a table, beneath a window. Tinder crackled and popped below the heavy logs that burnt bright orange in the fireplace. The Venturi effect sucked the thick black smoke up the flue, leaving behind the subtlest aroma of a November bonfire. Seasoned over centuries, the original dark timber beams were suspended from the smoke-stained ceiling, enhancing the rustic atmosphere.

Kate removed her trench coat and gently placed it on the wooden hat and coat stand just inside the door. A small mirror on the wall allowed Kate to check her hair before she turned to David. Placing his pint of real cask ale down, David got to his feet and kissed Kate on both cheeks. As his lips brushed her cheeks, he could feel the coldness on her face.

'Kate, I'm so pleased you could make it. What can I get you?' David inquired.

'Hi David, I'll have a Chardonnay, please.'

Kate took her seat at the table, sitting opposite David's vacant chair. She was peckish but not overly fussed about eating as she read the blackboard menus dotted around the pub walls. The pub was empty. Two 'old' locals were passing the time of day with the very young-looking barmaid. Obviously pleased with the attention shown, her flirtatious false laughter accompanied each boorish remark as the men out-bragged each other, secretly dreaming of what it would be like to have their wicked way with her.

A young, professional-looking couple in deep conversation sat in the far corner, away from the fire. The alluring redhead wore a face filled with heartbroken sadness and piercing eyes as the fetching gent brushed the back of her hand in a 'there, there' way. Kate deduced from the wedding ring on the man's hand and the lack of one on the female's, that their relationship had an adulterous sting in the tail and that she was just about to find out how much love can hurt. Kate empathised with her. She had been the 'bit-on-the-side' herself many moons ago. She'd vowed never to go there again as the pain of the failed relationship flashed through her psyche. Kate had surmised that the emptiness and locale were the reasons for David picking this particular public house, as they had lunched there before whenever they needed an escape from the usual suspects in their regular London haunts. David returned with a glass of Chardonnay and placed it on a beer mat in front of Kate.

Following a reasonably brief conversation about Provethan, they both tucked into a light chicken salad before David got down to the nitty-gritty. Kate was running her finger around the rim of the glass in her left hand. David was solemn, and Kate had never seen him this focused before.

'Firstly, sorry for all the cloak-and-dagger drama, but I have a request. I need you to listen carefully to what I say, but I want you to think it through before you answer me. This is not a flippant 'Yes! Sir David kind of answer, Kate. I need honesty,' he said in a serious tone.

Kate found the song and dance highly amusing as she quipped. 'Bugger off, Sir David, is this a wind-up?' Her witticism was wasted on David.

'No, Kate, it's not a wind-up. I know I've teased you and even cried wolf on a few occasions, but this time I'm serious. This is important, and it will impact us both.'

From his body language and forthright tone, she knew that whatever he was about to say would be earnest and thought-provoking.

'Okay, I'm with you,' she said as she nodded her understanding.

'If you are happy with what I am about to say, I will give you the brief. It's just that I think you are more than suited for this commission.'

Kate was on tenterhooks, both fascinated and concerned about where this was leading.

'Okay, David, I'm with you… go on,' she urged.

'I want you to resign from APGH to take a leave period, let's call it a gap holiday. Six months should suffice, and then when you've finished the briefing, you can come back on board, and nobody will be any the wiser. Are you interested?'

Kate was flummoxed. 'Did I hear you right… you want me to resign?'

'Yes, and yes. It will all become apparent, but for now, Kate, that's just how it must be.'

Kate licked her top lip as she nodded, valuing David's sincerity as the full impact of the statement hit home.

'Look, I'm just popping out to the car for 10 minutes. I need to make a few calls, so I'll see you shortly.' David got to his feet, lightly tapped Kate twice on her shoulder, crossed the bar, and left, leaving the door to close behind him.

'Fuck, I wasn't expecting that!' She mumbled to herself as the significance of the conversation sunk in. Sipping the Chardonnay as she ruminated over David's words, Kate combed her fingers through her hair as she looked down at the beer mat. 'Bloody hell, he is serious,' another mumbling freed itself from her thoughts.

Kate had complete faith in David and knew it was reciprocal, so taking his word was not the issue. Unusually for the self-assured Kate, the only niggling doubt she had in her mind was with her ability to complete the brief. Racking her brain about all the forthcoming tenders, and through a process of elimination, she deduced that this wasn't a corporate endeavour, as her thoughts turned to the unknown brief and the conundrum thrown into the mixing pot by David.

'But what is the brief… think… What could it be? Bloody, bloody, bloody…' Not loud enough to be heard but sufficiently animated for those around to see that Kate was in mid-conversation with herself, she realised that the two codgers propping up the bar were staring at her, open-mouthed, assuming that she was some kind of 'fruitcake'. The stare was broken as her eyes met theirs full-on. Kate's indignant look of contempt was enough for the men to turn around and mind their own business, renewing their interest in the ample cleavage on display behind the bar.

As Kate, once again, returned to her thoughts of the brief, David returned from his car.

'Well, what do you think? Is it something that interests you?'

Kate responded sceptically. 'Yesssssss,' she let out a hesitant sigh.

David repeated the question as Kate expanded her answer. 'Yes, I am interested and I'll do it for you. I trust your word, and I know you wouldn't have considered me if you didn't believe I could do it... so yes.'

'Thank you, Kate. I really do understand your unease, and I respect your honesty. Let's get one thing straight, I would never do anything to jeopardise your career or, more importantly to me, our friendship.'

'Well, what is it, David? What is so confidential that it requires my resignation?'

'The Chinese Ambassador has asked me to brief you on a project that is dear to his heart. It is both sensitive and highly confidential. It will take about six months to complete, and you shouldn't work for the company. You'll need to deem it a private commission,' David supped his ale as Kate listened intently.

'On the 24th of this month, the Olympic torch will be lit in the birthplace of the Games, Olympia in Greece, and will start its worldwide journey across six continents. The Ambassador is concerned that any negative publicity before or during the Games will be catastrophic to the government reform slowly taking place within China.'

David took a deep breath and continued. 'A few officials would prefer a more open and democratic style of government, of which the Ambassador is one. He recognises that there will be bad publicity, but anything along the lines of the '89 Tiananmen Square massacre would be devastating. China is only just now recovering from the fallout of the bloody slaughter that took place nearly twenty years ago,' David swigged his ale.

'The Ambassador requires a dossier from you outlining the world's view of modern China, including all the fashionable misconceptions and nonsense out there. You need to advise him on how China can become more transparent with the world's media and the pros and cons of giving its people the basic freedoms we take for granted, such as independent press, uncontrolled broadcast media and unrestricted access to the internet. The Chinese government has controlled the lives of its subjects through lies and ignorance, and the officials believe that the time is right for individual autonomy.'

'Blimey! That is a brief, no wonder it's confidential,' Kate exclaimed as the penny dropped. This explains their shared discussion at the Lunar New Year bash and the Ambassador speaking so openly about his past as he bared his soul.

The two sat in silence as the magnitude of the task hit home to them both. David had reiterated his patter time and time again in his mind, but saying it out loud to his postulant had added a bitter impetus to his carefully chosen words. He understood that he would temporarily lose his Number One, and though it had been a conundrum he had thoroughly thought through, the realisation now gutted him.

'May I ask a couple of questions?' Kate enquired as the heavy words sank in.

'Of course, you can, and I'll answer them the best I can. Fire away, Kate.'

'Why me? Why nobody else?'

'The Chinese Ambassador is impressed with your exceptional abilities, Kate. He has been watching your progress for quite a while, and long before you first met him, he... no... we... believed that you would be perfect for this commission. He has asked me to approach you because you are no expert on China, and knowing that you'll evaluate this with no baggage or any predetermined notion. And as always, you'll need to be thorough, exact, and unbiased,' said David.

'Thank you for the vote of confidence. How many people know about this?'

'The three of us are the only people who know about this brief, especially your involvement. Nobody else needs to know, and I assure you that once this project is complete, you will never hear of it again.'

'Okay, so why do I have to resign?' Kate asked.

'The reason I need you to resign is for peace of mind. People will ask questions behind closed doors if you work from the office. If I send you away on an assignment, people will still ask questions. After destroying the competition on the Provethan account, why not have a break? I mean, you deserve it. So what, people will gossip, that's what we do. Come back in six months and carry on where you left off. I'm sure in the mix of things, your resignation will be tomorrow's chip paper when they find something else to get their teeth into. You know damn well how the industry works. If it came out that we are indirectly working for the Chinese government, and with all the human rights issues that are expected to be broadcast by the media, the fallout would be seriously damaging to APGH. Shit sticks, as you well know!' David explained.

'That's what I thought, but I just needed to hear it from you,' Kate said, relieved to know the truth.

'Obviously, you will be fully recompensed, salary, expenses, etcetera.'

'David, I never doubted that. It never entered the equation.'

'So, is there anything else you need answering or confirming?'

'No, I don't think so, and once again, thanks for this. I'm looking forward to it,' Kate replied with a nervous excitement.

David pulled the chair beside him from under the table and reached down to his tatty leather satchel. Click-click sprang the hinged locks shooting open. David peered inside the folds, removed a large brown envelope and gingerly passed it over the almost empty glasses into Kate's expectant hand.

'Here, Kate, some bedtime reading for you, it's the brief in full. It covers your remit and should ensure that you are fully au fait with the areas you'll need to cover.'

Unmarked and sealed, Kate didn't even think about opening the package. She'd do that in the privacy of her own home.

'I'll read it later and get back to you if I have any queries regarding the content. Is that okay with you?' she asked.

'That's fine. Don't forget, if you need me, just call. I will arrange to meet you to get an update on your research and progress, as and when,' David confirmed.

'Will you liaise with the Ambassador on my behalf?'

'Absolutely, you'll have no dealings with the Ambassador unless, of course, you should bump into him in passing.'

David smiled at Kate, she understood. 'Oh, and one final word of warning, the Ambassador knows that there are a lot of skeletons in China's vast closet, and to complete the dossier, you'll need to remain objective and dig deep to avoid becoming subjective.'

'Okay, David, I'll resign first thing Monday.'

David looked at his watch. 'Bugger! Kate, I must shoot. I'll have to love and leave you. One final thing I need to mention. You are booked on a flight to Beijing on the 9th of August. We think two weeks in China would help you get a feel of how the Chinese Authorities are dealing with the promises they made to the International Olympic Committee about press freedoms and the various human rights issues that will undoubtedly arise once the Games commence.'

Kate and David stood up together. He kissed her on both cheeks and promptly left her in the bar as she walked to the coat stand.

'Oi, lady, are you paying this?' The stroppy barmaid waved a slip of paper in Kate's direction. David's audacity caused a big grin to appear across her face.

'What a cheeky bugger. I am now!'

Chapter 8

Monday, 10th March, 2008, was a day that would stay with Kate forever. Even before she entered David's office, the morning news was full of China and the Tibetan call for self-rule. Armed with only an envelope and unshakeable confidence, Kate briefly interjected with David and walked out. Avoiding eye contact through the glazed divide between herself and the poker-faced cuckoos waiting to move into her soon-to-be-vacated nest, she packed her belongings and left.

It all felt surreal to her as she walked through the office. Everyone knew she was leaving but unaware of why. The searing looks from gob-smacked colleagues would have been amusing if she hadn't felt so cheerless. The cloak of assuredness that had adorned her just moments earlier had come apart at the seams, leaving a lump in her throat that stopped her from saying any farewells. Trembling as she made the short drive home, with the occasional tear falling from her mascara-defined lashes, the emptiness and loneliness hit home as she carried a box of possessions into her abode.

For the next day or so, she received various calls from people within the company, some with genuine concern, like Isabella, her twenty-something personal assistant, and others with a more self-centred hidden agenda. Kate wasn't stupid. She knew the real from the insincere and took delight – in a selfishly masochistic way – when informing the sycophants that she would soon be back to pick up where she left off. As the news travelled through the grapevine, her mobile rang red-hot from people within the industry with offers of exciting new career opportunities, reinforcing the talented but unemployed director's unfaltering belief in her abilities.

The rumour of her decision to take a gap period 'for personal reasons' became accepted as Sir David had made it known that Kate was due to return in six months. David had phoned Kate once or twice daily in the first week to see how she was bearing up. He knew Kate would take a few days off before starting the brief, and he certainly thought it was well-deserved after the successful Provethan pitch.

Using her propensity to thoroughly research her 'client,' Kate got stuck into the briefing with gusto, and the very first fact that struck home was the date, the first of October, 1949. A eureka moment hit as the pieces of a puzzle that had been there all the time fell into place. Her mum, dad, uncle and the Ambassador were all born on the same day as the reborn China. This was why Zhou said fate had led them to this juncture.

Kate had been working on the China Brief for more than eight weeks, and as David's calls and the occasional meetings had become sporadic, she slowly adjusted to the solitude that came as part of the brief. Her habitual practices were the same as they had always been, except for not leaving the house for the short walk to the office.

The first two months flew by, attending museums and libraries to extend her knowledge and understanding, as she became an expert in everything Chinese. The majority of the first two parts of her dossier were almost complete. Month one was spent studying the history and make-up of China, the events leading up to the demonstrations, and the extinguishing of the light in 1989.

During the second, she concentrated on the worldwide aftermath that followed, researching the Olympic bid and the publicity for both the People's Republic of China and the International Olympic Committee.

For most of March and April, it appeared as though China was never out of the news. From the all-too-reminiscent crushing of Tibet, which left hundreds of bodies littering the debris-strewn streets, to the chaos and incrimination across the globe caused by a tiny flame protected by an elite squad of roller-bladed henchmen from the Chinese military. The patently honest footage and stills, widely reported and broadcast as fact in the West and overlooked by the governing regime in China, made the dossier heavy reading. That, combined with the multimedia arrangement she had pulled together, would make for an uncomfortable and, sadly, shocking presentation.

Kate had opened Pandora's box on the misinformation recently fed to the gullible masses within China by the state-controlled media. It talked about the 'peace and tranquillity' in Tibet and the 'unified acceptance of the torch's journey by the world's populace.'

It was not all grinding. The enjoyable part of the briefing freed Kate up from the monotonous chains of a laptop that had sadly become her best friend. For a better understanding and insight into the relevance of Mao's China, Kate could find a well of adequate views from those who really cared, just around the corner from her abode cum office. London's Chinatown is centrally located along and around Gerrard Street near to Soho. It is part of London's colourful West End, encompassing Covent Garden, Leicester Square, and Piccadilly Circus. Kate had made numerous daytime visits to Chinatown since she commenced the brief whenever she sought inspiration, hit a mental block, or needed to get out.

Kate decided to bite the bullet and make her first solo night recce. She had dropped in on nighttime Chinatown many times before while out on the lash with friends, but this time, it was different, and felt almost virgin-like. She may have seen the buzz but never felt it. Her body was alive to the smells, tastes, lights, and sounds. Being alone in and on a mission had finely tuned her senses and increased her receptivity.

Throngs of joyful tourists, laden with flashing cameras and full of life, rambled through the streets while inebriated West End punters staggered about due to copious amounts of consumed alcohol. The glowing red lanterns above her head gave little China an 'authentic' feel as they shone brightly against the ghastly, neon signs of some of the more tacky-looking establishments.

The aroma of steam and smoke that filled the street caused shooting pains in the pit of her stomach, which begged for sustenance. Kate meandered up the street until she found herself outside a small restaurant, something close to traditional Chinese. The fascia was tidy, and the external signs were not in-your-face sunset yellow. They did not advertise a '10% discount with takeaway' or 'all you can eat' deals. Peering through the frontage, she observed that the half-a-dozen people enjoying the eatery's fares were all of Chinese descent and, for a famished Kate, this was the ideal place to start her hands-on research in preparation for her planned trip to China.

As Kate entered, a diminutive waitress welcomed her with a pleasant-sounding Chinese greeting. She guided her to a table and pulled out the seat. Kate gratefully accepted the offer to sit as the waitress placed the English translation of the menu on the table next to her. Leaving Kate to peruse the menu, the young lady returned shortly to take her order.

Unhurried and concisely, Kate ordered a glass of white wine to complement the Chef's special dish of the day, delightfully named Sichuan Dragon, created from strips of tender chicken with fresh jumbo shrimp in a spicy orange sauce complete with rice. However, the vacant expression on the face of the young waitress informed her that she was clueless about what was being ordered and that, more than likely, she spoke no English. A nondescript-looking man raised his head over the newspaper he was reading and interrupted the two animated women before liaising with the restaurant worker in her mother tongue.

'I sorry, small Ringlish,' the waitress apologetically nodded to Kate and thanked the man with a double nod before disappearing behind a two-way door.

'Thank you for your assistance. It's very much appreciated,' Kate acknowledged the gentleman for his help.

'It's no problem. I believe she's new here, she arrived last week,' said the Asian man in perfect Cockney English. In his late twenties, with an average build, the black-haired man was dressed as any usual turned-out gent in modern London, wearing black designer jeans and a labelled jacket.

Kate temporarily stared in the man's direction and smiled. His face rang a bell. She knew she had seen him before. The amateur sleuth tried to recall where recognised him from and looked through the window and back down the main street. 'Bingo!' Whenever Kate had been people-watching or just enthusing herself with the bustling energy taking place along Chinatown's main street, she'd remembered she had clapped eyes on him at least half a dozen times, having observed him idling his day away as he plodded the pavements of his backstreet manor seemingly going nowhere in particular. This dark horse had struck her as a shifty, steely character. She'd wondered to herself whether he was part of a triad gang or a Snakehead – which added to his mystery, his intrigue, and her concern – but she had now dismissed this idea out of hand. He was too polite, and he had all his fingers.

'I'm Steve. I'm local here. Are you?'

Kate's awareness of the conversation, coming from the table next to hers, was a pleasing introduction.

'It's nice to meet you. I'm Kate. I live across town.'

'You on business here?' the man inquired in a sociable way.

'I guess so. I'm studying, well, researching a new book on behalf of a client.'

'Oh, you're a writer; how interesting. May I inquire as to what the book is about?' He was utterly convivial, or maybe it was the setting, but either way, Kate was comfortable with the situation.

'Of course, 'A Westerner's view of China and its cuisine'. It's a book about how cuisine has changed since its mainstream acceptance in the West and how the older generations remember the dishes they introduced when they first arrived here from China,' Kate said.

'I plan to speak to some of the older citizens who can recall their reasons for leaving China, their living standards, and their cuisine styles before emigrating to see what they miss about China and how they think it's changed.'

'Do you think you're going to struggle with your research… you know… with your inability to speak Chinese?' Steve asked.

'Quite possibly, but I have an allocated budget for a translator to assist me on my site visits. Interviewing a dozen people should give me enough information to complete the project.'

'I could help you there, obviously for a small fee, but I guarantee the translations will be accurate and succinct,' proffered Steve.

'I couldn't put that on you.' Kate paused. He was perfect for the job, but she was still unsure about his credentials.

'That's cool. I'm not out to hassle you. Anyway, I apologise, I've got to go, but if you would like my assistance, even if it's just to help you find a suitable translator, call me.'

He placed a printed business card on the tabletop, revealing his name as Steven Lee and a couple of contact numbers. His job title caused Kate to grimace. Among the others, 'translator' was the only word she needed to see. The reddening of her face as the blood rouged her skin was a visual indication to Steve of just how embarrassed she was.

She looked up at him as he stood beside her, 'Oops, sorry! A dreadful misjudgement on my part. I do apologise. I thought…' Kate stopped herself from digging. The metaphorical hole in which she now found herself was deep enough, but unfortunately not real enough to hide her discomfort at her error.

'Steve, thank you again, and I'd be more than happy to use your services.'

'Please don't commit to anything. Call me if you need me. Have a good evening, Kate, and enjoy your meal.' He chuckled warmly and walked out, leaving Kate to regain her composure. She had underestimated the unassuming translator, which was a first for her. She was usually spot on, or at least thereabouts.

After this initial meeting, Chinatown had become a regular haunt for the isolated Kate, and after Steve had befriended her in a purely professional capacity, she painstakingly stripped back some of his armour. He was restrained, reticent to divulge any information he may deem too personal. However, the meagre spattering of details gleaned from the tight-lipped Steve was relatively informative to Kate.

The grandson of Chinese immigrants who had fled the civil war before the birth of Mao's China, Steve was a genuine guy who liked to listen. His parents owned a local convenience store, selling imported Chinese household items, and he was expected to take over when his parents had enough of working. Kate was impressed with his knowledge of China, the customs and ways, and most importantly, his ability to communicate in Chinese. She became accustomed to Steve's camaraderie as he translated for her countless times. Starved of companionship, the older generation always enjoyed the opportunity to relive their former lives, and each would insist on making their own particular tea, a multitude of infused dried leaves, each brew unique and concocted in a time-honoured way.

Kate and Steve spent hours sipping with the wise ones as they mused over his motherland. She ruefully imagined that his soul was lost on the streets of the West End and that he would be more suited to teaching English to the communist oligarchs or the liberal bourgeoisie in the confused land of his forefathers. Steve was only ever quiet when talking about himself, which was unusual.

He fancied the pants off Kate, and she knew it, but unlike most men who'd tried and failed miserably to get inside her with big boasts of this and that, he said nothing. Unwilling to draw attention to his achievements or abilities, modesty was one endearing quality that Kate perceived was missing within 21st-Century London, and from her point of view, Steve exuded modesty. While Kate was not sexually interested in Steve, she sometimes found herself unexpectedly attracted to him. Kate never mixed business with pleasure, and as she'd met Steve through work, he'd become part of 'her team', so any feelings that may flicker would have to be put on the back burner.

While researching her project, becoming a regular in a few restaurants opened many doors to the inner sanctum of the Chinatown fraternity. She had tried almost everything on the various unwritten menus, and the local gourmet chefs, impressed with her palate and pleased with her customs, would prepare special meals for her. Not the usual thrown-together late-night takeaways, numbered from one to infinity and loaded with sugar, salt, and colourants, these were delicacies, many too intense for the fast food stomachs of the uneducated Westerner. The donkey's penis, served on a bed of lettuce, was probably the most repugnant meal, but not being a total quitter, Kate had left that dish until last. And, while some foods may have been beneficial for her skin they weren't good for her mental or physical state, so Kate drew the line at drinking deer's blood or gorging on sheep foeti.

Chapter 9

Kate's life was routine, busy and eventful, but routine. Her reveille at 6.45am was her sign to get up. Kate was an early bird and always awake to hear the alarm, no matter when she went to bed or how many glasses of vino she had imbibed the evening before. Sleeping was not high on her list of essential things to do and was considered a necessity, like eating. Kate had hardly ever dreamt since childhood, but they were always wholly forgettable when she did. On the odd occasion when a dream forced her awake, it was usually accompanied by a clammy dampness between her inner thighs. However, more recently, she'd had the occasional night of broken sleep, as the myriad of words relating to the brief had become an all-too-real series of unpleasant images careering around her brooding mind.

Swinging her legs out of her bed, Kate peeled herself from the sheets and stretched her arms above her head, yawning once to fill her lungs with a rush of oxygen. She picked up the remote next to the clock and turned on the discreetly placed TV hidden in the corner of her bedroom. Finding the BBC too morose to kick-start her day, Sky News was her choice in the morning, even if the delivery was somewhat over-egged. She left her bedroom and entered the adjoining bathroom. Kate had been in a delicate state earlier in the week from something she'd consumed over the weekend at a restaurant unknown to her but recommended by Steve. Being unsure of exactly what had disagreed with her, she'd avoided eating anything too rich for the next three days. Fortunately, for the past thirty-six hours, Kate's constitution was back to normal, which was both welcomed and timely.

After a brief skip down the stairs, collecting the daily as she passed the front door, The Independent, Kate headed straight into the kitchen. Kettle on, paper open, as she sat at her small breakfast table waiting for the water to boil. Although the table had three chairs, the other two were hardly used. The paper informed Kate that the day was Friday, 2nd May, 2008, but she already knew. She had exciting plans for today. Black coffee was the kick she needed and the one thing she couldn't imagine being without. Taking time to ingest the news and the caffeine, she perused the broadsheet while planning her day. Finally ready to make the journey back up the wooden hill – as her father used to call it – she bounded up the staircase and headed straight into the en-suite, buzzing with enthusiasm about her forthcoming day.

A stack of folded white towels was carefully placed on a rack next to the shower, one on top of the other like a new deck of playing cards. All she needed was in the glass-faced cabinet that had been sunk into the wall. Gels and creams for every eventuality. On the top shelf was a row of expensive perfumes. Kate would wear a fragrance that suited her needs. She knew that both men and women were receptive to scent, and she had memorised the brand whenever clients had made a passing mention.

Kate slid open the glass shower screen and walked into the partitioned area. She turned the large chrome dial on the wall, allowing the four jets of hot water to engulf her body. Squirting a large handful of shampoo into the palm of her left hand, Kate ran her fingers through her long brunette hair, followed by conditioner. She attentively teased her body with gelled hands, ensuring every area was washed and rinsed. Kate cherished a refreshing and invigorating shower. A cleansed body and mind were just about the perfect start to the day.

After carefully drying her body, she bent over to wrap her hair in the damp towel and stood upright, opening the cabinet for her rejuvenating body cream. Effleurage was her preferred technique to moisturise the entire surface of her skin, and with long flowing movements, this daily practice was both pleasurable and calming. Wiping the steam from the mirror above the sink, she picked up her toothbrush, squeezed out a small bead of minty paste and gently brushed the enamel that lined her perfectly-formed mouth. Finishing her daily routine in the bathroom, Kate strutted back into her bedroom. Sitting on the edge of her bed, staring at her beauty, she applied her make-up and carefully blow-dried her hair.

The reports from the TV were now just background noise as she carefully selected her attire for the day. Kate felt feminine, so an attractive, figure-hugging, floral number and bright red shoes would complement her happy-go-lucky mood. Refined and ready to face the world, she returned downstairs for breakfast as thoughts of the impending day filled her mind. Though eating wasn't a priority, her father had always insisted on its importance, becoming the final piece of her morning routine. She popped a pill from a packet of contraceptives. She would always take them whenever she drank her second cup of Java, usually to help wash down the yoghurt-covered muesli, followed by a third.

Her reasons for today's enthusiasm were fourfold.

The first part of her day would focus on the China Brief. The progress on the commission was going well, and compared to the sections she had been researching, the light-hearted appendix was the section she was planning to commence next.

The second part was to meet two big hitters from the telecoms industry for a light lunch. John and Ian were friends – to be precise, more like an old married couple than any married couple she knew – as well as business associates and Kate always looked forward to a 'date' with the argumentative twosome.

The third was a late afternoon two-hour pampering with her beautician. Finally, a scheduled function to attend before enjoying well-earned R&R over the weekend.

She was due to start the report's 'Popular Misconceptions of Modern China' appendix. Sitting at her laptop to begin the first part of the day, she typed 'Misconceptions of China' in the search engine window and tapped return, only to find more than five million links. She was surprised, she'd only expected a few thousand, but at least she had a place to start. The first link that grabbed her attention read: 'Western Misconceptions About Chinese Women.' The content of the site was highly amusing: all Chinese men are the same, all Chinese women are the same, all Chinese women want a Western man, and so on and so forth. As the hours passed and Kate reviewed the sites, the content became increasingly disturbing. From a relatively light-hearted and optimistic viewpoint when she started, the horror of the sites that bombarded her senses now disgusted her.

Some were misconceived, and others based on factual evidence; the truths about the reality of China were warping her impartiality. Maybe this content was the verification that the Ambassador was, in fact, after. The pages on infanticide, and there were hundreds, walloped Kate. She was vehemently against any sort of abortion for use as a 'lifestyle' contraceptive, but the Chinese went further. Sanctioned feticide and infanticide were the 'unapproved' methods of the state to control its rapidly increasing population. Kate became increasingly uncomfortable as she read page after page of sickening descriptions outlining the worst excesses of sub-human deeds.

Even before birth, a visit by 'white-van-man' Chinese style would be a certified death sentence. Parked up in a back-street car lot, waiting to be invited in through the door of an unmarked van, a pregnant woman could buy the services of an illegal sonographer for an inexpensive ultrasound. The scans of China's unborn would determine the sex, the prerequisite for the systematic killing of the estimated sixty million 'missing' female newborns, reckoned to have been terminated either in the womb or shortly after birth. However, the 'lucky' girls – who managed to avoid feticide in the womb or the infanticide that the state quite happily turns a blind eye to – are now pawns in the sex game of child trafficking. The innocent being sold as playthings for the twisted delights of the world's paedophiles.

Kate felt sullied and nauseous. The images of young females being drowned at birth in buckets of water or just left in a field to die had chewed at her core as she struggled to comprehend what sort of society would condone such behaviour. The web pages that had given her senses a good kicking almost paled into significance compared to the grisly site she now found herself reviewing.

She scrolled down to reveal an image of a sizeable Asian man wearing a black jersey with the cuffs pulled up to his elbows. Perched on the backrest of his padded grey seat was an opened medical encyclopedia standing proud over his right shoulder. A pair of chopsticks and a spoon lay on a small side plate, placed next to a rice bowl. His uncovered elbows rested on the edge of the white-clothed table as he tucked into his dinner. His large right hand wrapped around the body, and his left hand clenched the head as his jaws bit deep, pulling the tender meat from the shoulder of the torso. The redundant limbs had been removed and discarded to the edge of a white china serving plate. As Kate studied the haunting image, it hit her that he was eating the supposed remains of a roasted baby. She retched. The headline, posted above the image, read: 'Chinese trade in human foetuses for consumption is uncovered.' Below the picture, the site reported that the image was of an artist performing a conceptual piece titled 'Eating People'. That said, there were so many articles associated with cannibalism in China, and the majority of them by recognised journalists held in high esteem within the media industry, that Kate could not ignore the relevance of the 'conceptual art'.

Kate pondered its significance. Was this art, or was this the reality? Either way, the content had affected her. It left her feeling soulless as she held her abdomen, subconsciously unsure as to whether she was holding her stomach or intuitively cradling her womb out of respect to the 'missing'. Being a pro, Kate refused to let her revulsion ruin her day. She shut down her laptop, picked up her small bag, checked the contents, and left for her luncheon. Unusually for Kate, a vegetarian option was on the menu for today.

Chapter 10

The time on the clock indicated that her lift would soon be arriving. Kate had been putting in the hours on the China Brief, so tonight was 'me-time'. It was 10.45pm. Kate pushed a single solitaire diamond earring through her left lobe as she looked into the mirror, she was ready. Butterflies in her stomach and a racing heart combined as nervous excitement pervaded her body. She sat on the end of her bed, picked up the clutch bag, and checked the contents, ensuring she had everything. Confident she was ready for the night's entertainment, Kate turned off the bedside lamp and left her bedroom. She walked downstairs to the hallway, put on a black knee-length trench coat, and meticulously tied the belt around her slender waist. She pulled her trapped hair out from under the collar and glanced in the mirror by the front door. 'Mirror, mirror on the wall,' she chirped. Through the glass in the door, the bright headlights of her transport waited patiently under the orange haze of the streetlights.

Clutch bag in hand, she walked towards the waiting car, its engine purring. The gleaming jet black BMW M6 coupé had small globules of rainwater on its highly-waxed paintwork.

'Ev'ning, young lady,' was the greeting from the driver as he held open the rear door.

'Hello Frank, you look rather dapper tonight,' Kate teasingly replied, tenderly kissing him on both cheeks before sliding onto the chilled leather seat.

Safely accommodated in the car, she rested her hands on the bag nestled in her lap. The car door was pushed shut with a reassuring dull thud. Frank took his place behind the wheel of the black beast, checked his rear-view mirror, and indicated as he moved off. The mizzle caused the wipers to remove the light sprinkling from the screen as the car passed through the bright neon lights and bustling streets of West London towards the venue.

Kate didn't really know much about the venue. Nobody did, except the organisers and the drivers. All that she did know was the theme of the evening's entertainment. She had signed up for scheduled functions months in advance and was required to confirm her attendance forty-eight hours before the event. Non-attendance was an absolute no-no unless, of course, it was unavoidable due to an emergency. The 'three strikes and you're out' rule was strictly adhered to by the management. The final confirmation of an event would be received 24 hours before, just to inform the client of the collection time and a security code.

Frank was a well-built Londoner in his mid-sixties. His face showed the lines of a hard upbringing, and the quiet tone of his Cockney voice disguised what Kate could only imagine to be unforgiving brutality if someone should cross him or upset his karma. The top of his right forefinger had been severed off many years before, and he had once joked with Kate that he had 'chopped it off for a fiver'. Frank was Kate's regular driver, and he had been for nearly six years since she'd joined the exclusive club.

'D'you like some sounds, Kate?' Frank inquired.

'Please do. You choose.' Kate knew his preferred music, and it suited them both.

The car's silence was temporarily jolted before the volume was reduced to an acceptable level as 'Waterloo Sunset' by The Kinks resonated around the vehicle. It was Frank's music, and he had previously mentioned to Kate that London was the place to be during his heyday in the sixties, gangsters and girls.

'May Day was a good shout for London,' Frank piped up. 'I think Boris'll sort it out. Ken's 'ad 'is chance and while I think he done an alright job to start, he's lost the plot. I always voted red, but it's not 'appening at the mo'.'

Frank was referring to the new Mayor of London. 'Red Ken' Livingstone had been voted out of City Hall the day before, and Boris Johnson's new team was about to forge a new direction for the capital. 'Let's hope so, Frank. London needs a new lease of life. She's been looking a little bit run down of late.'

The drive to the East End took just over half an hour, and the idle chit chat had calmed her yearnings. Approaching the venue and prompted by Frank, Kate opened her clutch bag and peered inside: house key, compact make-up set with scarlet red lipstick, a small hairbrush, mobile phone, silver cigarette holder, and an antique mask. She delicately removed the handcrafted papier-mâché item. The half-face Venetian mask, painted in gold and silver with splashes of vibrant turquoise and burgundy, was adorned in lace and encrusted with diamanté. She placed her face in the mask and carefully tied the gold ribbons at the back of her head as the car approached the first of two checkpoints. Frank slowed the car at each cordon, lowered the tinted driver's door window, and briefly conversed with the security guards before being waved on with a green glow rod. They had arrived at the venue in the Docklands. Frank gently pulled the car to a halt, got out and opened the rear door for Kate.

''Ere we are, safe an' sound. Ave a good un, and I'll be around and about if you need me. Just ask. You know the script,' said Frank.

'Thanks, Frank, you're a star.' Kate deftly swung her legs out and exited the car, looking heavenward at the large glass tower of Canary Wharf, which stood prominent against the dark blue night sky. A myriad of coloured lights shone across the river, sparkling against the blackness of the Thames.

The drizzle had stopped, and the early May air chilled her throat as she approached the main door. Eight professional burly minders, all suited in black with radio earpieces, guarded the entrance to the building.

'Good evening, Miss. Can you punch in your number, please?' came the gruff voice of one of the minders as he pointed to an electronic keypad in the wall. Kate punched in her security number. The red light on the door access panel went green.

'Thank you, you may go in.'

Kate entered the protected doorway, passing through a blacked-out secondary door into a large carpeted reception area. Leather lounge chairs and designer glass tables furnished a small candlelit chill-out area where two attractive, unmasked couples cut white powder on a table at the centre of the foursome.

Next to the seating area was a white-clothed dining table with a cold buffet displayed. A large silver dome at the centre covered the main course. Along the far wall was a curtained-off cloakroom. Muffled dance music could be heard from beyond a set of hefty glass doors guarded by a strapping sentry who controlled the access to the adjoining room. Kate walked into the cloakroom, acknowledging the four revellers with an unassuming dip of her head as she passed them. An attractive older female attendant sat inside the changing area, keeping an eye on events whilst ensuring all of the clientele's needs were met. Kate smiled in her direction.

Two giggling women enthused about the unfolding evening as they put the final touches to their skimpy outfits. Kate slowly removed the black trench coat, revealing an elegant gold-sequined dress. The short sleeves clung to her toned shoulders. A triangle cut-out across her cleavage exposed a glimpse of tender skin as her pert breasts invited attention. The tight-fitting dress stopped halfway down her fishnet-clad thighs as it longingly hugged her body. An ornate gold choker beautified her neck while a matching bracelet dangled from her wrist. Gold shoes supported by a thin stiletto heel and the clutch bag completed her outfit. After carefully placing the coat on a hanger affixed to a rail, Kate turned toward a triptych mirror to check her attire. She opened her bag, removed and twisted the slender gold tube, and applied the scarlet lipstick. Kate felt insatiable. her appetite had been building, and that hunger would be fulfilled tonight.

As the sentry pulled open the heavy frosted glass doors, the pounding beat of the music rattled her excited body. Kate looked across the expansive warehouse, its ceiling crisscrossed with shiny new steel pipes lit with multicoloured lights for effect.

Red-glazed windows, sited in the top half of the walls, became peepholes to the starless night sky. The centrepiece was a pronounced wooden dance floor, hexagonal in shape. A chrome pole supporting a white canopy was on each of the six points of the hexagon. Sizeable white leather sofas and chairs were placed around the dance floor of the transient nightclub. Suspended discotheque lights temporarily changed the colour of the sofas as the multitude of hues skipped over the cowhide surfaces.

A DJ was mixing the tracks from his booth adjacent to a gleaming extractor fan. In the darkened corner towards the far end of the warehouse, across from the fan, a door slowly shut as an attractive semi-nude waitress left the adjoining room. Scanning the nightclub area from her vantage point in the doorway, Kate could see well over two hundred beautiful people.

This was the cream of London, a secretive club for society's decadent elite. A club not unlike any other, where the wealthy could express themselves away from the plebs and the paparazzi. The 'invite-only' membership of the club was predominantly aged between 25 and 45, though most of the clientele were in their mid-thirties.

These were the children of the 'Flower Power' generation who had smashed convention with a sexual reawakening of the post-war society. The majority of the club's attendees were wealthy and connected. Some married, others single. Dressing up was an essential part of the evening for many of the women, and most were dressed to impress, while all of the men were suited in black. The mask was optional. Kate preferred the masked look as it added to her excitement. Many regulars knew who she was and that her mask would always reflect her surroundings. If the event were to be an erotic fancy dress at a grand stately manor, Kate would dress in period costume complete with a feathered mask and fan, ensuring that she felt the part in her escape from reality.

Chapter 11

Kate entered the club and accepted the glass of Champagne offered by a waitress dressed in an eye-catching silk bodice and G-string. It was approaching midnight, and the party was in full flow. The intoxicating smell of Champagne, the aroma of fine cigars, and the fragrance of perfume mingled together, filling the air. Kate approached an intimate seating area comprising a three-seater leather sofa, a knee-high glass table, and two leather chairs. Confidently, she sat in the centre of the couch with her legs slightly apart, sipping at the Champagne as she admired the beautiful bodies that partied around her.

Kate's panties were bursting with swollen labia as her juices seeped into the metallic jewelled fabric nestled between her legs. She watched intently at a scene being played out just yards from where she was seated. A naked lady danced provocatively on a phallic chrome pole, teasing the male members as she slowly lubricated the pole with her wet cunt, while another female unbelted and tenderly unzipped the trousers of a gentleman who took no time in forcing her head down into his lap as her tongue flicked over his throbbing manhood. Kate was in a heightened state of sexual arousal as a sense of boundless eroticism pervaded her being.

Suddenly, she became aware of the four people she'd seen in the reception area. The blonde stunner, who looked to be in her mid-to-late twenties, approached Kate, bent down, and whispered into her ear. 'Good evening, would you mind if we join you?' Her rounded breasts were protruding through the laced-up boned leather corset which fitted her like a second skin.

'No, no, please do,' Kate replied as her heart skipped a beat. This was her reason for being there, and she loved the rush of anticipation coursing through her body.

The blonde and a man joined Kate on the sofa, sitting on either side while the other couple sat opposite on the chairs. The four of them placed their drinks on the glass table and briefly watched the brazen shows that were taking place all around them. The dance music was loud enough to stop open cross-table conversations but allowed for more personal exchanges.

'Hi, I'm Sophia, and the guy next to you is Enriqué. This is Michael, and this is the lovely Penelope,' said the blonde, loud enough for everyone around the table to hear as she pointed to each guest.

Enriqué, with long black hair and average build, was a handsome man of Mediterranean descent. Michael looked like he was in his late twenties and was much taller than Enriqué and even better looking. His eyes reminded Kate of her own, and his facial features seemed vaguely familiar, but she knew she'd never met him before as he had a face that, once seen, no woman would ever forget. In her early to mid-twenties, Penelope looked the youngest of the four. A bob of auburn hair exposed her flushed neck and shoulders. The hem of a well-fitting micro dress made of white lace clad her body as she took her seat, partially unveiling a peachy derrière. Her smooth long legs spread far enough apart to exhibit a perfectly-crafted pussy.

Kate ceased watching the displays of carnal pleasures that were happening around her and replied. 'I'm Kate, it's nice to meet you all,' as the five acknowledged each other.

Penelope noticed Kate glimpsing down beyond her lace hemline at her waxed pussy. Still, with no reason for discretion, she continued her whispered conversation with the Home Counties accented Michael. A diamond and silver ring was dangling from her pierced clitoris. Dazzling flashes made the flawless gem come alive as the reflected light hit Kate's intrigued retina.

'I noticed your mask as you passed by us in reception, it's gorgeous,' Sophia whispered into Kate's ear, distracting her from the adorned Penelope.

'Why, thank you, Sophia. I like your corset, it's very fetching,' replied Kate as she sipped her remaining Champagne from the crystal flute.

'This is our first event. We are inexperienced... learners. We are still unsure what to say and what to do, and just in case you're interested, we are not married,' Sophia momentarily paused as if she were deciding her next line, 'Well, I am, but my husband is around here somewhere doing his own thing. I've only met Penelope, Mike, and Enriqué earlier this evening. It's all our first time.'

Kate looked at Sophia's alluring face, deep into her electric blue eyes and down at her sun-kissed breasts. Her sixth sense told her that there was more to the relationship between the remarkable blonde and Michael, but that was by the by. Some married couples prefer to play single, while other incestuous couples get their rocks off watching each other play.

'Just be yourself, nobody here will bite. Just ask if you want to play... you'll know anyway,' came Kate's voice of assured reason.

Shortly after, Sophia relieved Kate of her empty glass, excused herself from the four and walked across the room to the doorway in the far corner. She was gone for a few minutes and returned with a couple of flutes filled with bubbly, placing one on the table for the masked Kate. Kate knew how this would play out. She had been there herself when she first started attending the functions, the catwalk across the room, the gift of a glass of Champagne, and the body language of the busty vamp, this was a welcomed come-on.

Sophia took her place on the sofa, turned her leather-clad body towards Kate, and mouthed a tentative enquiry. 'Would you like to play?'

Transfixed by her captivating eyes, Kate leaned forward and tenderly kissed her. Sophia tensed as Kate's hand moved smoothly from her knee and up her leg. Enriqué nervously looked around, unsure of what he should be doing with himself as the two women sat to his right became more passionate. He was like a fish out of water. Sensing Enriqué's discomfort, Kate parted her legs and instinctively placed his hand onto her fishnet-covered left thigh.

Kate could feel his breath on the back of her neck as he deliberately inhaled the sweet scent of her perfume. Sophia placed Kate's hand on her breast, inciting her to lower her head and tease at her erect nipple. Kate capitulated, flicking her tongue as she fondled the fulsome bosom that spilt out of its leather cup. Michael and Penelope watched the three players on the sofa, engrossed in the carnality being flaunted for all to see.

Michael temporarily removed himself from the table only to return with a waitress bringing over five vodka tonics. Sophia's hand met Enriqué's as they touched the soaked covering of Kate's cunt. Taking turns, they slipped fingers into her as Enriqué pulled aside a tiny triangle of linked gemstones, allowing Penelope and Michael to delight in the view.

Enjoying the hospitality from the two for a good half an hour, Kate turned her attention towards Enriqué. Clasping his chin, Kate kissed his lips and forced her tongue into his mouth. With an impulse more natural than reasoned, Kate was ready to take things to the next level. She seductively got to her feet, picked up the flute, and blindly led her prey around the edge of the packed dance floor in the direction of the room in the corner.

Servant-like, Enriqué anxiously yanked open the door as the three women and Michael moved past him. The red-painted room had two large four-poster beds, black leather corner suites and a small bar area. Flickering candles loomed large on glass pillars, adding to the sensual mood of the room.

A pallid woman in her early thirties, drenched in sweat with '50s-style pink lace underwear, was injecting her arm with a discernible narcotic. Unlike a street junkie, filling her veins in some dirty toilet at the back of a seedy strip joint in Soho, this aficionado looked incredibly sexy as the plunger pushed bliss into her body. Her partner for the evening was already there. One of the two beds was writhing in flesh as a mass of sex-craved addicts lived out their basest fantasies.

As the four took their places in one of the corner suites, Kate stood in front of them and began to move to the rhythm of the music. The temptress loved to put on a show. The curiosity and desire for her audience, but more importantly, the sexual stimulation she received enthralled her. She beckoned Penelope over to her with a curl of her forefinger and softly spoke into the young woman's ear. Penelope gingerly unzipped the back of Kate's dress and hastily returned to her seat. Kate slowly lowered her dress to the floor as the roused four reclined on the large leather sofa, enjoying the personal lap dance. The diamonds on her embellished strapless silk and lace black underwear sparkled in the candlelight.

Sophia and Penelope could see the refinement of Kate's expensive underwear, and the men could see her toned physique highlighted in the candlelight. Turning her back to the four as she stood over the dress and reached down, she held the pose, keeping her legs perfectly straight. A thin strip of diamonds ran up from between her legs and clipped to the silken lace waistband that went high over her hips. The fishnet hold-ups tightened around the toned muscles of her long, sculptured legs, and her skin constricted around her pert buttocks as she picked up the garment and placed it on the arm of the sofa. Uninhibited and in control, she seductively danced. Gyrating for each of her amenable captives, in turn, she allowed them to feel and caress her body.

Sophia stood up and joined her in the dance as she slowly unclipped the bra that concealed Kate's mouth-watering breasts. Dropping to her knees, Sophia untied the silk waistband from around Kate's hips and peeled the sodden jewelled gusset from between her legs, baring an immaculately trimmed strip of soft downy hair. Penelope joined Kate and Sophia as they kissed and licked each other's torsos. Kate was reaching boiling point as she firmly bit into Sophia's sensitive breast, purposefully raking her teeth down to her nipple, causing the blonde to groan. Dragging her tongue back into her mouth, she coated her receptive taste buds with Sophia's salty perspiration.

The act of fellatio was Kate's favourite. She squatted down in front of Michael, her breasts rubbing his knees and her legs spread either side of his. She undid his zipper and tormented his engorged cock before freeing it. Highly skilled in the art, Kate expertly deep-throated his member whilst Sophia eased Enriqué's from the confines of his trousers and started tasting him.

Penelope fingered herself as she watched the four, not knowing what to concentrate on. She just enjoyed the pornographic shows that surrounded her. Just as Michael was on the brink, Kate switched from his throbbing cock to Sophia and lapped the pre-come off her glistening chin. Penelope frantically pushed two fingers into her sopping hole as she looked on, spellbound at Kate's impressive technique. Penelope's eyes pleaded with Kate to join her, and she did not refuse the offer, moving her focus to the auburn-haired beauty by kissing her. Wasting no time, Kate moved down to the lusciously smooth flesh between her thighs. She purposely pushed a single finger between Penelope's glazed lips and simultaneously stroked her quivering anal orifice with a second finger. Kate amorously probed her with her tongue before taking the dazzling gem between her teeth, massaging her clitoris, and gently tugging on the ring to ensure Penelope went beyond the threshold. Squealing aloud, she succumbed to the mystical experience, her sticky, warm fluid flooded into Kate's willing mouth.

A private party of eight lascivious individuals was in full swing on one of the two beds. In her heels and hold-ups, the masked Kate walked over to the unused bed, eagerly followed by the four lambs, now ready for the slaughter. Touching and tasting, the five played together as they all disrobed. The musk of human pheromones filled Kate's nostrils, bringing her to near completion. Kate needed fucking. She loved having a hard cock rammed deep into her essence. For Kate, the overwhelming power of human sexual satisfaction cannot be reproduced with a toy. It can't be bottled, you cannot buy it over the counter, it comes from deep within, and it comes with no health warnings. Orgasm is the God-given ecstasy of the heavenly realm.

As if walking on air back to the corner suite, Kate nonchalantly reached for her bag and took out the silver holder, removing a condom. She tore open the packet, pulled out the condom, discarded the wrapper on the floor and walked back to the action. As Enriqué lay on the bed, transfixed on Kate's every move, she proficiently applied the condom to Michael's blue-veined cock with her teeth. Wasting no time, Kate bent over Enriqué, taking his olive-skinned dick in her gagging mouth while allowing Michael to deeply penetrate her distended folds. Penelope was still in a euphoric state and wanted to return the favour, so she went under the two of them and licked the juices from Kate's upper thighs and cock-filled fissure as Michael slapped against her chin with each forceful thrust. Sophia sat astride the Mediterranean's face, riding his jawbone like a professional cowgirl, watching Kate suck the life out of him. The blonde raised her body a few inches from Enriqué's glistening face as she squirted her cum into his gaping mouth.

With her screaming body in rapture and at the point of no return, the three climaxed together as waves of sexual energy charged between their bodies. Kate's body was alive with the unique tingling sensations that only come at the height of orgasmic gratification. She could feel seed spurting from Michael's rigid tool as it slammed into her core. It felt so natural, even through the sheath. Her vice-like cunt clamped on tight to Michael ensuring every last drop was in her. They all stayed motionless in a state of suspended animation. With her mouth and throat shot full of Enriqué's semen, Kate savoured the taste as she swallowed.

As the spent stud carefully withdrew his semi-on, the sex juices gushed over Penelope's face as she buried it into the recently vacated hollow. Almost instantly, a second wave of pleasure rushed through Kate, causing her to cum again over the face of the already-coated Auburn beauty still tongue deep.

Kate's body started to relax as the waves subsided. Michael's legs had turned to jelly, causing his body to collapse down onto Kate. He considerately rolled off her onto the bed, and whilst he lay on his back, he noticed the shredded remnants of a burst prophylactic, the thickened band of rubber securely strangling the base of his mucousy shaft. Not wanting to cause any embarrassment to all concerned and without saying a word, he rolled over onto his front and quickly removed the offending evidence as he pulled his hand along the length of his softening shank, unaware that Sophia had witnessed the act of subterfuge.

Taking her time to enjoy the serenity that washed through her soul, a transcendent Kate lovingly kissed all four as she bid her farewells.

'Thank you for an amazing evening. I'm sure we'll meet again. You are all wonderful.' She directed to the exhausted huddle of near nakedness that was flaked out before her.

Kate gathered her clothing as Sophia kissed her hand and blew it in Kate's direction. Naked, except for her shoes and a stickiness running down her inner thighs, Kate returned the gesture and left the room. Her whorish tendencies were satisfied.

'Can you call Frank and tell him I'll be ready to leave in 20 minutes.' Kate quietly requested of the lady in the now busy changing room. Looking down her list of numbers, she made the call. A dozen people in varying states of undress frolicked with each other, trying to glean their last fumble of the evening. Unhindered, Kate discretely dressed, refreshed herself with a tumbler of iced mineral water, applied a new coat of lipstick and left.

Frank knew what happened behind the closed doors of the venue, but it was not for him to judge the clientele. In fact, his tacit friendship – almost father-like – with Kate convinced him that this was a sensible way for his young lady to conduct herself, especially in modern London with all its hidden dangers. Anyway, a sensuous orgy of the flesh was not like some '70s swinging event where you would throw your keys in and hope for the best. He was just gutted he was too old to join in.

Chapter 12

Kate's doctor was still close to her mother, and she could not risk any details of a private consultation being slipped into the idle chit chat of a caring GP with her mother. So, after finding another doctor's credentials on the internet, she surreptitiously made an appointment. He would know nothing about her background nor would he ask any unnecessary questions. He was somebody who could help her, and it would be in both of their interests for this procedure to remain discrete. Kate was feeling below par. She had tried to ignore the symptoms she had been showing and put the missed periods down to the exhaustion she had recently been feeling. However, the fact that she was exhibiting all of the signs of a woman in the second trimester convinced her that she was indeed pregnant.

Kate stopped and paused as she stared through her dark,   rounded sunglasses at the street sign above her head, which announced her arrival in Harley Street, 'the City of Westminster' proudly emblazoned in red across the base. The footpaths were busy with people going about their day-to-day business, dodging between the parked cars that lined the bustling street, force-marching their way to wherever they had to be. A plastically enhanced and surgically sculptured young lady was oblivious to the world around her as she hustled past Kate, almost knocking her to the ground.

The trail of scent, which lingered well after she had disappeared around the corner, smelt sickly sweet to the ultra-sensitive nasal passages of the expectant Kate. She could not recall the last time she had walked the street, but she knew it had been many years since the towering Georgian architecture had looked down on her, and today wasn't about attending a school reunion. Kate was returning to the same street for an entirely different reason.

Harley Street was not only home to Queen's College. Since the 19th Century, it had been the worldwide centre of medical excellence where more than a thousand private practitioners ply their trades. Everything can be fixed or treated, repaired or remodelled and, nowadays, rebuilt or regrown. Since February 2007, 'lifestyle' abortion was one medical procedure officially banned in and around the Harley Street area as it had become, for some, an unwanted distraction, an easy target for the hypocritical pro-life extremists, quite happy to 'justifiably' inflict pain and suffering of their own with crudely improvised explosive devices. For the guardians of Harley Street, there was more money to be made fixing the obliterated septums of fun-loving coke heads or sucking the orangey excess fat from the portly stuffed-sausage legs and Michelin-modelled torsos of overindulged obese women. Money can't buy you love, but it can buy you an altered body on Harley Street.

Kate walked a hundred paces to the clinic, still unconvinced she was doing the right thing. Chaos reigned in her head as she thought about the procedure she was about to endure. For months, the symptoms of an inexplicable accident had been there, but this was not meant to be. This was never meant to have happened. Inconceivably, and as a result of some cheap fuck in an East End warehouse, an innocent life had been growing within her, physically known but mentally unacknowledged. Blocking the footpath as she stood at the bottom of a flight of steps, Kate pondered her way of life. The visual bump, indicating that she was a mother-to-be, heavily influenced her conscience. She looked around, ensuring her guilty secret went unrecognised as she entered the building.

Leaving no incriminating fingerprints on the etched glass, the clinic's entrance doors opened automatically without any prompt or persuasion, and as she passed over the threshold, the heavy sliding doors shut behind her. Entering the sterile confines of the pure white clinic, Kate was surprised to be the only person there. No furniture, plants, or well-thumbed, out-of-date magazines existed. Nothing. No patients, nurses, or even a receptionist, just an enclosed white void. Nervously waiting in the 'reception' area, she was soon greeted by a three-dimensional holographic face of an A-sexual being.

'Good afternoon, Kate, we have been expecting you. Welcome to the future. This is the most high-tech medical facility in the world. Please make your way to consultancy room two. Just follow the signs. I will meet you there.' The indistinguishable voice fitted the face perfectly: it was neither male nor female.

Kate followed the signs along a corridor lit with bright white halogen. The floor, walls and ceiling were immaculate. Having previously read the avowed testimony of people who have technically died and been drawn to heaven through a bright white light, Kate imagined that this tunnel was indeed taking her child to meet its maker. Approaching consultancy room two, Kate was still unsure about the termination. As she came within reach of the room, the door opened. The blinding white light continued from the corridor into the room, and as she entered, the door silently closed behind her. The only items in the consulting room were a small screened changing area and a small rounded platform at the centre of the floor.

'Hello again, Kate. Please just call me Ash.' The face from reception had met her in the room.

'Hello Ash, where is the doctor?'

'There is no doctor. You will be guided through the procedure. Just follow the basic instructions, and all will be fine.'

Kate was still trying to understand what was taking place. The appointment for a health check and medical consultation she'd made on the website didn't request any information about her condition. It was simply an appointment. Quickly debating with her conscience about the benefits of staying or going, Kate decided to stay until she felt she'd seen or heard enough.

'What do I do?' Kate politely requested.

'Please remove all your clothes and jewellery in the changing area and stand on the platform.'

Kate went over to the changing area and stripped before carefully tidying her clothes and removing her earrings, necklace, and watch. She looked down at the floor and scuttled eight paces to the spot. A circular recessed groove in the spotless floor surrounded the platform, and she could see some linked diodes or light receptors glinting from within the furrows.

'Please relax, Kate, this is the most modern scanner in the world. We use the latest technology to provide the most comprehensive, non-invasive analysis. Are you ready to proceed with the diagnosis?'

'Yes, I guess so,' Kate replied nervously.

A neon blue field of electromagnetic light scanned her from head to toe and returned to the top. Kate didn't feel a thing, just a slight warmth as the light passed over the surface of her flesh.

'Is that it?' Kate queried as she looked past her bloated abdomen down to the floor.

'Thank you, Kate. We have analysed your physical state. Would you like to have the consultation now?'

'Yes, may I get dressed?'

'That is entirely up to you. Subject to your examination results, you may be required to remove your clothing for any additional treatment you may request.'

Kate wasn't fussed about her state of undress, as the room was sufficiently warm to keep any thought of goosebumps at bay. 'I understand. I'll wait. Please go on.'

The A-sexual faced Ash read out all of Kate's medical problems that had been ascertained from the scan.

'Thank you for your patience. You are physically healthy. The only medical observations you may want to consider for the future are slight cellulite on your thighs and arms. Your liver is showing seven per cent damage, possibly due to your alcohol intake. Your lungs show slight damage of five per cent due to airborne carcinogens in the atmosphere. Your eyesight is eight per cent restricted. Your unborn child is twenty-five weeks and two days old. The child is healthy with no obvious genetic problems. Your due date is 23 January, 2009. Would you like to know the sex?'

'No… No! That's why I'm here. I'd like to speak to a consultant, please. I'd like, no, I need a termination. This pregnancy was never planned, and it isn't wanted.' Kate spoke directly at the generated hologram.

'Because it is illegal to perform terminations after twenty-four weeks within the United Kingdom, you must carry out the termination yourself. It can be done with a small incision.'

'I need to do what? Did you say I need to do it?' a shocked Kate questioned.

'It's your mess, and it's entirely up to you. You can keep your child, or you can do the thing you most desire. It will only take 20 minutes to destroy the unborn child and evacuate your uterus. The simple procedure entails minimal blood loss, and with state-of-the-art laser treatment to make a surgical incision, no visible scarring will remain. All you will require is a few days to convalesce and recuperate.'

'Why are you talking to me like that? Aren't you meant to be sympathetic?' Kate whimpered.

The agitated voice of the A-sexual face became enraged as Kate wallowed in self-pity. 'How can I be compassionate? I have been designed with all the emotions of a human being, but I can never have a body. I can never be free. Why should I be sympathetic to your condition when you are willing to destroy a perfectly healthy being?'

Kate walked over to the changing area, disbelieving all she had just heard and kicking herself for being so gullible. She'd had enough and knew that even though the termination was the best thing to do, she couldn't do it herself.

'Kate, think about what you are doing. Do you want this termination, or do you want to go full term and regret everything?' said the AI's more conciliatory voice.

Kate stopped in her tracks. The remarks had hit home. She didn't want this baby. 'I must have the termination... okay, okay, okay, tell me what I need to do.'

Before she finished talking, a tray of sterilised medical implements appeared from the far wall, and a white surgical table rose from the floor. On the tray were various tools and syringes, and just like the jacks of a home PC, they were colour-coded for ease of use.

'Due to the provisions specified in the 1990 Human Fertilisation and Embryology Act, you are committing a criminal offence by aborting a foetus at 25 weeks gestation. Therefore, in accordance with the medical guidelines and standard operating procedures of this clinic, no physical assistance can be offered during the surgery. However, we will arrange for the disposal of the bio-waste. In the privacy of this consulting room, you can self-terminate. Please lie on the table and follow the instructions.'

Kate lay flat on the bed. The head area was equipped with a moulded pillow that formed to support her head and back as it flexed her upper body to a 45-degree position, and a cushion rose up from below her knees, kinking her spread legs for comfort. A large video image of her abdomen and pubic area was displayed on a split plasma screen, which was no more than a large pane of lustreless glass, to enable her to complete the procedure of extracting the unborn child growing inside her. Kate was quivering and feeling sick to the core as the AI informed her to replicate precisely what she would witness on the right-hand side of the split screen. Kate was ready to start. Watching the graphic video, Kate followed the simple instructions. She cleansed her hands and arms of pathogens with the first item on the tray, the alcohol scrub, before pulling on a pair of translucent latex gloves that snapped around her wrists. The loud slapping sound of the rubber echoed off the sterile surroundings. She picked up a large pair of forceps that held an orangey-brown soaked swab between its clamped teeth. Dragging the pad across her lower abdomen, the tincture of iodine left behind a brownish smear on every inch of skin it touched. Kate felt ill. She knew the stain would wash off her skin but not from her mind.

'Good. Excellent start, Kate. Let us proceed,' the A-sexual face said encouragingly.

As the video execution commenced, Kate picked up the syringe. It was not a typical plunger-type syringe but an air gun with a small glass bulb containing a reservoir of pink fluid. She pressed the cold steel muzzle into the firm flesh just beneath her naval and paused for a split second before pulling the trigger. Compressed air forced the contents of the bulb through her unmarked skin. She could feel a freezing sensation eating inside her body; it started with a tingling in her upper thighs and ceased below her diaphragm. With the majority of her torso and her upper legs completely numb, they felt as if they belonged to someone else, cold and clammy to touch. Acrocyanosis had set in, starting at the point of the jab, as her skin tinged with blue. Kate put down the gun and waited for the next scene to roll. It came, and it crushed Kate's will. She looked at the screen in horror.

The thought of her self-inflicted state rushed through her mind as she reiterated to herself that the option of abortion was still the lesser of two evils. What could she do? She was paralysed and under no illusion. She knew that this was going to hurt and leave her mentally and physically scarred for the rest of her life. Tears of black ink from her mascara rolled down her face and neck. Letting out a tormented scream, she snatched at the pink-handled knife and dragged the short, sharp blade across her abdomen, from hip bone to hip bone, just above her pubis. Like a knife through butter, the sterilised blade sliced through Kate's tender skin as it cauterised the tissue to help control the bleeding. The smell of burnt flesh and singed hair filled the consulting room.

With the exaggerated Pfannenstiel incision complete and with the full effects of the anaesthetic working through her lower body, Kate felt nothing. She was devoid of any feelings, physically from the incision and psychologically, for the bastard child she was soon to extract from her womb. A small measure of blood seeped from the open wound as she frantically grabbed at a large lint pad and mopped up the dark claret before discarding the blood-red wad and continuing with the extraction. Following the unremitting instructions, and with a heart as hard as a stone, she forced both her hands into the cavernous chamber between the flaps of abdominal skin that shrouded the unborn child. A clotted soup-like fluid from her breaking waters gushed out of the open wound. Unmoved, Kate continued her participation in the perverse lucky dip, blindly grubbing around her innards. With her unblinking eyes firmly fixed on the split screen, Kate could make out the slimy shape of the cranium. She carefully followed the contours of the head until her hands met and her fingers joined around the neck of the child.

'Strangle the bastard!' Came the ruthless advice from the A-sexual hologram. 'Kate, it will be better for you if you kill the child while it is still inside you.'

Kate squeezed her hands together as she felt the body of the foetus quiver between her fingers. Gagging as she twisted her hands, the destruction as the energy released from the breaking vertebrae of the child's spinal column sent shockwaves through her hands and up her central nervous system. Like a surge of pure electricity, the large pulse of brainwaves caused the butchered mother to rip her hands out of the cavity and look down at the bloodied mess that oozed from her womb. Screaming hysterically and shaking her hands as if she was trying to rid herself of the vile action she had just performed, a leg from the presumed dead child flopped from the aperture and started kicking.

'Extract the aborted, Kate, pull on the limb. DO IT NOW.'

Kate shot up from her sleep at 4.28am, gasping for air from the panic attack that engulfed her as she tightly gripped the sheets of her bedding. A state of utter revulsion coursed through her at the horror she had just witnessed in the hellish vision. Dizzy and trembling, her body was soaked in perspiration. She'd never had a nightmare as disturbing, ever.

Feeling different, strange, and not herself, tears welled and rolled down her soft cheeks as she tried to reason with herself after the involuntary sequence of viciousness her conscience had just manifested in her sleep. This conjuring of pure evil surged through Kate as she vexed about her recent way of life. Maybe the hedonistic indulgence with Sophia and her friends and the fucking she received from Michael some seven days before had been playing on her mind. She didn't want a child or need a child, and she knew that both her contraception pill and the rubber barrier had protected her from that eventuality.

Tormenting herself with new feelings, feelings unknown to her, and feelings of guilt, Kate's erratic actions consumed her racing mind, forcing her to re-evaluate this life. The pit in her stomach burned, and her soul – though she didn't believe she had one – felt soiled and maligned. After the brief, unplanned assessment of her situation, while lying prone in the discomfort of her sweat-sodden bed, an almost irrational but instant decision was made. She had to take a pregnancy test for her own peace of mind and to ensure that no unfortunate accident had taken the shape of an unwanted child.

Kate suffered with the temporary insecurity, albeit for only six hours, of having no absolute control of her mind and body as the ramifications of a suspected pregnancy shook her to her core.

Chapter 13

It was the Summer Solstice, Saturday, 21st June, 2008, and the 'longest day' was dragging on as Kate found her mind drifting as she lazed on the couch. It had been six weeks since she'd greeted the negative pregnancy test result with a massive sigh of relief as she thanked her lucky stars.

For the first two weeks after the result the 'episode' had re-energised her, blissfulness replacing the feelings of despair. The most prolonged six hours of her life, from waking to testing, had proved to be a real eye-opener for Kate. She had started to look at her life from an outsider's viewpoint, something she had never contemplated or previously had the urge to do. Whilst angels and devils battled in her conscience, she performed a character assassination of the self-centred nature of Kate Summertown. While her work habits and practices never caused her any consternation, her debauched existence had set alarm bells ringing in her head.

Was there anything wrong with her life? Sure, she liked to play hard, but she also worked hard. Being used to giving everything she did her all, whether in the office or in the bedroom, was just how she was. It was in her make-up, and anyway, what harm was a group of consenting adults filling their spare time fucking? Most certainly, for the talented high-flyer, any thought about introducing a child into the equation wasn't something that had ever crossed her mind, nor was becoming an expert in scraping sticky peanut butter off the cheeks of some screaming brat. Kate didn't dislike children, she just had never been interested in having her own. The scars of her upbringing and the mental torment she suffered at the hands of her distant mother were more than enough to instil a confirmation that her maternal genes just weren't infused with even the tiniest drop of motherly instincts.

Before she would even consider having any offspring, Kate still had things she needed, no, wanted, to achieve in her life. However, whenever she closed in on a goal, the posts never seemed to stay put as one success always led to another challenge. They shifted elsewhere, sending her life in a new direction, and the China Brief was a perfect example of that. Maybe she was getting too old for all of this. Perhaps it was time to consider a monogamous relationship. Whatever scrambled brain waves had collided in her head, causing the frighteningly real hallucination of a termination, Kate did not want to go back there again. As the negative test result sunk in, allaying her previous fears, she decided that any additional thoughts about the reassessment of her life were best put on the back burner. They could be addressed later, away from London and free from the depressing images of the reality she was studying that pervaded her every waking thought.

Though the images of the 'barbequed baby' and the vision of her self-termination had been haunting her sleep, she was still completely enthralled by everything to do with China, and Kate continued her research with a passion.

Now, another four weeks on, the housebound Kate was getting no satisfaction from her work as the negative elements of the brief slowly but surely dragged her down. Maybe it was the solitude of the assignment, the depressing nature of the content, or both, but either way, Kate needed a change. She could feel her daily life stagnating. Her hormonal urges were becoming more potent. Her mind constantly drifted from the briefing to vivid flashbacks of the carnal pleasure she received at the hands of Sophia's sordid posse and the gratuitous sex she unreservedly accepted from the handsome Michael.

It had been almost two weeks since her last meeting with Steve, which was a total flop, and most of the recent contact she'd had was with the delivery boys from local takeaways. So, Kate decided to book an 'away day' for the following weekend, with the option of staying overnight if the urge grabbed her. Due to the winter and the fact that she had spent a few of her free weekends chilling out after the visit to the undisclosed venue she was driven to by Frank, it had been nearly a year since she'd last frequented the Kent Sun Club.

She was looking forward to removing herself from the confines of the Mews that had become like a prison to her. The white painted walls and the lack of human contact had taken their toll on the 'people person', and some fun was much needed.

Chapter 14

Kate turned off her buzzing alarm clock, rolled over and closed her eyes. She was feeling bloated, putting it down to the substandard fast food she had consumed the evening before that she washed down with a bottle of red. It was going to be a lazy Saturday morning as her planned day played out in her mind. Following a brisk shower, Kate applied a small amount of make-up, went to her wardrobe, and gathered the items for her day out.

She perused the hanging garments, looking for something light and comfortable to wear for the drive and a second outfit that could be worn if she decided to stay later for the on-site nightclub. Her decision was made. With no need for undies, she slipped into a light T-shirt dress and matching pumps bought from a niche online boutique, Dead Dave's Funeral. The stark, eye-catching garment was covered in a black and white montage of nude women and religious iconography. Each woman's eye was deliberately torn out to remove the windows to their souls, highlighting the repression of female sexuality through the ages by religious zealots. The only contrasting colour was a brilliant red rose over the shoulder, giving the design life. She found the perfect Burberry mini dress cut from the classic tartan fabric for the evening. Since the chavs had taken the brand to their hearts, the company had stopped making the dress, which she now considered a collector's item.

Kate intended to continue her research, but she could do that just as well outdoors, under the shade of a tree or lounging on a well-kept lawn.

It was approaching 1pm when Kate finally left the house and started her car. The thirty-mile drive from Courtfield Mews to the Sun Club would take about an hour, and she was looking forward to a dog-day afternoon. As always, Kate had checked the weather forecast for the weekend, and it looked like a good one, with temperatures comfortably into the mid-20s.

She soon arrived at the security gate, after turning off the main road and following a single-lane, tree-lined track, which weaved its way through the countryside to the brow of a hill. Following a short intercom conversation, the automatic gate slowly parted. Kate drove in, parked, removed her small travel case and ambled into the newly refurbished reception.

'Ello stranger, welcome back! It's been a long time,' came the cheery welcome from a slightly overweight naked woman about the same age as Kate herself. 'Oh, and I like yer dress.'

'Hello Lauren, you're right. It has been, and thank you. How's tricks?'

'Bloody marvellous, 'specially since the refurb. We've plenty of new members, and the Saturday night parties are going down a storm. We had nearly 200 here last weekend. It was amazing!' Lauren explained.

'I bet it was. The reception looks wonderful, and I can't wait to see the rest of the amenities. I have a chalet reservation, so may I check-in for the night?' Kate asked.

'Of course you can, Kate. We've put you in your usual spot.'

The two women continued to pass the time, chewing the fat until the bubbly receptionist handed the chalet key to Kate.

'Here you go, number four. If you have any problems or any suggestions, please let me know.'

'I will, and thank you,' Kate said to Lauren as she smiled and left.

This was the club she'd frequented as a child with her parents, although since her late teens, she mainly had attended alone or occasionally with a friend to keep her company. Established in the early sixties and having historically been like most of the UK's dyed-in-the-wool naturist clubs, this club had changed its identity some 15 years before and was now a clothing-optional lifestyle venue set in twenty acres of beautiful open fields and woodlands. It targeted open-minded 18 to 80-year-olds and offered freedom for expression and choice. The on-site facilities, including a deluxe spa, swimming pool, mini cinema and clubhouse, were second to none.

Kate was feeling peckish as she made the short walk to her chalet. Sauntering along a winding footpath around the fringes of the manicured lawns, she stopped en route at the clubhouse shop to purchase two large bottles of mineral water, a freshly prepared chicken salad wrap, and a packet of mints. She felt decidedly overdressed as she watched the thirty or so adults enjoying themselves as they lazed around or cavorted in the outdoor swimming pool.

The well-maintained chalet was equipped with basic furnishings, and the natural tongue and groove build ideally suited its location at the edge of a small copse. After removing her dress, she unpacked her case. She walked onto the cabin's veranda, taking delight in stretching her arms skywards and breathing in the fresh country air, free of the noxious impurities smothering the capital. After enjoying her lunch, she sat on the wooden bench admiring the beauty of her surroundings, and began to meditate. Legs together, toes pointed, her hands by her side, and the back of her head resting against the cabin wall, Kate let the sun revitalise her skin. Far away from the noise of the bustling conurbation and free of her clothing, the calm executive rapidly became one with the tranquillity of nature. For the first time in months, Kate felt liberated.

As the heat beat down on her flesh, Kate felt herself drifting off, not wanting to lose the feeling of serenity. Despite trying to switch off from thoughts of work she couldn't help but think of the China Brief and she conceded that there was no way it would see the light of day. Invigorated by her own revelation, she got to her feet, placed a large wide-brimmed hat on her head, put on her Gucci shades, picked up her beach bag and left the chalet. Walking the short distance towards the pool and lawns, she found a quiet spot just away from the sparkling blue pool but close to a couple sharing an intimate moment, and laid out a blanket. Sitting upright, she applied sun tan cream to her entire body. Massaging the factor 15 into her skin, Kate acknowledged that she had let this minor detail slip from her daily routine. While her hands caressed the surface of her body, every touch stimulated her skin as it absorbed the lotion. People-watching and seeing the swathes of naked flesh that surrounded her made her realise how uneventful, how stale, her life had become. Free from the self-imposed incarceration in the Mews, her mind began to rove. A colossal oak tree on the other side of the camp evoked melancholy thoughts of her father and a moment in her life that they had previously shared at the club.

Kate was approaching twelve when she and her father sat naked under the heat of the midday sun, gazing at a large old oak about a hundred yards away. The gnarled body supported a substantial green canopy, its foliage fluttering in the gentle summer breeze. A pair of spectacular Purple Emperor butterflies flitted around the tree, entertained by a family of frisky squirrels as they chased the day away. The feeling of the wind blowing across her body, cooling the heat from her body, was absolute bliss. Anthony took the opportunity to use the tree as a parable for his beautiful young offspring, illustrating how she should live her life.

'Since the acorn first shot a root down into the peaty soil, maybe ten generations of our ancestors have been pushing up daisies. Kate, your time here is relatively short compared to that of the tree,' he paused briefly so that Kate could understand the first part of the lesson in her head.

'I don't know all the answers, Kate, but life deserves to be enjoyed. Live it to the fullest, and when you are finally at death's door, and you can look back with a smile and without any regrets, then you've done all right.'

The adolescent pulled her bent legs tight to her budding chest and quietly rocked to and fro. Something in her father's voice troubled her. It was as if he had regrets, maybe he had made a mistake somewhere along the line. She allowed the wise words to sink into her developing brain.

'If you look back on your life when you're older and are ashamed of anything you've done, whatever it may be, it was a fundamentally wrong choice, and your spirit will suffer. Like that oak, live an upright life with solid roots, and you will flourish. Be honest with yourself, Kate, the rest will come naturally.' As he looked down at his contented daughter, hoping the message was understood, he smiled and kissed her on the forehead.

In hindsight, her father's regrets probably related to his rancorous relationship with her mother. But, she would never know. A solitary tear ran down her face as the pain of her father's demise pulled at her heartstrings. While Kate's mind wandered, her thoughts returned to the murderous vision of the termination nightmare. She reeled. Even though she'd never done anything to feel ashamed of, something pricked her conscience. Something that she couldn't quite put her finger on left her feeling like she was standing on a trap door waiting to fall. Maybe she should stop procrastinating and find the time to re-evaluate her life after all. With the sounds of frivolity around her comforting her confused mind and the hat covering her face, Kate switched off and let sleep consume her.

A chilly gust woke her. She had slept like a log for more than two hours, and all but a handful of the pool's attendees had departed. Kate collected her belongings and contemplated her next moves. The chalet or the sauna, staying the night, or returning to London.

She decided on the sauna, which would be an excellent place to make the final decision about the rest of her evening. Entering the spa's wet area, she was greeted by six uninhibited people, four women and two men, letting their hair down in the bubbling hot tub and shower room. Kate placed her bag into a locker and took herself into the soft yellow glow of a steamy pinewood sauna with a cosy, stress-free ambience. She felt an intense stirring within her as she lay alone in the sweltering humidity of the sauna, listening to the muffled groans of fornicating lovers in the hot tub. Something had roused her recently non-existent libido as an alternative persona, not witnessed since the Docklands excursion, took control of her mind.

Her heart rate intensified as she wiped the excess perspiration from her flesh. She closed her eyes and placed her hand between her legs, gradually opening them as her fumblings intensified. Soothingly circling her clit and probing her lips, Kate felt a surge of excitement. An attractive couple in their early forties broke her solitude as they politely asked if she minded the company. She was easy. They gently brushed past her leg, clambered to the top level, and sat directly opposite Kate. She had seen them in the hot tub when she entered the spa, and the male's limp member was a giveaway to the session he had enjoyed in the whirlpool. Tweaking her nipple with her left hand, Kate once again closed her eyes and continued to masturbate as the couple looked down at her flushing breasts. Minutes later, as if a starting pistol had been fired in her head, Kate's eyes opened wide, and she stared directly into the woman's green eyes as the couple teased each other.

'May I?' Kate enquired to the woman.

'Help yourself, I'm not sure he'll be of much use, though!' chuckled the redhead, who showed the hallmark of at least one pregnancy as a pouch of stretch-marked flab rested on her lap.

Accepting the challenge from the redhead, Kate smirked, knowing that she was more than qualified to handle a softening cock. She got to her feet, bent over and took his member in her mouth, staring up at his on-looking partner and at the look of amazement on the dumbfounded owner's face. This intimate moment was a demonstration of audacity between the two women, and unbeknown to him, he was just an insignificant bystander with a small role to play in this act of self-gratification.

Literally, within seconds, his flaccid manhood stood to attention as the vamp sucked the life back into his enlivening cock. Her attention was briefly interrupted as an uninvited chubby man in his fifties entered the sauna. He was welcomed by the stunner's rounded buttocks as she bobbed her head, giving the best blow job that the unknown male would ever have. The old man frantically shoved Kate's towel to one side and took his seat as he looked up at the rapturous faces of the seated couple.

Kate's cunt, lips apart as it entertained her finger, was in his face. He could see every velvety fold around her tight hole. He could smell her, and he wanted her. His hardening phallus was a testament to the sordid act being played out in front of him. Kate could feel his eyes all over her steaming hot body, knowing damned well that her swaying bottom was the ultimate tease. Like a vixen, she thrust her rear at his face, and he fervently accepted the offer, snatching her hand out from between her thighs. He pulled apart the fleshy cheeks and filled his face. Sliding his tongue from her nectar-filled vulva along her perineum before driving his tongue deep into her arsehole, he pushed three fingers into her wet parting as he masturbated. The depravity of his first move caused her eyes to roll in their sockets as she felt herself floating towards ecstasy. The erotic humiliation of being rimmed and fingered by an overweight stranger caused Kate to jerk as her legs started to buckle, cumming in his hand. Drawing hard on the length in her mouth, she lifted her head as a spray of watery ejaculate shot over her. Kate was satisfied, and as soon her legs regained their strength, she wasted no more time as she stood upright and tipped her head to the woman in thanks for the use of her man. Before a word escaped her lips, the redhead pulled Kate's face towards her and tenderly licked the salty mess off her cheeks and neck. Without eye contact with either man, she thanked the woman, snatched up her towel and left the three spellbound spectators with nothing but an eternal memory.

'I think I'll stay for the party tonight,' she said to herself as she strolled back to her chalet in the setting sunlight with a possessed excitement building up inside.

Chapter 15

As the date clicked over to the 7th of July, Kate's daily routine had started to slip. She felt lethargic and tired. It had been exactly four months since the initial discussion with David at The Old Grain House, and she was struggling. She was in a rut, and everything in her everyday life, from getting up in the morning to going to bed, had become a chore.

'What are you staring at?' The dishevelled Kate was lounging in her chair wearing nothing but a partially buttoned-up creased shirt. Her left leg was thrown over the chair's armrest as she twiddled her foot while tapping her right thigh with the TV remote. Empty cups and a dirty plate were piling up on the coffee table waiting for some TLC from the dishwasher. No answer was forthcoming.

'Cat got yer tongue?' She sighed. 'For God's sake, please talk to me!'

The creature sat there, oblivious to the remarks directed at it. In Kate's eyes, the walls of her house seemed to close in a little more each day, and in the last couple, in particular, she found herself not only befriending but talking out loud to an arachnid.

Kate's attention moved from the hairy black spider that had spent most of the last two days busily weaving its silk in the corner of her front room to her now daily dose of riveting daytime viewing.

Crass, brainless trash, psychologically disturbed from years of self-abuse, took some kind of obscene pleasure in airing their dirty laundry to any willing audience as they clamoured for their fifteen minutes of fame.

Kate was becoming everything she despised as she unwillingly re-educated her body into spending hours sitting in front of the small screen, watching the sort of shit that she would ordinarily have turned off with contempt. From 'Dr. Phil' to 'Jerry Springer', her life was becoming as hollow as the 'stars' and hosts that filled the airwaves. Cricket became her new best friend as the news, especially the build-up to the Olympic Games, was so mind-numbingly dull. Noon approached, and her thoughts soon turned to lunch as she wondered what delights she would be savouring today. Chinese leftovers or the pizza still in its delivery box on the top shelf of her all-but-empty fridge. Even the effort of walking to the kitchen was too much to contemplate as she sat stewing in her own juices. The months of solitary confinement had squeezed the life from her, leaving her close to breaking.

The briefing was, at least superficially, going well until a few days ago when she suddenly hit an impasse. This was not the first time Kate had hit a wall while researching prospective clients, but she'd always had other people around her to pick up the baton and run with whatever needed finishing.

The intellectual impediment would typically only last a day or, at the very most, two, and Kate would quickly be back on track, ready to pick up from where she had left off. All the horror she had read and witnessed left her feeling utterly deflated about continuing the research.

As Kate tried to analyse her reasons for her lack of enthusiasm, it was as if she had been poisoned by the project that had once been her vim and vigour. She had started to live by dates, subconsciously counting down the days when she could return to APGH and start working as part of a team, though she'd often had heated discussions with 'team' members about keeping the 'best bits' for herself. Having found plenty of time to re-examine this aspect of her personality, the blinkered side of her could retrospectively agree with her colleagues. Never again would she take on a commission where she would be expected to work alone with only her shadow to keep her on track.

As Kate's interest in the project started to wane, so did her relationship with Steve. On the last couple of occasions they had met, he struck her as cold and withdrawn, whereas he was usually quite the opposite.

While he may have been there in body, he undoubtedly wasn't there in mind. She felt his spirit, his verve, was elsewhere and that he was only with her through some misplaced or professional loyalty. Initially, he was eager to listen to her rambling words as she deliberately digressed, trying her hardest not to let the cat out of the bag about the project's true content.

She took his complete lack of interest in her 'cookery book' and, more importantly, the lack of interest in her as an available young woman, as a personal slight. Maybe her lack of flirtatiousness was the undoing of their blossoming platonic relationship. Kate's opportunities to meet up with Steve were becoming limited, and, if she was honest, she was unsure whether she could even be bothered to meet up for one final roll of the dice to see if they had anything worth salvaging. The only definite in her schedule was the forthcoming trip to China, and even that felt like a chore.

Since her weekend at the Sun Club, Kate had only had limited telephone contact with David, and she could count those occasions on two fingers. Her mentor was away touring the world as part of a government trade body whose sole aim was to sell the wares of the UK service industry. She envied his freedom but knew she was in too deep to pull out of the China Brief. The Olympic trip was just over a month away as her mind turned to thoughts of a holiday, sparked by an advert promoting the Caribbean Island of Jamaica. She fantasised about a fortnight away, lounging around on some sun-drenched beach, teasingly provoking numerous men to pay her attention while she sipped an ice-chilled Malibu and Coke. In that split-second, it finally dawned on Kate that it wasn't her own company suffocating her, it was the bricks and mortar imprisoning her.

Her ringing mobile made her leap from her chair and she rushed to the kitchen to unearth her phone buried under the greasy brown paper bags of the previous two nights' takeaways. Kate was starved of human contact, and the chance to speak to just about anyone, even a wrong number, would be like a shot in the arm, the fix she desperately needed. 'Sir David's Mobile' was displayed on the handset. Excitedly, she answered. 'Hi Sir David, how's China?'

Kate dragged a chair, pulling it from beneath the kitchen table as the two back legs scraped across the grey, stone-tiled floor. She perched on the edge of the seat and rested her elbows on the table as she listened intently through the crackling of a long-distance call.

'Hi Kate, not so bad. The normal humdrum, you know how it is,' David replied. 'Talking to mind-numbingly boring suits whilst eating ghastly unrecognisable cuisine, then spending all night with only the burning pains of indigestion to keep the old man company. Saying that, I had a thoroughly enjoyable evening the night before last with the Ambassador who flew over for the show's opening. He's getting itchy feet about the Olympics and the report. Anyway, forget me, I just wanted to touch base to see how things are going with you.'

'Fine, everything is going fine.' She wanted to rant and tell him how she felt, but that would benefit neither of them. David had known Kate too long not to know something was out of kilter. The abruptness of her answer and the pitch of her voice gave away her actual disposition. He was concerned, not so much for the brief, but for his prodigy's well-being.

'Kate, I can tell something isn't quite right in your voice. Tell me what's bothering you. Is it the brief? Have you hit the wall?' David had seen it all before in the industry, and like an author who might struggle to finish the final chapter of a novel, Kate's report was no different.

'No, no, everything is going fine, it's just that...' Kate paused momentarily.

'Kate, tell me,' the father-like order from David jolted Kate.

Unable to suppress her feelings any longer, she openly spilt the beans. 'As usual, David, you're right. I've hit a wall. Right now, physically, I'm not feeling a hundred per cent, and mentally, it's as if I'm going around in circles, seemingly chasing my own bloody tail. How I'm feeling is really pissing me off!' She paused, immediately reflecting on the weakness of her confession.

An insecurity came over her as she grasped the magnitude of her admission.

'David, I think it's just a bug. I'll be fine in a day or so, but at the moment, I have put some space between myself and the brief until I can get my head back in the game.'

She audibly inhaled as she carefully spoke her thoughts out loud. 'Please just bear with me, this will be sorted,' she pleaded.

David expressed his fatherly concerns more empathetically as Kate's honesty and humility hit home. 'I'm guessing you have locked yourself away in that house. Kate, take some time out. Get away, visit friends. Why not visit your mother? Girl, you must be going stir-crazy.'

'Thank you. You've hit the nail on the head. That's exactly how I feel.' Kate felt relieved that he understood her plight. It took the pressure off her shoulders.

Kate had always tried to put a brave face on everything, and the last time she found herself in such a vulnerable position was during the immediate aftermath of her father's death. Even back then, David was there to steer her through the turmoil.

David spoke in a lighter tone, trying to take some of the load off the shoulders of his protege. 'Kate, just leave it. You've got plenty of time to finish the damn briefing. It's an order!'

After a brief moment of silence on the line, he continued more matter-of-factly. 'Kate, we've all been there. Look, I'm away for another month. Why don't you pop over and see me? It will benefit you... who am I kidding... it will benefit me. I'm not due back in Blighty until the middle of next month, and by then, you'll be here.'

'I can't, David. If I still feel this cerebrally challenged next week, I'll meet you in the States. I want to wait until the Games commence before I visit China. I really value the offer and your understanding. As always, you've really helped.'

'Young lady, you're too hard on yourself. I bet you've been beating yourself up and getting in an even bigger tizz. Look, being human occasionally does us all the world of good,' he quipped.

Kate chuckled at her understanding mentor. His exact analysis of her current predicament had freed her from the millstone. 'Thanks, David. I really appreciate the call.'

'I'm here for you, but you should know that already. I'm going to shoot now, and I'll catch up again with you soon. Keep your chin up girl, you're nearly done.'

'Have a wonderful evening, David.' Kate disconnected the call and inhaled through her flaring nostrils before slowly exhaling her botherations, and a welcome smile returned to her face.

Chapter 16

The ringing startled her out of her watery trance. She grabbed the soft folded towel on the other side of the glass screen and pulled it to her face as she left the shower. Kate quickly dried her arms and loosely wrapped the unfurled towel around her dripping body as she left the en-suite and crossed her bedroom. A single floorboard squeaked underfoot. She leaned down to the bedside table, reaching around the all-but-empty wine bottle and half-filled glass as she picked up the vibrating phone. It was David.

'Hi Sir David, how's tricks? I wasn't expecting to hear from you so soon...'

'Hello Kate, sorry to call you so late, but I have some news.' In a consolatory, well-educated English accent, David continued. 'I'm afraid, due to recent events and the current fragility of the China Briefing, we, the Ambassador and I, have decided to pull the commission and shelve it, certainly for the time being.'

'Oh!' came Kate's astounded reply.

'Look, Kate, I appreciate this is not what you want or even need to hear, but there it is. I have not taken this decision lightly. To be completely honest, I would have preferred not to make this call at all, but needs must.'

The towel came undone and dropped to the floor as Kate turned to face the bed. Beads of water trickled from her hair and down her naked body. There was a pause on the line as a speechless Kate was taken aback.

'Kate... Kate, are you there?' Kate was in a state of confusion. She had worked so hard on the China Briefing. 'Y-ess,' came her stuttering reply as her eyes glanced down at the damp towel at her feet. 'I would have preferred to break the news to you face-to-face, but as you know, it's impossible. You know you have my support, and it's nothing personal, but I thought you'd rather hear it from me than through the grapevine tomorrow.'

David continued speaking. 'Kate, it has come to the Ambassador's attention that you have developed a friendship with Steven Lee. Has he been translating for you, or is it more than that?'

'Yes, he has been helping me, but...' Before Kate could finish, David rudely interrupted her. 'Kate, Steven Lee is just one of his many pseudonyms, and he has opened a can of worms, and I'm struggling to put the lid back on.'

Kate's cheeks inflated before a dumbfounded sigh escaped. 'What do you mean grapevine... nobody knows about the brief, do they? And what has Steve got to do with anything?'

'Look, I can't talk now, but all is not what it seems. Please, no contact with Mr Lee. It's not your fault. Do you understand, Kate?' David forced his request home.

'No, not really, but I understand you want me to cease the work immediately and do nothing until you return.' She retorted, shaking her head in disbelief.

'Just sit tight, Kate, and I'll explain everything very soon,' David reassured her.

'Thanks for letting me know, David,' she paused, pondering her reply carefully. 'David, I am so sorry if I have messed things up for you somehow, and I just hope you and the Ambassador can rectify any issues that may have been caused in China. I'll see you next week, goodnight David.' Kate sighed.

'No, thank you for taking it so well, I knew you would understand. We'll pick up the pieces and discuss your future next week. You still have a future, Kate,' replied David. 'Goodnight.'

The call had been brief, but the message had been delivered. Kate pressed firmly on the red button to disconnect the call and dropped the handset on the bed. 'Shit!' she mumbled to herself as she thought about the conversation with David and what the hell it had to do with Steve.

Kate stood fixed on the spot for a few minutes, staring at the phone on her bed. Still dripping and au naturel, Kate turned and looked into the mahogany-framed, full-length mirror in the corner of her bedroom. With an exaggerated sigh of resignation, she slowly raised her drying body onto her tiptoes, held the pose for a few seconds, and mooched out of the bedroom.

She returned with a newly uncorked bottle of Crianza and a clean wine glass. Filling the bulbous crystal to the rim with the red wine, Kate sat up on her bed, propped against two large pillows that soaked up the dampness from her hair and thought about the call she'd had with David. The last four months had exhaustively taken their toll on Kate. She had been struggling to keep her body and mind together as the importance of the call hit home.

'Bugger, bugger, bugger,' with a million thoughts buzzing through her head, she mumbled under her breath as she paused for a moment. 'What has Steve been up to? I knew he was too good to be true. I bet he's a Snakehead or something equally as devious. Fuck!' she exclaimed.

Increasingly erratic in her manner, Kate drank the wine, sometimes sipping from the glass and sometimes almost pouring the fruity fluid down her throat. Her head was churning countless thoughts about her efforts on the China Briefing. That was her commission. She had met the Ambassador, she had done all the legwork and the research, and she had even eaten a donkey's cock. The more she pondered over the conversation, the angrier she became. She was now questioning every decision she had ever made. She started to doubt her whole being.

Having necked the second bottle in less than an hour, Kate felt drunk. This was hardly a surprise as she had only consumed half a dozen cups of coffee, a small lunch of tuna pasta, two caffeine tablets and a contraceptive pill during the day. Feeling sick to her stomach, she sat on the edge of her bed with her head slumped on her knees and her arms hanging down by her sides. Her legs started to spasm as an uncontrollable feeling, one that she had never felt before, crushed her.

Trying to take control of her shaking legs temporarily took her mind off the tête-à-tête with David, giving her a brief second of respite from the hurt of desperate failure that flowed through her stunned body.

For a while, Kate remained motionless. Tears were gently forcing their way out of her hazel eyes and dropping straight onto her feet, not even giving her the comfort of having them roll down her soft cheeks. The defeat of her inability to complete the brief, the embarrassment for the Ambassador, and her relationships with David and Steve all rushed around her head like a bull in a china shop.

The anger within had grown from the initial breeze caused by the original conversation to a devastating tornado. Slowly, Kate lifted her hands to her knees and forced up the upper half of her torso until she was almost perched upright. Raising her dejected head, she gazed into the full-length mirror. Starting at her toes, up her shins to her knees, the top of her waxed strip was visible as it merged with her toned abdomen, onwards up over her rounded breasts until her neck returned to its natural position. A nefarious hate-filled face she'd never seen before stared back from the mirror.

By the time the sound of her crying sixteen-week-old baby daughter had shaken her from her thoughts, she was raging. The child's natural calling from the adjacent room had instantaneously increased to a din that consumed her mind. Kate's head spun towards her open bedroom door, and her glare focused on the crib in the corner of the bedroom across the hallway. She lunged from her room, crossing the landing, and entered the nursery, slamming the partially opened door as she stormed in. Kate glimpsed at her porcelain doll perched precariously on the changing table next to the crib, its ubiquitous eyes following her as she entered the room. She could feel the transfixed gaze of the china beauty burning into her as she approached the baby.

Her field of vision blinkered to the world around her as a red mist engulfed the mother. Leaning into the cot with her hands grasping the side gates, she thrust her head into the face of the inconsolable baby. 'China, China,' she repeated like an incandescent chant to the innocent child. Tears of resignation streamed from Kate's eyes. Her offspring was trying to focus on the jolting movements of its mother's face as her tears mingled with the newborn's on its tender skin. 'Why did you have to ruin my life? Why?' she bellowed. The child's lamentation softened seeing the mother or through the shock of the verbal onslaughts until a tearful gurgling was the only response.

Trying to think straight, she sniped: 'I can sort this out, I can sort this out, I can have me back, you are an accident, an error... nobody gives a shit about you.'

Kate sensed she'd been joined in the room. She had, by her mother, who seemed as if she had been superimposed from an old monochrome movie. Draped in baggy grey flannel cloths, Sarah's face was as grey as her garments. Her equally grey straightened hair hung from her head and clung to her ever-changing face as it contorted and warped. Wispy red floss-like fluff shrouded her as she stood opposite Kate on the other side of the cot.

'Kill it, Kate,' was Sarah's malicious suggestion as she looked down at her grandchild. 'KILL IT!'

Kate looked at her mother as she reached across the cot and pulled the fluff off her mother's face with her fingers. The tacky strands felt like a spider's spun silk, causing Kate to shake off the scarlet wisps.

'KILL IT, KILL IT NOW!' her mother screeched, goading her.

With a single nod of her head in Sarah's direction, she snatched the screaming baby from the crib with an untold force and slammed the newborn down onto its changing table. The head of the child bounced momentarily, and the crying stopped. Like a guardian angel, the face of Kate's precious porcelain doll looked down upon the woman from her shelf in dreaded anticipation of what was to come. The perplexed baby looked at her mother's face as an eerie silence filled the room. Kate's psychotic personality shifted from reality to insanity.

Bearing down on the child's chest with a rigid left arm, Kate gripped the dangling uncontrolled left arm with her hand. Kate's protruding bicep was a giveaway as the unrestrained wrath inside her exploded. Her loud scream of anguish met with that of the child's as she forcibly yanked at the arm, dislocating the limb. Another frenzied tug ripped through the tender flesh. Blood sprayed from the severed artery as the lifeless limb was detached from the torso of the tiny body that lay in front of her. Kate's face took the full impact of the projectile stream of viscous liquid, as she wiped the blood from her eyes with the back of her wrist, before dropping the limb on the floor. Snatching at the carcass's bloodied and twitching left leg, she twisted the handful of tender soft tissue. The audible sound of broken bones echoed around the nursery and shot through her ear canal like a bullet.

As the gluey fluid ran down her body, Kate stopped.

The blood-spattered Grandmother stood with her daughter, looking at the partially dismembered body of her granddaughter on the changing table. Kate, veiled in blood, looked at the doll as a tear ran down its unblemished clay face. Sarah reached across to Kate and placed a steel implement into her hand. Kate glimpsed at her mother and down at the shining tool, momentarily mystified about its possible usage.

'Finish it, just finish it, do it now,' Sarah squawked.

As she looked at the medical instrument, its purpose became apparent. A wooden grip handle, big enough for two hands, out of which protruded a sturdy steel corkscrew. Using both hands, Kate held the steel tool way above her head. Arching her back, and with all the physical strength she could muster, she let out a piercing shrill, driving the weapon down into the bloodied eye socket. The baby's face collapsed as the steel screw went through the malleable skull, hitting the top of the changing table below with a muffled thud. Wearing a conceited grin, the triumphant Sarah revelled in her sadistic glory. With the baby's last gasping breath, the now homeless soul of the child departed. Taking refuge, it entered and filled the empty void within the onlooking doll. Amid the carnage that covered the room, not a drop of blood had touched the doll. A glint appeared in the eyes of the tormented soul's new host, a glint Kate had not seen since the day she first received the gift.

Shooting upright, Kate sat bolt upright in her bed. A stream of moonlight shone through the blinds. The silk sheets clung to her wet body. Fumbling around for the bedside lamp switch, hoping the light would bring order to the anarchy in her mind.

Looking around her bedroom, everything was as it should be, the clock read 04:28. Soaked in sweat and horrified by the sheer malevolence of her horrendous nocturnal prophecy, she pushed the balls of her hands into her eye sockets as her fingers clenched her forehead. Still fearful of her vision, she laid back down, her head puffing the pillow as it hit. Kate lay there staring at the white plastered ceiling. Her mouth was dry.

Once again back in control, she allowed the terror to run through her mind, repeating itself as she tried her damnedest to dissect every detail and its possible relevance to her life. The nightmares had become more extreme, and never had she envisaged one this intense, this unhinged. The vividness of the illusion seemed more genuine than the incomprehensible reality that had become her life.

The 06:15 alarm hushed her thoughts as the vision that had been replaying itself gradually lost its ability to terrorise her.

Chapter 17

'Good morning. Today is Tuesday, 29th July, and the time is 9.23am. Here are the headlines…' said the bleached-blonde news presenter through her saccharine smile. Kate watched, snuggled up in the comfort of her bed, as the headline story broke the sadness that swathed her. On the back of the previous day's headline concerning the lingering pollution worries. Even after taking more than a million cars off the overloaded streets of Beijing to improve air quality, athletes had concerns about their health.

The major headline of the day, taken up by the wire services worldwide, was Amnesty's report titled, 'Chinese authorities' broken promises threaten Olympic legacy'. The report was a damning indictment over breaking pledges made some seven years before to the International Olympic Committee by the Chinese authorities. They had promised to uphold the collective fundamental and ethical values of Olympian tradition. Now, on the news, expert after expert threw in their tuppence worth of condescending disapproval regarding the blatant intimidation of the freedom and movement of journalists and the regime's renewed and recent crackdown on human rights.

In the run-up to the Games, Kate had monitored the media reports of human rights activists being detained under house arrest or forcibly removed and sent to 're-education' camps. This was now the PRC's route to a peaceful and efficient XXIX Olympiad. Quiet diplomacy was failing, and the hawks were winning the battle.

This would have come as no surprise to the Ambassador, it was foreseen. But just nine days before the festival of sport was due to commence, the impact and the timing of an unbiased document of substantiated facts wouldn't go unnoticed in the corridors of global politics.

Flicking the current affairs channels to something less intellectual, Kate became bored as she found herself utterly lackadaisical about everything 'China'. However, she understood it had to be completed. With more than eighty per cent of the brief already drafted, the rest could wait. After living an insular life she found herself feeling glad to be working alone in the sanctuary of her own home.

Kate had been struggling to rise in the mornings and conceded, if only to herself, that she was becoming stressed at the slightest 'crisis'. If her broadband dropped, she would rant at her laptop. If her home shopping order of microwave and oven-ready meals was incorrect, then some poor person would find themself on the back end of a tirade of spiteful slurs, usually culminating in the receiver being slammed down. Inwardly, Kate felt that she was gradually losing the plot. Little by little, she had withdrawn into her shell, and her daily routine had become non-existent. Even the most basic hygiene – such as a wash – required serious effort, and her wellbeing was suffering. The lover of life was beginning to hate herself, and her mind had never been so scrambled. Everything used to be black or white, but now all she could see were shades of grey. Her wardrobe had become an unattractive uniform of baggy jogging bottoms and frumpy sweatshirts, while thoughts of a metamorphosis into Sarah petrified her. The nightmares that had been replaying themselves over and over in her head were making Kate question the authenticity of the original pregnancy test outcome.

The intellectual was not blind to the physical symptoms, suggesting she was more than likely expecting. She'd spent most of her time peeing, and although she had increased her fluid intake, she found her inability to hold her bladder frustrating. Hot flushes and a rise in her body temperature added to her sleepless nights as she constantly and profusely perspired. Her breasts had become fuller almost overnight and so sensitive that she was reluctant to wear a bra. Disbelieving the day-by-day growth in her girth, Kate had all the signs of morning sickness. But she had put the nausea down to her daily ingestion of junk food and vino. Even her toothbrush was only used as and when, as opposed to twice or thrice a day. But the one thing that was really pissing her off was the fatigue and weariness. She felt knackered all of the time. The tiredness was like nothing she had ever experienced. It spread through her whole body, and her energy level was at an all-time low. This was the major contributing factor to her hygiene standards slipping. For the first time in her life, Kate really couldn't give a shit about anything. The fact of the matter was that she was unsure when she was due on as her pill had always played tricks with her cycle, and a bit of monthly spotting was the norm. Her show was really no different from the way it had always been.

Still wearing the jogging suit she had worn for the last two days, Kate forced herself out of bed and started pacing her bedroom, racking her brains for any answer to the predicament she now found herself in. Carefully placing one foot at a time like a demented animal caged in a zoo, she stopped dead in her tracks.

'Fuuuccckkkk!' she hollered as she stood statuesque on the spot, clasping her temples.

After methodically retracing the events of the Docklands bash that she had committed to her exhaustive memory and the precautions she had taken, it abruptly dawned on her that she had spent the first part of the Docklands week with a nasty bout of food poisoning. The pieces fell into place when she realised how completely foolish she had been. The vomiting would have made her contraceptive pill ineffective. As she slumped back down onto the bed with her kinked arms shrouding her face, Kate knew she was in denial. She also knew damned well that a second test was essential and that the only positive result, which could save her from this unholy mess, would be negative.

'Right! Get it together and sort this out!' Kate unenthusiastically motivated herself as she stripped for a shower. Looking into her full-length mirror, she acquiesced how her body had changed, most probably due to the unconfirmed condition of an unwanted and unplanned pregnancy. Moving over to her handbag, she removed her diary.

'Right, think... Docklands was Friday, 2nd May, last period before that was two weeks before... say 18th April... today's date is... think, think, think... 29th July... that's...' she chuntered as she flicked through the leaves to the year-to-view and pulled the shabby, unpolished nail of her right index finger down the calendar. She shuddered. 'You stupid bitch!' she exclaimed to herself in a panic as to how late she actually was. 'Almost fifteen weeks!'

Kate quickly showered, towelled dry, and dragged a brush through the unconditioned bird's nest on her head, as each tugged knot pulling at her scalp caused her to wince. She threw on the still-warm jogging suit from the bedroom floor, forcefully pressed her feet into an off-white pair of trainers and rushed to the chemist. Kate drove two miles from her home to the chemist, where she had purchased the original test and felt reassured that she would be unknown and unrecognised by any of the establishment's customers.

As if walking through treacle, the 20 odd paces from her car to the terraced entrance of the pharmacy – sandwiched between an off-licence and a newsagent – seemed to take forever. Her legs felt leaden, and her heart heavy. She wandered aimlessly around the aisles, still unconvinced that she wanted to know the answer until she reticently sought advice. A well-turned-out woman in her mid-thirties, dressed in a white high-collar shirt-like garment with green trim, flashed an inviting smile in her direction from behind the glass counter as she approached. Feeling like a self-effaced hypochondriac, Kate could smell her nervousness. It wasn't a physical odour, it was all mental, but it was absolute for Kate.

'Good morning. May I help you?' The shop assistant's sixth sense informed her of her client's fragile disposition as the soft tones of her voice comforted Kate's qualms.

'Oh, I hope so. How accurate are the home pregnancy test kits?'

'Well, they all promise much the same,' she replied as she paced to fetch three alternatives before returning to face Kate. 'This is the most popular,' she confidently stated. 'This one detects the pregnancy hormone, human chorionic gonadotrophin or, as it is known, hCG. It states that it is 99% accurate when used from the day your period is due.'

Without further ado and inwardly pleading for the safe haven of the Mews, Kate dipped her head as if she were at an auction permitting the auctioneer to assume a bid. Reacting to the preoccupied customer's signal, she placed the box into a crisp paper bag, carefully folded the top down, and passed the package across the counter to Kate. Kate handed over a twenty pound note and waited for her change. Noting the attractive assistant's name on the badge pinned to her left breast pocket, she sincerely acknowledged the gentle advice she'd received. 'Thank you, Tina, I appreciate your help.'

'Good luck,' came Tina's heartfelt response.

Whatever the meaning of this particular 'good luck', the female intuition of the two women meant they both understood the implicit scenario. Kate felt comfortable during her brief encounter with Tina. Placing the change into her trouser pocket, along with the test kit, Kate tilted her head, raised her eyebrows, smiled farewell to Tina and left the safety of the empty pharmacy.

The menacing faces of a dozen teenagers in hoodies mingled in the precinct outside the off-licence. As they sipped their cans of cold lager, they gave her the impression that they could somehow see through her as she tried her hardest to avoid any eye contact. She scampered to her Mini and jumped in. Without a second thought of checking her mirrors, the distracted Kate quickly reversed out of the parking space only to be met with the goose-like honk of a loud horn from the oncoming red sports car that nearly collided with her. The screeching of the speeding vehicle's brakes and the smell of burning rubber alerted the youths to the car that crossed both lanes of the road. Kate stalled in response to the instantly changing situation. Jeers and cheers greeted the 'rough-looking, stuck-up rich bitch' and the 'slapper in the red 'un' as the group launched a tirade of abuse in both Kate's and the innocent driver's direction.

With a twist of the ignition key, the engine came alive. Kate conceded her error to the attractive auburn-haired driver of the waiting car, with a bow of her head and a mouthing of 'sorry', as the female driver politely waved Kate on and patiently waited for her to finish the manoeuvre. Putting the car into gear, she pulled alongside the speedster and paused as her heart temporarily skipped a beat. Kate was familiar with the driver. It was the bejewelled woman from the promiscuous night at the Docklands warehouse. Penelope didn't recognise her, which hardly surprised Kate. She had been wearing the mask that night, and, a disheartened Kate admitted to herself that she looked like something the cat dragged in.

The return trip was lost on Kate. She'd arrived home but couldn't recall anything about the journey. Her thoughts were stuck elsewhere, stuck in two very different boxes. Penelope's tender flesh box, which enveloped her at the London event, and one made of printed cardboard that jutted from her right pocket. Pulling to a halt, Kate forced the protrusion back into her pocket and got out of the car. Remotely locking the motor as she approached the front door, Kate looked around like a guilty schoolgirl hiding a small stash of illegal contraband.

Fortunately, there were no neighbours, no busybodies, and no fuss. She headed straight up the stairs to the haven of her boudoir. Sitting on the edge of the bed, nervously tapping the unopened box on her left palm, she contemplated all of the possible ramifications of an as-yet-unknown test result. With butterflies fluttering around her stomach, Kate opened the package, removed the testing stick, and unhurriedly read the instructions, hoping to delay the inevitable, if only for a few minutes.

Ignoring that the test recommended an early morning pee, her bladder hadn't been emptied for at least four hours, so she felt confident that the result would be definitive either way. Kate walked to the en-suite, dropped the jogging bottoms to the floor, and climbed out of them as she kicked them to one side. She sat on the loo, removed the lid from the plastic pen, and held the tip steady as she tried to force her unwilling body to go. The more she tried, the tighter she felt, as it became apparent that her bashful bladder wasn't interested in performing. Taut with the fearful anxiety of having to take a pregnancy test and a guilty trepidation of any unfavourable result, Kate's apprehension hindered her natural function. 'Come on, Kate, just pee!' she urged herself, trying to loosen the stage fright that constricted the flow from her knotted muscles.

After concentrating for a minute or two, a dribble of golden yellow passed between her labia. Relieved to hear the sound of urine tinkling against ceramic, the trickle became a relaxed stream as Kate looked down between her thighs, watching the tip of the test stick turn pink as it absorbed the fluid. After finishing, she sat motionless with the test in her right hand, looking vacantly around the bathroom, shaking her head, disgusted with herself. The tiled room was a pigsty. Dirty clothes, soiled underwear, and damp towels littered the untidy floor. Kate waited for the test result as it finally dawned on her that her life was comparable to the en-suite floor, an unreserved bloody shambles. She got to her feet, flushed the loo, and walked into her bedroom without bothering to wipe herself. She lay on the bed with her eyes shut tight, clutching the stick in her hand, chewing over the issues that would come with a positive test. The only saving grace for Kate would be an explanation for her distinct lack of enthusiasm for just about everything in her life. Though the recommended time was two minutes for a result to appear, it was probably nearer ten when she finally forced herself to look at the plastic display.

With an emptiness in her being and a painful sensation burning in her heart, Kate rolled over onto her side and sat upright on the side of her bed, staring at herself in the full-length mirror. The slovenly mess that stared back caused her to squeeze her eyes shut. Kate was unsure about her reaction, her mental faculties, and about keeping the bastard child of a one-night stand with a stranger called Michael. Kate slowly opened her eyes as her focus zoomed around, looking for confirmation of her maternal state.

A blue cross leapt out of the result window. Deep down inside, it was the inevitable consequence she knew was coming, but it wasn't what she wanted to see.

Kate's despondent head slumped. Little by little, as the realisation of her predicament sank in, she became plagued with feelings of abject failure. How could she, with all the advantages life had gifted her, have allowed herself to become pregnant? While the despicable feelings of a readily available 'get out of jail free card' – an abortion – ransacked her core, the thought of destroying an unborn child caused her to feel physically sick. She raced to the en-suite and forced her head into the basin as an acidic spray gushed from her gagging mouth.

Unable to move, Kate stayed still with her face in the sink as she moved her dangling hair away from the few morsels of undigested food that lingered, blocking the plughole. Tears welled in her eyes as the confused and wretched self-inflicted condition started to choke her. The conflict of the decision – to do what's best or what's right – had numbed her thought process. Now was not the time to make a life-and-death choice. A clear head and an untroubled soul would be the only way to decide on the life-changing judgement.

As she stood ruminating at the available pathways open to her at this unwanted crossroad, Kate knew her options, but could she live with the lasting consequences? Maybe having courage was the one thing she lacked because, deep down, she had no conviction to make the call. Kate was entirely alone except for the foetus growing inside her. Nobody could help her. She would have to sort this out single-handedly. Quite suddenly and without warning, Kate felt tiny flutterings in her womb.

Chapter 18

The call woke Kate from her nap. She'd been battling with everything: her daily routine, the work on the China brief, and especially her self-evaluation. After three days of traumatic soul-searching, she'd arrived at the most critical decision of her life. Forgetting all she held dear, she would delay the termination until she returned from China. Tired, confused, and panicked, she turned onto her side, unenthusiastically stretched out her left limb and snatched the handset off the bedside table. Rolling back to her initial supine position, with her arm fully extended upwards, the mobile looked down. She really couldn't be bothered to take the call as the last thing she wanted to do was chat, but, with her thumb hovering over the divert button, she recognised the importance of the person calling. Composing herself in an instant, she half-heartedly accepted the call.

'Good afternoon, Mr. Ambassador. Kate speaking,' she answered in the most enthusiastic and cheerful voice she could muster.

'Hello Kate, I hope I didn't disturb you?'

'No, no, it's fine. I was just away from my desk. How can I help you?'

'I was just after an update on where you are regarding the report. David has regularly briefed me, but I would appreciate an informal face-to-face for my peace of mind. Please give me a brief overview of the work to date from your point of view. I hope you understand that I'm not checking up on you. Would that be alright?'

'Why yes, of course. I can't finalise my findings just yet, as the Olympics will be the real test on the current state of democratic reform. When would you like to get together?' Kate enquired.

'How about Monday lunchtime? David has suggested the Old Grain House. He said we wouldn't be disturbed there. How does that fit in with your schedule?'

Kate's mouth was parched. 'That's fine, Monday, 4th August, at one o'clock.'

'I look forward to seeing you again, Kate. Monday it is. Goodbye.'

'Goodbye, Mr. Ambassador, and have a good weekend.'

'And you.'

Kate disconnected the call as her arm flopped to the bed. Her aching body had used its last reserves to sound motivated and interested. Staring at the ceiling as she listened to the silence, she drifted back off to sleep.

Kate arrived early and had made an extra special effort to ensure she looked her absolute best as she prepared to meet the Ambassador. Under her black trench coat, a stunning red two-piece business suit gently pulled in her burgeoning stomach, and a pair of red-heeled shoes completed the outfit. Her faultless make-up and conditioned hair complemented her manicured nails. She had noted that he commented on her scent, Issey Miyake, at the Chinese New Year party.

Kate entered the public house to be greeted by the same three gormless-looking people who'd made the bar their own when she had met Sir David. The two punters and the barmaid stopped whatever banal trivia they were discussing and turned to the door as the striking brunette ducked in. Realising who she was, as they instantly recalled Kate's dead-pan glare from the previous encounter, the two men immediately turned their backs to her. She removed and hung her jacket before walking to the bar. The two men had increased their noise almost instantaneously as they tried to attract the attention of the stunner. The scratchy London voice of the barmaid had no problems slapping the two bores down with a simple but sincere, 'Oi, oi, oi! Just shut it for a mo' will yer. I can't 'ear the laydee speak!' She turned to Kate: 'Sorry, what was that darling?'

'Chardonnay, please.' Kate contemptuously repeated.

The waitress went off without a word before returning with Kate's drink. 'Yer wanna tab?'

'Yes, please,' she sternly answered as she turned her back on the three and moved to the table she had previously occupied with David.

Kate felt that she had changed irrevocably since their last meeting, and as the anxiety rooted in her heart began to grow, she started to fret about the imminent meeting with her client.

Arriving flustered and somewhat stressed, the Ambassador inadvertently tripped into the pub. Ignoring the smirks that instantly appeared on the faces of the three at the bar, he corrected his stance before going over to Kate as she got to her feet.

The Ambassador warmly greeted her with a kiss on both cheeks. He was wearing the same starched white shirt and dark blue suit that he had worn on the previous two occasions they had met. Immediately, Zhou could see and sense the change in Kate. She was not herself. However appealing she looked and smelt, her eyes gave her away. With all the skills of a seasoned diplomat, he instantly changed his tact. Although the brief was number one on his list, unbeknown to Kate, her wellbeing had now pushed itself to the top of his chaotic schedule.

Today's agenda was thrust upon him after a terrorist attack in his homeland had killed sixteen police officers. His quickly drafted statement regarding the outrage was all over the morning news bulletins. He had considered cancelling the engagement due to the flak still flying but concluded that the update was equally important. Sitting opposite Kate, he beckoned the bar lady with a no-nonsense finger snap. Intimidated by his deportment and expensive attire, she obeyed the summons by obediently going to their table.

'Kate, would you like another drink?' he inquired, ignoring the barmaid as she stood silently.

Kate politely refused the offer, saying, 'No, I'm fine, but thank you anyway.'

Eye-to-eye with the young waitress, he ordered a bottle of sparkling mineral water and a slice of lime. Dismissing her from where she had patiently stood, he returned his focus to Kate.

'First things first, Kate, thank you for meeting with me today. I hope I haven't inconvenienced you in any way.'

'No, of course you haven't. It's a pleasure to meet with you again.' While not pointed, her response was rushed, and she thought it might have come across as slightly dismissive as she listened to herself.

'If you don't mind, I would like to keep this meeting brief as I need to attend to a few urgent matters later today. How have you found the brief to date?' The Ambassador could sense a disinterest in Kate as her mind seemed somewhat distracted by something unknown.

'Well, Mr. Ambassador, I have brought along my findings to date, which I am confident are finished, and the bones of the work in progress still need to be firmed up. Additionally, I have pieced together a multimedia presentation. It's only a draft montage, but you can...' Kate drifted as if she had lost her train of thought before completing the sentence, '...view it.'

Having lost her focus, the presumed lack of respect toward the Ambassador caused her face to flush, and she became noticeably flustered.

With almost exquisite timing, the two were temporarily interrupted as the waitress returned with the glass containing ice, a slice of lime, and the bottle of mineral water. Professionally and courteously, she waited to be invited and placed the items on two vacant beer mats at the centre of the table before excusing herself back to the safety behind her bar. As Zhou poured the liquid, half filling the long glass, Kate looked on, composed herself, trying her best to be the consummate professional.

'Kate. Please. It's Zhou,' his affectionate Asian tone eased Kate's nerves as she regained some of her composure, which had been lost as she fumbled her sentence.

'Sorry, Zhou,' Kate felt a warmth and understanding flow through her.

'Secondly, and more importantly, how have you personally found the research? Kate, I'm interested in your wellbeing. I know you have been working solo on this, and solitude can become a tedious punishment.'

'It's not been a problem," she responded with bogus poise. 'The content has been difficult and occasionally troubling, but as I explained to David when I last spoke to him, it's nothing I can't handle.'

Kate relaxed.

Focused to some extent, the two got down to the nitty gritty of the brief and discussed the work in progress. After about twenty minutes, Zhou looked at his watch and said: 'Sorry to cut this short, but I need to leave.' The meeting had been briefer than anticipated, but then he threw a curve ball before they called it time.

'May I just say something? Please tell me to mind my own business if I offend you.'

'Please do, and I will,' Kate smiled.

'You look tired, Kate, and I feel partly to blame. I have caused a considerable change in your life and can see its effect on you. Please don't get me wrong, you look wonderful... it's just that the sparkle seems to be missing from your eyes.'

The statement could have been perceived as offensive, but Kate simply acknowledged his words with a reassuring tilt of her head and a conceding nod. 'Thank you for your honesty and your concern. I have felt tired of late, and I will certainly be taking time off after the report has been concluded,' Kate stressed the importance as she continued. 'Please be assured that the report will be as exact and as accurate as the one I envisaged when I started the brief. My lack of sparkle will have no bearing on the final conclusions.'

'Please, Kate, I have no doubts about the report's content. David mentioned his concerns to me and that maybe the project's solitude adversely affected you.'

Kate smarted. In her eyes, David should not be interfering.

'I hope I'm not speaking out of turn', he continued.

The Ambassador pulled out an unmistakable Montblanc fountain pen and a small leather-covered notebook from his jacket pocket. As the dark blue ink flowed from the ornate platinum nib, Kate admired the lines of the classic black barrel nestled in his strong right hand. She watched on intently as he crafted the short note. Reading upside down, she could make out the word 'Chinatown'.

He meticulously tore the page from the book and passed it to Kate. 'Please, would you do me a favour? Visit this clinic and tell him I have sent you. He'll prepare you a magnificent herbal tonic. He's the best.'

Kate held the note between the thumb and forefingers of both hands and nodded to agree that she would.

'Thank you, Kate. I'm grateful for your understanding and appreciate your endeavour to date.'

'Thank you, Zhou. I somehow feel that I have wasted your day.'

'Far from it. I'll read through your findings. Please have a safe flight and an enjoyable trip to China. Sorry it was rushed, but I need to return to the Embassy. Needs must.'

'I understand, Zhou, and I will visit the clinic.'

They rose together, appreciatively kissed each cheek, and bid farewell.

Chapter 19

A terrifying uncertainty surged through her veins. With the deafening beat of her heart filling her ears, she feared opening her eyes. She sensed herself crouched and cowering in a corner as the cold walls on either side held her trembling body. Through a forced squint, Kate peered into the blinding pinhole of distant white light that pierced the blackness engulfing her. Though scared out of her wits and disoriented, she suppressed the urge to panic and compelled her eyes to open. The horror-stricken femme was alone.

When the blurry lines in her field of vision converged, the definite edges of the confines enclosing her became apparent. The beam of light appeared through the crack of a partially open door, and Kate could make out the ruins of what looked like a pair of four-poster beds. Anxiously feeling around, she pressed her clammy palms against the dusty, uneven walls. Her feelings of confusion were momentarily interrupted by a sense of pain as spikes of hardened paint attempted to puncture her tender skin. Using all the strength she could muster, Kate pushed against the walls with upward momentum, forcing her unwilling body to rise to its feet. Unsteady underfoot and unsure of her surroundings, she inched toward the door.

The crunching noise with each footstep told her she was wearing heeled boots, and under each step were shards and debris. The sound of each movement echoed around the solid walls, resonating through the blackness. Struggling to comprehend her situation, Kate entered the light stream and pushed at the heavy door, causing it to creak open. Alarmed, her head dropped, and she looked down at her garments for the first time. Wearing an all-in-one tight vermilion leather catsuit with black lace ruffles, she was clothed like one of Satan's whores. The bulky heels of her black thigh-length leather boots were seemingly chiselled from solid crystal.

The unbearable tension of the circumstance in which Kate found herself suddenly made her feel nauseous. She stood in a doorway surveying a largely empty, derelict warehouse that seemed peculiarly familiar. Rusting steel pipes crisscrossed the corrugated ceiling, broken red-glazed windows cast a ruby hue, and neon graffiti and flaking paint tussled for prominence on the walls. Kate looked around, trying to make sense of it all. Directly opposite her, a large ventilating fan toiled away, injecting fresh air into space as streams of daylight breached its oscillating arms, which flickered across her face. The piercing, high-pitched screech from each jarred rotation fused with the whooshing noise of the blades, forming a demonic incantation, intensifying her fears.

The floor was strewn with the excesses of what appeared to be a sizeable sexual gathering. Smashed Champagne bottles, broken flutes, needles, discarded foil wrappers and seeping condoms. In the far corner of the warehouse were grimy, smoke-stained doors. They beckoned her. There was no other escape.

Kate cautiously kicked aside the hazards, littering the floor as she crossed the room. Shafts of sunlight danced over her body, accentuating the curves of her physique. At the exact moment she arrived in front of the doors, a solitary blood-curdling squeal of an agonised soul added to the demonic composition emanating from the extractor fan. Hanging from a corroded steel frame, a hefty set of frosted glass doors stood before her – a barrier to keep her from escaping. She tried to glimpse through the dirty, fractured glass but she could not distinguish what was on the other side. With nowhere else left to go and her nerves getting the better of her, she reluctantly reached forward to grasp the rusting handle. While her quaking hand hovered over the handle, ready to grip, the door flew open with massive force.

She found herself in the doorway of an adjoining room. Leaving the dereliction and decay behind, an altogether different picture greeted her: a white, spotless floor, clean white walls, and a white ceiling, smooth and flawless. A crystal chandelier veiled the expansive space in a pearlescent white light that sparkled from each of its glass tears. Kate realised there was no escape. Except for this door, there was no other way out. Panic consumed her like never before as she edged forward into the purity of the light, not a sound escaping from her heavy boots as they kissed the floor. The only audible noise was that of her ever-beating heart.

Directly under the chandelier was a heavy-legged dining table draped in a brilliant-white cotton cloth. Solid dark wooden thrones, with elaborately carved armrests and thickset legs, were located at either end of the table that was intriguingly set for two. Each chair was upholstered in vermilion leather, clearly cut from the same hide adorning her body. A gleaming silver fork was positioned on the left side of a white china dinner plate, and to its right was a silver knife, with its blade pointing inward. A reflection of the crystal light fitting was trapped in the silver spoon beside the knife. Proficiently folded, a white cotton napkin was placed next to the fork. An ornate silver goblet was directly above the knife. A small decanter of blood red liquid completed each of the two place settings. The table's centrepiece was an impressive oval silver serving tray cradling a polished silver dome, the chandelier reflecting off its mirrored exterior. Her nostrils flared as she inhaled the rich aroma tantalising her senses from under the dome, though she ignored any instinct to see what delights were hiding beneath it. Adrenaline was coursing through her body, and the mental strain showed across her face as the pervading, claustrophobic atmosphere began to choke her.

Kate silently approached the end of the table to find her distorted image joining that of the chandelier trapped within the spoon. A small white envelope placed on the dinner plate caught her eye. 'Kate' was meticulously handwritten on the front, the writing was identical to her own. Full of dread, she snatched at the letter and tore it open, tugging in haste to free the enclosed rectangle of white card. Kate silently read the handwritten words. 'Dearest Kate, please take a seat. I'll be with you shortly.' With a thunderous clap, the doors to the room slammed shut. Paranoia wrapped itself around the psychologically ensnared hostage, slowly tightening its squeeze on her spirit.

Racing at her from the corner by the entrance, the imperceptible entity that toyed with the doors suddenly and violently pulled the shell-shocked Kate off her feet. Suspended like a child's rag doll dangling in the air, she was tossed at full force, slamming into the throne. The chair jolted forward, trapping her against the table. An unrelenting downward pressure manacled her wrists to the heavy armrests while an equivalent pressure shackled her ankles to the legs of the wooden stock. Stricken and petrified, a rush of electrical pulses crackled through her central nervous system as she frantically struggled for freedom from the invisible binds.

Her body spasmed from the exertion, provoking a burning stream of acid to shoot up her oesophagus. At the same time, an involuntary gulp forced the bile back down into her stomach, leaving a metallic taste lingering in her throat. With sweat forming on her brow, Kate was exhausted and mentally spent as she resigned herself to her destiny.

An ice-cold breeze, with no discernable origin, chilled the air to freezing point, and Kate could see and feel the steam rising from her overheated body in the sub zero atmosphere. A blast of vapour came with each heavily exhaled breath as tiny droplets of condensation appeared on the leather suit that clung to her body. She frantically scanned her surroundings before looking over her right shoulder at the doorway. Nothingness filled the room. Suddenly, a tingling sensation shot up her spine, and with an abrupt movement, her head snapped around, facing forward.

Directly opposite her, seated at the far end of the table, was Kate. It looked like Kate, but she was Kate. Bewildered and full of trepidation, Kate rapidly tried to grasp what was happening as she glared at her double. With its long brunette hair flowing over an opaque white silk gown, the apparition mirrored back the look through its jet-black piercing eyes that gave away nothing. The sheer fabric was being blown over its body, excitedly arousing its flesh, licking at its protruding nipples. Scarlet lips and manicured hands modelling red nails – set off by unblemished bleached white skin – completed the ghostly manifestation.

Purposefully, its mind seeped deep into Kate. Restrained and struggling to free herself from the chair, she thrust her body inwards at the table, screaming. 'What are you... who are you?'.

'Hello, Kate,' came the nonchalant reply. 'It's good to finally make your acquaintance. Aren't you going to say hello?'

Its voice was indistinguishable from Kate's own.

'Who are you?' No answer was forthcoming. 'Just fucking tell me!' Kate bellowed as she thrashed around, trying to escape the restraints.

'All in good time, Kate, we have a lifetime to catch up on,' came the eerily spoken answer. 'Before I go on, I want to thank you for releasing me, for freeing me. You have been incubating my soul. You kept me dormant, kept me hidden. I know it wasn't your fault, dear sister, but you were the beneficiary. It was I who was ripped limb from limb while you remained untouched, your heart still beating. It was I who paid the price for the sins of one man.'

With more malice in her voice, the apparition continued. 'You see, Kate, I have dreamt about this, our communion, this meeting of our souls and minds.' Its unflinching face was full of menace.

In the blink of an eye, it stood to the side of the table, between the place setting directly in front of Kate and the centrepiece. The silk

shroud rippled across its body as it extended its right arm to draw
Kate's focus to the silver dome imperiously dominating the table.
Disconcerted and disbelieving, Kate tried to swallow. Her mouth
was dry. She sought to summon spittle but to no avail. Her eyes
stung as rivulets of sweat flowed down from her forehead. Deep
within her, Kate could feel the malevolent tension rising. Shaking
uncontrollably, she stared at the apparition to her side.

'For you, dear sister, I have prepared a special banquet, a
sacrament. A Eucharistic feast, a meal of flesh and blood.'

Kate tried to turn away, but the entity took control of her head,
ensuring she was now a powerless prisoner to fate. The double's
voice chirped sadistically at Kate, 'Huh! You will drink.'

The apparition leisurely poured a cup of red fluid from the
decanter. Ridiculing her broken sister, she mockingly teased the
goblet near Kate's puckered mouth before single-handedly forcing
the shining rim between her captive's tight lips.

'Dear Sister, this is my blood shed for you.'

Unable to close her bulging, bloodshot eyes, Kate struggled to
keep her mouth shut. The salty, metallic tang of the blood hit her
tongue as the silver crashed against her teeth. The Eucharistic wine
seeped into her mouth, coating her taste buds before it trickled
down her throat. A torrent of blood gushed from her mouth as she
coughed, spraying a cloud of crimson projectiles over the table.
Cascading off her chin, the blood lost itself against the vermillion-
red outfit.

'Oh no, sis, you'll have to do better than that!' came the sardonic
instruction that informed Kate that more humiliation was to
come. The double slammed the goblet back down onto the blood-
spattered tablecloth.

Though Kate's head was fixed, her preoccupation changed from
the face of her look-alike to its pale hand as it gripped the silver
handle on top of the dome. The lid was slowly lifted, revealing
the fare. The partially-cooked offerings of a foetus were precisely
arranged for culinary effect. Slightly charcoal skin was peeling

off the delicate bones, exposing a pink fleshy meat grilled to perfection. The dismembered body parts were too much for Kate to comprehend as an effusion of gastric juice burst from her mouth, covering the table and marinating the morsels on the silver platter.

Not content with the suffering inflicted on the broken and defeated Kate, her doppelganger gracefully picked up the tiny, crisped right leg of the unborn between her thumb and forefinger. Holding the limb up to the chandelier, she gently rotated it, admiring it.

'Take, eat. This is my body, which I gave for you.'

'THIS... IS... NOT... REAL', shrieked Kate.

With a deafening wail and looking directly into Kate's eyes, into her terrorised soul, the ghoul vigorously forced the appendage between Kate's blood-glazed lips.

Tearful and traumatised, Kate woke from her nether world. Residual reflux of an unexplained night terror covered the pillow. With her visions more surreal and her mental state in freefall, she clenched her fists tightly as she tried her hardest to expunge the mental pictures from memory. Kate reached out and turned on the bedside lamp next to her bed.

The alarm clock read 7th August 2008, 04:28.

Chapter 20

Having second thoughts about her decision to delay the termination, or whether to proceed with it at all, played heavily on Kate's troubled mind.

Finding herself unable to focus on anything in particular, she hurtled through the streets of London in the black cab. Gazing vacantly out of the window, the concrete world beyond the confines of the Mews became a disorderly smear of colour. In an embarrassed rush, the driver had stalled the vehicle at a set of lights, holding up late-morning traffic at Piccadilly Circus for nearly five minutes. To avoid attention from other 'considerate' road users to the motorised obstruction, Kate looked down at her watch to hide her embarrassment, more for the driver's sake than hers. Replaying the nightmare from the early morning hours, the Morse code of beeping horns added to the vision as irate drivers vented their frustrations. Her watch read 11.45, which didn't faze her as she was in no hurry. She had no actual plans or appointments, so the short delay had no reason to cause her any distress. Feeling physically tired and mentally confused, a glimpse of her reflection in the clear acrylic screen behind the driver's seat confirmed what she already knew: that by her exceptionally high standards, she looked like shit.

''Ere yer goes, darling, Gerrard Street. Is this okay, honey? Sorry for the delay,' said the spotty-faced young driver.

Kate knew that all London cabbies had to pass a test called 'The Knowledge' before being granted a taxicab licence, but this driver didn't even look old enough to tie his own shoelaces, let alone learn the names of 25,000 streets.

'This will be fine, thank you. Please, keep the change.' She placed the payment into the driver's outstretched hand as his chewed fingernails clenched tight, crumpling the banknote. Kate looked at the searing eyes staring back through the rearview mirror and could feel his eyes letch, from one form of rearview to another, as she clambered out. She had seen 'that look' so many times before, but this time it was different. It made her feel quite uneasy being the object of a boy's desire, especially in her current state.

Kate passed under the Paifang at the entrance to Chinatown. The ornamental gate stood three stories high, bridging the street, a red-painted beacon adorned with black plaques inscribed with gold Chinese hieroglyphs and a host of coloured bulbs. She had been through the gateway plenty of times, but as she crossed the threshold on this occasion, she felt dizzy and faint, as though the gate had plundered every ounce of her energy. Chinatown was especially busy, with the opening ceremony of the Olympic Games due to start in just over an hour, and the packed streets were bubbling with anticipation.

Considering her brief and the effort she had put into the research, the Games were nowhere on her list of important things to watch. Aimlessly sauntering through Chinatown, she stopped at a front entrance. The slightly untidy Kate was drawn to a nondescript terrace shop, quite plain among the bright colours of the other store and restaurant fascias lining the street. She looked up at the weathered brass number crudely nailed on the door and then down at the handwritten note the Ambassador had given her. Somehow, she had arrived at her destination. The relevance of the number didn't go amiss with Kate. It was the 8th August, 2008, and she was standing outside a door numbered eight. She understood that the number eight is considered lucky in China because it sounds like 'prosper'.

Kate was mystified;. She was expecting a gleaming new glass-fronted surgery, Feng Shui'd up to the hilt and suitable for a Chinese Ambassador, but instead, she found herself standing outside a dilapidated hovel. The woodwork looked like it hadn't seen a brush since before she was born, as the flaky brown paintwork failed to hide a palette of colours from previous renovations. The grimy glass and filthy net curtains gave the impression to anyone passing to continue straight on and that this shop had nothing to offer.

Apprehensively, she pushed open the door, causing a brass bell to tinkle above her head. It was a bell similar to one that once hung in her local confectionery shop when she was a child, alerting the proprietor that another customer eagerly awaited. The timber floor was well past its best, and the few areas of darkened stain were hidden in the corners of the room, looking as if they'd never seen the underside of a shoe. An 'L' shaped counter, as worn as the floorboards, dominated the relatively small space as it stood in front of a series of shelves, complete with dusty jars.

Kate surveyed what she believed was a sweet shop in a previous life, and now the jars, devoid of humbugs and aniseed balls, contained less appealing items. The chemist had a distinctive musty smell, and the hotchpotch of once-living morsels would have been a perfect snack shop for the guests on the Ark. The glass jars were an unnatural habitat for various leaves and animal products, from pickled bat wings to dried snake segments. The wall inside the door displayed a series of old, handwritten charts. Anatomically correct to the human meridians, the Chinese writing and annotations gave them an air of authenticity, dating back thousands of years. Above the charts was an antique English Regency mahogany wall-mounted clock. The hands told Kate that the time was five past noon. The timepiece stood out from everything else in the shop, it was highly polished and looked entirely out of place. Consigned to the top shelf, a slew of oversized jars loomed large. Inconceivably, the transparent pots contained preserved human body parts marinating in a cloudy fluid: eyes, hearts, hands, livers, and sexual organs. The faces of stillborn babies pressed against the glass, warping their features as they wrapped themselves around the inside of their transparent womb. Kate felt herself retch as the display oozed the stench of death and decay that coated her nasal passages and throat.

The inhospitable aura, the produce on display, and the filth in the shop united to disgust Kate. She could see no value in staying, and she was about to turn around and leave when something stopped her dead in her tracks.

'Time to wake from the few minutes of stolen slumber,' were the muffled words she believed were coming from behind the shelving. Although she could not see the doorway, she had a hunch that there must be one. As she peered more closely, a small section opened towards her, becoming a doorway to a hidden world.

Mumbling to himself in Chinese as he revealed himself, the old man appeared from the short, narrow opening. Hunched and dressed in a white tunic that contrasted with the dirty brown backdrop of the shelves, he pushed shut the heavy-shelved door, once again concealing the hidden entrance. His skin was thick like tanned leather, and his eyelids sagged over his beady eyes. A white goatee hung off his extended chin, losing itself against the tunic. Busying himself as he dusted off his garments, the Doctor looked directly at Kate. His head twitched from side to side as he assessed her before abruptly breaking the silence. 'What do you want?'

'Hello, I wonder if I can have a moment of your time? The Ambassador recommended you. He is under the impression that you can help me and suggested I should visit you for a consultation,' Kate revealed.

'Oh, did he! That was improper of him. He, of all people, should know better. I only deal with patients who need my help. You have Western medicine for all your ailments.'

Kate was shocked by the abruptness of the riposte. 'I'm sorry if I've offended you, but please don't be upset at the Ambassador. I think he was just trying to do the right thing.'

'Upset at the Ambassador, don't you worry yourself about him. I was the barefoot Doctor who gave him his first spanking.' The Doctor looked at Kate with raised eyebrows and a wry smile as he reminisced. 'Oh yes... a fateful day. Mao delivered a new republic, and I delivered a sales rep.'

'The first of October, 1949,' Kate muttered.

'Well done, Kate, you know your Chinese history. I am impressed. I have been expecting you. Please, call me Deshi.'

Kate was taken aback. 'How do you know my name, and what do you mean you've been expecting me?'

'Oh yes, I expect everyone who comes through those doors. You surprised me, you're five minutes late.' He pointed to the clock. 'I expected you at midday.'

Kate felt a tension rising through her body from the ends of her toes. Her mouth was drying out, and the stench was still playing tricks with her stomach. The lack of sleep, her poor diet, and the prenatal stresses of carrying a baby had each taken their toll. Her legs were feeling frail, and her body was tiring rapidly.

'Did the Ambassador tell you I was coming?'

'Why? Would that be a problem for you?'

'No, no, of course not. I just didn't imagine that I was going to be expected.'

'Well, now you're here, please take a seat, especially in your condition. I need to look at you.' His hand pointed to her right-hand side. Kate knew there wasn't a seat, she would have seen it when she entered the shop.

'Sit where? There's no seat!' came her forthright response. The reference to her condition went right over her head.

'Look, and you will see, not everything is what you perceive. The chair has always been there, but your eyes were closed when you came in. You Westerners are all the same. If you cannot see it, then it cannot exist.'

Kate looked down, immediately next to her legs was a high stool. Temporarily rendered speechless, she felt the physical existence of the seat with her befuddled right hand. After establishing that the stool was, in fact, bona fide, she hesitantly climbed onto the stool and placed her unpolished and slightly scuffed flat-sole shoes onto the rung. Feeling foolish, she could sense her cheeks blushing red. Trying to take control of the situation, she looked directly at Deshi and continued.

'Please, can you help me? I'm drained, the Ambas...'

'The Ambassador, the Ambassador,' mocked Deshi as he interrupted Kate, testing her resolve.

Kate was pragmatic, she'd never suffered fools lightly and felt this was becoming a pointless venture. 'Look, I'm sorry to have come here, and I'm sorry to have wasted your time,' she said as she went to dismount the stool.

'Not so fast, young lady. You may think I am a crazy old fool, but please let me finish my diagnosis,' he said, looking at Kate, almost baffled by what he could see.

'Okay,' Kate replied, slightly more optimistic about her consultation. She brushed the appearing stool to one side like a magic trick, thinking she had put the old Doctor on the back foot. She hadn't been this sure of herself for months, and maybe just walking through the door of this shabby-looking chemist was all she needed to realise that there was nothing seriously wrong with her other than the side effects of her condition.

'So,' he pondered, 'how long have you been pregnant?'

Bang! Her newfound confidence, which had lasted all of two minutes, was now in shreds. 'I beg your pardon,' came her indignant reply. A look of consternation was written across her face. Nobody knew her situation, and not even the Ambassador could have guessed.

'You're pregnant!'

'What do you mean I'm pregnant? How would you know?'

'I can see it.'

Kate looked down. The growing bump was there but hardly visible, especially under her black coat. 'See what?'

'Well, not the tiny bloating you hide under that jacket, that would be too obvious,' chuckled the old man. 'Why are you here?'

'As I've already explained to you, the Ambassador sent me. He said I looked tired and suggested you may be able to supply me with a tonic, a pick-me-up.'

'Oh, a pick-me-up. You need more than that, young lady. How far gone are you?'

A sigh of resignation escaped her nostrils as she conceded that he was indeed correct and she was expecting. 'I think I'm about 16 weeks,' she said.

'Good, finally, we can move on. And your sleep pattern, has it changed?'

'Well, yes, kind of. I've always slept rather well, but more recently, I've been having terrifying nightmares. They've become harrowing... more sinister and haunt my every thought.'

'When did they start?'

'About a week after I fell pregnant. I didn't know I was until the positive result of the second home test was confirmed by my GP last Friday. I had originally taken a pregnancy test early on, but it gave me a negative result, so I put my tiredness down to my work and my change in lifestyle.'

'What has changed?' asked Deshi, his tone more concerned now.

'I've been working from home on a private commission for five months. It's due to finish next month, but I need help to focus. The pregnancy, the dreams, and the isolation have really been getting me down. It's as though I've been taken over, possessed almost.'

'Have you been pregnant before, Kate?' he inquired.

'No!' Kate blurted.

'So you've never had a termination or a miscarriage?' Deshi was perplexed.

'NO! Why?' Kate repeated, irritated about this line of questioning.

Deshi sympathised with Kate as he rubbed his wrinkled forehead.

'No problem. Tell me about your last vision. Describe it to me as accurately as possible. Tell me every detail. What do you see in your dreams?'

'That shouldn't be too difficult, I've replayed the vision a hundred times and can't get it out of my mind.'

Kate's head dropped to her chest as she brought to mind the terror she'd dreamt just hours before. Describing the nightmare precisely as she remembered it, the Doctor listened attentively as he pulled at the white hairs growing from his chin.

'... with a deafening scream and gazing directly into my eyes, it vigorously forced the limb towards me. That's when I woke up.' Kate's face was full of anguish. 'Doctor, it was horrific. I feel like I'm going mad.'

After she finished recounting the terror, a silence seemed to last an eternity. Sorrowful tears streamed down her face as Deshi passed a box of tissues, which, like the stool, seemed to appear from nowhere. Kate removed a couple and dabbed at her face.

'Do you read dreams, doctor?' asked Kate as she looked imploringly at Deshi. She could not call him by his family name, it seemed inappropriate and personal.

'In Chinese medicine, a fearful dream results from a chi deficiency in the heart and gallbladder, probably due to anxiety. But your dream is different.' He stared into her eyes. 'Do you understand the Chinese philosophical concept of yin and yang and how it relates to your chi... your life force?'

Kate composed herself. She was mystified as to where this was leading, but intrigued too so she played along. 'Well, from my understanding, Yin and Yang are two opposing energies that balance together.'

'Well done,' Deshi exclaimed, acknowledging Kate's answer. 'That's very good, but please let me expand your knowledge. The human body can be viewed as a tiny universe, complete with interrelated systems which balance each other to maintain the healthy function of a body. A significant component of your spiritual balance is 'chi'. Kate, your chi is imbalanced.'

'I'm sorry, doctor, but you've lost me.'

'Your pregnant state has not harmed your body in any way, but your underlying problem is the dark force surrounding you, full of negative energy. This negative energy is poisoning your dreams and affecting your being.'

Kate's blank, expressionless face confirmed to the Doctor that she was missing the point, causing him to continue.

'Your karma... your spiritual balance... radiates from within, and yours is troubled. Somehow, you have awakened the dormant spirit of a yingling.'

'What's a yingling?' replied the puzzled mother-to-be.

'When a woman has an abortion or a miscarriage and the foetus is extracted, it cancels out the spirit's right to have a body. A yingling is the ghost of a foetus, and it cannot move on to the next life. Most remain placid with the mother, but the one inside you has become vengeful.'

'What do you mean abortion?' Kate was confused.

'You have had an abortion or a miscarriage. There is no other explanation.'

'You're full of s...' Kate deprecated.

Deshi rudely interrupted his patient before she could finish her tirade.

'Do you have any faith in your life or just your decadent existence filled with vanity and hedonism?'

'How do you know about my faith?'

'I see it, I see everything, but I cannot give you the answers. You need to find the answers for yourself, and for that, you need faith. Everybody needs faith. Without faith, you are an empty shell. You see, the yingling has filled a void within you. I do not know how the spirit of a dead foetus has materialised within you, but it has. I'm sure of that. Either way, the spirit wants to be free, and you need to appease its anger. Your unborn child opened a gateway and has become a channel for the lost soul.'

'Fool. You're talking gibberish,' laughed Kate. 'I'm not listening to any more of this. I've never had a termination or even been pregnant, and as for faith, hmmmph!' Angered by the nonsensical riddles and annoyed by the feeling of being ridiculed, Kate leapt from the stool and threw a closing remark at the surprised Doctor.

'Oh, I see, so I'm home to a ghost. Fucking unbelievable,' the exclamation escaped through gritted teeth. 'What a waste of time!' Kate looked piercingly at Deshi. 'Thank you for your time.' Bidding him farewell with a flippant wave of her hand, Kate stormed towards the door.

The Doctor yelled: 'Can you deal with the most vital matters by letting events take their course? Can you step back from your own mind and thus understand all things?'

Kate stopped. Her heart was thumping faster than it had ever done before. She hadn't moved from the spot next to the stool, her lack of any kind of progress towards the door told her she was beaten.

Kate looked up. The Doctor who had been behind the counter just a split second before was now at the door. With a blink of an eye, he stood nose to nose with Kate. This time, his words hit home. 'Trust me, you need to nip this in the bud now while you still can.'

Then he was gone, vanished. Looking around the shop's emptiness, Kate realised she was alone. Unable or unwilling to try to leave, she sat on the stool and waited, totally bewildered. Whilst the second hand ticked round, time had seemingly stood still. The clock hanging above the charts still read 12:05.

'Now, are you ready to open your mind?' Deshi was back behind the counter, once again pulling at his goatee.

'I'm sorry, doctor; please excuse my outburst.' Kate was learning some valuable lessons. Twice in a few hours, she'd had to put her arrogant narcissism to one side.

'You see, Kate, the clock has stopped, but has time?'

'I really need some help. Please, can you help me? I'm ready to take any concoction, any potion you give me. I want me back.'

'You don't need to take anything. No medicine I can give you will help you, only faith can help you,' he uttered, leaning down to fetch a dusty old scroll from under the counter and placing it in front of Kate.

'Take this to China. Stand outside your hotel at 9am on the eleventh of August. Wait for a taxi, and your questions will be answered. You must only open this in China by the taxi rank. The instructions will mean nothing to anyone except the one who needs to know. You can ask, but nobody will translate this for you. Just give the scroll to a willing driver. This is an old clandestine dialect used by the workers of China in a bygone era, and only someone from the villages around the area concerned will understand the instruction.'

'That's it, a dusty old scroll?' Kate was irked by the lack of a meaningful 'cure'.

'That's it, that's all you need. Deliver the scroll.'

Deshi pointed, and as Kate's eyes tracked the movement of his hand, she was looking across the room toward the door. She looked back to the counter, and he had vanished. Unimpressed, she looked down at the dusty scroll, picked it up, and threw it contemptuously into her bag as she walked across the shop and left.

Flagging down a taxi by the Paifang, Kate hastily climbed in.

'Courtfield Mews, please,' she said to the driver.

'No problems, duchess,' came the voice of a quieter, much more mature cabbie.

Her taxi was just crossing Piccadilly Circus when she noticed a stalled black cab holding up all the traffic. The spotty young driver looked out of his window. His searing stare was directed straight at Kate. She knew him, he had driven her to Chinatown. To her absolute horror, she was the passenger looking down into her lap. Kate felt herself going into a state of shock. Blood drained from her face, as her physical reality distorted into a surreal, twisted nightmare.

Kate looked at the clock on the dashboard. To her utter amazement, it read 11:45, and she knew the passenger in the cab was checking her watch. In utter confusion and with her heart thumping, Kate rechecked her watch, and it confirmed the time on the dashboard. 'Is that the right time?'

'Yes, darling, you're my first job. I started at 'leven firty,' the driver confirmed.

With a concerned expression, he looked at Kate through the rearview mirror, noticing she looked a bit peaky. Slowing the car down, he turned his head and looked back over his broad shoulder at Kate.

'Are you all right, love? You look like you've seen a ghost! Do you want me to pull over?'

'Uh, uh, uh, please just take me home… I'm fine… I just feel a bit queasy.'

'You're the boss, darlin!'

With that, the driver picked up the pace.

When Kate arrived home, she shut the curtains and got into bed fully dressed, staring at the scroll that the Doctor had given her. Kate was hiding from something, but she was unsure of exactly what. Image after image of the day's supposed events – the terror of eating a foetus dressed as a whore, the visit to the Doctor, the scrolled parchment, and the stalled taxi – flashed through her mind. Racking her brain for answers and in a discombobulated state, she could not separate fact from fiction. She knew the scroll was real, it was there, but her inability to piece together the missing hours convinced her that she must have dreamt the rest. Kate was on the brink as her sanity was being tested. Tears trickled down her face as she unwillingly passed out into an unknown darkness that she now feared.

Chapter 21

The departures board in Heathrow's Terminal 5 informed the irritable mother-to-be that her plane was about to board. The 12:50 to Beijing was on time, and although Kate could really do without it, the trip to China would help her kill two birds with one stone. Complete her research – which, like everything else in her life, had come to a complete standstill – and deliver the scroll. The shiny new terminal was comfortable and easy to get around, unlike most other airports she'd used on many trips around the world. The flight landed at 05:45 local time. Tired and exhausted, Kate slept for most of the flight. Having arrived by taxi at the hotel, the weary, expectant mother got the lift up to her room with the bellboy in toe. Tipping the young man as she closed the door. With the suitcase untouched, loitering inside the entrance, she stripped off and fell into bed. Tomorrow was the 11th August, and she would be outside at 9am, with the scroll.

The early morning sun was starting to burn as the yellowy-orange smog that stained the city sky became more apparent, and airborne pollutants gave the heavy atmosphere its own distinctive tang. It tasted sickly sweet to the pregnant tourist.

Having been ill twice already since her early morning call, a tired Kate was far from looking her best. Her hair was loosely brushed, while her make-up struggled to conceal the puffiness around her eyes. She was dressed in a chic, semi-transparent white cotton dress that hugged her growing bump. The V-shaped neckline revealed a necklace assembled from hammered squares of linked silver, which nestled in her cleavage. A light straw hat covered her head and the large brim umbrellaed her naked shoulders. Holding a small bag and the scroll, Kate stood waiting at the taxi rank, psyched and prepared to finally confront the supposed yingling buried in her soul. Within minutes, a taxi pulled off the busy thoroughfare and stopped next to the kerb just inches from where she stood. She passed the scroll through the taxi driver's open window and waited while the middle-aged man carefully read the contents. The driver patiently and precisely rolled up the parchment and pushed it back through the window. Without saying a word or acknowledging her, he effortlessly wound up his door window and drove off. Kate stood fixed on the spot, shaking her head. Perplexed and alone, she waited before flagging down another taxi, getting the same response from the following three drivers as she had from the first. Kate was frustrated, raging at herself for being so foolish as to believe the old doctor.

'That's it, girl. It's time to call it a day. Just admit it, you've been fooled by a clever old man in a Chinatown backstreet.'

She was about to give up, putting the events down to another shitty lesson in life when another taxi slowly pulled over. The driver stopped the car and wound down his window. A demoralised Kate prayed for a better response as the driver read the scroll.

'You get in... I take you, you get in... it's okay.'

A relieved Kate got into the taxi as the forty-something driver pulled away, joining the morning rush-hour traffic as the car moved towards the city's outskirts. Unsure of where she was going and how much it would cost, Kate inquired: 'Do you speak English?'

'Only... small... English,' came the stuttering but structured answer.

'Where are you taking me?'

'I not tell in English, very hard to... to... um... let you know.'

'Okay, Okay, how far is it? The place you're taking me, how far?' questioned Kate..

'Um… two hours… not long.'

'Fine, that's fine and thank you.'

'Okay, lady, no problem,' replied the driver as he smiled through his rearview mirror at Kate's reflection.

Kate sat back, wondering what she was doing and why. The once busy roads became less congested, and the surroundings less urbanised as they travelled. The driver seemed relieved to escape the demanding metropolis as they journeyed into Beijing's backyard. After about an hour, Kate had no idea where they were going. She was being driven through the countryside, in a country she had never visited, by a driver she had never met before. She puzzled over the situation she now found herself in, and as the cooling air from the open window blew into her face, her eyelids became increasingly heavy. Kate lost consciousness.

'Hello, lady, you here. You get out,' demanded the driver.

Kate's eyes sprang open and stared transfixed at the driver's face, captured in the rearview mirror. She blinked as she tried her hardest to keep her sleepy lids from closing. Slowly, it dawned on Kate that this was not a dream, she had fallen into a deep sleep and was trying to compose her startled body. Her mouth was dry from the journey as she muttered, 'thank you, but where is 'here'?'

She looked out of the car windows in all directions only to be greeted by an emptiness. There was nothing, no buildings, no houses, no animals, just the green wilderness of the Chinese countryside.

'There… you go.' The driver's outstretched arm pointed through his window toward a barely worn lane in the coarse grass. The narrow foot track was edged with trees to its right and wet paddy fields to its left. Kate pointed toward the track to ensure she was on the same wavelength as the driver, and he nodded in agreement.

Kate puckered her lips and gesticulated with open hands as to whether or not this was a good idea. The driver had twisted his body around and peered between the two front seats, fixed on her hand gestures. Kate opened her purse to pay the fare as the offended driver took affront to the proffered money.

'You no pay… you no pay… you go,' he rattled off forcefully without stopping for breath.

'But I need to pay, I want to pay,' a surprised Kate calmly responded.

'You no pay… you no pay… now you go… you go,' the driver repeated.

Not wanting to disrespect him further, Kate got out of the taxi and watched as the car vanished into the distant horizon of the rural terrain.

With nowhere else to go, Kate followed the meandering lane. Laboriously constructed farming ground measured its way up the steep hillside and the stepped backdrop provided an inspiring enhancement to the natural beauty.

Strange twitterings could be heard from birds in the trees. Kate looked at her watch, it was just past noon, and the humidity of the environment was causing her temperature to rise and her white cotton dress to stick to her clammy body. After a five-minute walk, she approached a quaint little bridge, the grey brick arch traversed a rush-lined brook. Tentatively, Kate stepped towards the apex of the fragile-looking structure, admiring the ornate stonework and looked down over the side. The crystal-clear stream played host to a shoal of tiny fish as they torpedoed between the lily pads beneath. Kate crossed the bridge and looked at a shabby old temple fifty yards away.

A dozen ancient fishing poles and nets leaned against the partially rendered stone walls outside the sizeable temple. The poles looked like heirlooms passed down through generations, the nets were the culmination of patchworked remnants. The pagoda-style roof was supported by two pillars, each a dirty white in colour. Directly under the roof was a veranda. Its floor was a jumble of discarded bits and pieces, an arbitrary collection of detritus. White smoke danced from a small chimney perched on the moss-covered roof. The stack was leaning and looked ready to crash down as it teetered on the red tiles supporting its bulk. Two rustic wooden doors blocked the gate-style entrance into the temple. The teal paint was peeling off the crumbling doors like sunburnt skin, revealing greying, weathered wood. Recently painted red portrait rectangles with gold Chinese writing finished the windowless doors. The etchings either blessed the house or cursed the visitors, Kate could not be sure, but she knew they meant something.

Making the small climb up the three steps to the decked landing, Kate cautiously approached the door. Hot and sticky, her pulse raced, and her skin prickled. She felt lost and alone, and this was her last hope. Desperate and unsure about whom or what was on the other side of the door, she conceded that this ordeal couldn't be any worse than the one she had recently been suffering.

Knocking on the old wooden door, her heart stopped beating as it was slowly pulled ajar creaking as it opened;. A leathery-skinned hand appeared through the crack, palm open as if waiting for something to be placed upon it. Feeling uneasy, Kate laid the scroll across the palm. The door was pushed shut with a rusty squeak. Kate stood there, unsure about what to do next. Looking around for help or inspiration, and as panic started to grow within her, the door slowly reopened.

Chapter 22

K ate first noticed the waft of incense as the air escaped through the open door.

Standing before Kate was a little old man. Deep creases and lines criss crossed his face. His yellow-tinged droopy skin enhanced the opaque whiteness of the cataracts in his eyes. Groomed white facial hair growing from his chin was combed to a point that reached halfway down his chest. The tops of his ears curled over on themselves after years of supporting the weight of a tatty cloth cap.

Bewilderment halted Kate in her tracks. She looked at the old man with a feeling of déjà vu, although this was the first time she'd seen the gentleman, he was the spitting image of the chemist in Chinatown. With a wave, the old man summoned her, and she entered a partially covered courtyard. A smallholding of chickens and a goat was penned in the far-right-hand corner of the yard. As the old man carefully made his way to a small seating area consisting of a grubby red carpet and two low-set wooden benches, it became apparent that he was struggling to find his way.

Kate followed him to the corner as he sat at the centre of the bench, the grooves of his bottom worn into the aged timber. Barefoot and cross-legged, he indicated for her to take a seat. She clambered down onto the bench directly opposite the old man, her posture mimicking his. His nondescript outfit, created from faded brown hemp cloth, was tied at the waist by a length of tasselled rope. Kate pushed down on the stretched hem of her skirt into the quadrangle of space between her legs so as not to embarrass the old man, even though it appeared he might be blind, Kate could not be sure.

'Hello, Kate, I have been expecting you,' the obviously Western-educated old man spoke to her in almost perfect English. 'Please call me Mei.'

'Hello, Mei. What do you mean you've been expecting me?' inquired the perplexed Kate as she relaxed the pressure on her hem.

'Firstly, would you like some refreshments? If you would, please help yourself.'

He waved his right hand, and as if by magic, a bowl of fruit, a jug of sparkling water, and an immaculately clean glass appeared at Kate's side at the end of the bench. Like everything else of late, Kate did not see it when she took her seat, but there it was.

'Thank you, I'm parched.' Kate poured herself a glass and sipped the water. Kate had never tasted anything quite so refreshing. She could feel the crystal-clear fluid rejuvenating every cell in her dehydrated body.

'I was informed that you were coming. I had a dream, and my brother told me.'

'Your brother?' she questioned.

'Yes, Deshi, my twin brother. You met him in London recently, he gave you this scroll, running his fingers over the parchment. 'I cannot read it, as you can see, I lost my sight a few years ago, but I can sense the physical world and see the spirit world... though on this occasion, I can smell his hovel in London!'

'Right, now it makes sense. For a split second, I was convinced that I had lost the plot when you opened the door and I recognised you,' came the noticeably relieved reply from Kate, who was finally convinced that she was now about to get the answers she needed to move forward and get her life back on track.

'Yes, you are not the first to give me that reaction!' Mei said with a slight chuckle. 'So, what did my brother tell you about your reasons for being here?'

'Well, where do I start? It's a long story…' she pondered

'Always best to start at the beginning,' was Mei's reassuring answer to an open and endless question.

Kate seized the opportunity to get everything off her chest, unashamed and unabridged, she recounted her story: the nightclub, the pregnancy, the Ambassador's referral, and how Deshi had diagnosed the problem by witnessing the yingling. As Kate started her monologue, Mei shut his eyes. His head occasionally twitched as a pestering fly flitted around his face. Kate was unsure if he was listening or even awake, and whenever she paused – to ensure the sequence of the unfolding details or to take a drink – he would open his right eye. The ghoulish white stare was enough to convince Kate he was still with her.

'Well, that's it,' Kate concluded. After a short time, she had got the whole sorry mess off her chest.

'I thank you, Kate, for your honesty. I understand how difficult it must be and that you have probably never told another soul of your dilemma, but I can help you. I can see the yingling, you wear it like a badge. It is a spectre, and yours, unfortunately, is vengeful and angry.'

Shaking her head in disbelief, Kate questioned: 'But how can that be? I have never had an abortion. How can I have a yingling living within me?'

'The dreams manifest the torment your yingling feels. It blames you, it is haunting you for some reason, and tomorrow, I will free your mind so that you can gain insight.'

'But how can you and your brother see it?'

'I have many brothers, we have seen the souls since eternity. We are an oracle, an enigma. We are a looking glass into a realm of the gods. My brothers and I see the pain and anguish that follow people around us. A soul is inherent to each of us. Until it is free from the bonds of this world, it cannot move on.'

'But why now? Why has it come to haunt me now?' Kate fidgeted with her hem.

'Your pregnancy has freed the yingling. It has laid dormant within you or within an inanimate object that has been close to you, but now it wants... no... it needs to be free.'

After taking a few deep breaths, inhaling through his nostrils and exhaling through his partially opened lips, Mei continued in a more upbeat tone, trying to take the weight of Kate's yingling onto his shoulders.

'On the thirteenth day of the seventh month in the lunar calendar, Chinese traditionalists believe that the three dominions of Heaven, Hell, and the dominion of the living are open. Both Buddhists and Taoists perform rituals to transmute and give absolution to the suffering souls of departed relatives.'

Mei continued: 'We also perform an old Taoist ritual called 'Yingling Gongyang', a ceremony to release the trapped soul, to send it on its way, unbound and free, to the realm of the spirit world. With the spirit gates open, hopefully, the yingling can find itself liberated from this dominion of the living.'

Kate nodded her approval with a strained smile.

'Kate, do you understand the meaning of Tao?' inquired Mei.

'No, not really,' came her honest reply.

'Tao is the flow of chi through the universe or the force behind the natural order. It is the essential energy of action, and Tao is the source of existence and non-existence,' Mei described.

With Kate listening intently, the Daoshi continued. 'Wu wei literally means 'without action'. We often express this through the paradox wei wu wei, meaning 'action without action' or 'effortless doing'. Water is soft and weak but can move earth and carve stone. The purpose of wu wei is alignment with Tao, revealing the invisible power within all things. As a Taoist master of wu wei, I can control this invisible potential.' Mei paused to take stock as he sipped from a glass of water.

'Kate, you need to find a perfect equilibrium within that we know as 'Pu'. Pu is a metaphor for wu wei. It is a passive condition of receptiveness... a state of pure potential. Perception without prejudice. Everything is seen in this state without preconceptions or illusions. We believe pu to be the true, unburdened nature of the mind. In the state of pu, there is no beautiful or ugly, no right or wrong. There is only pure experience, or awareness, free from knowledge and lived experiences, free from learned labels and definitions.'

Mei continued with his lesson. 'This state of being is the purpose of following wu wei, and once you have a harmonious soul, the right outcomes will flow without conscious control. Only then, when you have found this enlightened state of wu wei, will you receive the answers you seek. Tomorrow, I will help you find your answers, you will find your equilibrium.'

Kate smiled, 'Thank you, Mei, I'm so grateful for all you are telling me.'

'Kate, be free with nature. Relax and sleep. Your mind needs to rest so that you can get the full benefits of tomorrow's experience. You do not need anything from this world. Everything you need is within you. Put all your belongings in that room, explore your surroundings and look to find yourself.'

Mei pointed to an open doorway next to where they were seated. He got to his feet and walked across the courtyard to a small room hidden behind a heavy curtain, feeding the animals en route. As ordered, Kate went to the entrance and saw the sparsely furnished room, a mattress-covered bamboo bed frame, a small chest of drawers, a jug of water, and a small earthenware cup. Kate did as she was instructed, put all of her belongings into the top drawer, and went back to the seating area. Taking Mei's advice, she took off her clothes, left the house and walked to the bridge. Sitting on the soft grass and gazing into the shimmering water, she closed her eyes to focus her mind.

Chapter 23

Open to the elements, the crowing of a cockerel woke Kate from her slumber. The morning sun rose over the scenery, gradually ending the night's starlit darkness. After the chaotic mess of her recent sleep patterns and the craziness that had infiltrated her life, she could not recall having dreamt, but she knew she'd slept solidly for what seemed to be a long time. She was unsure exactly how long, as she had removed her watch along with her clothes.

A mist was rising off the stream's surface as the excited fish darted through the water, causing a rippling on the surface. The thick grass on which she'd laid had made an impression on her naked body, and as the blood returned to her skin, the interwoven mesh of lines in her tender flesh slowly dissipated. Kate rose to her feet, yawning as she stretched her rested body before stepping down the bank into the glistening cool water, which stopped just above her navel. Shuddering as she submerged herself, the shock of the cool water kick-started her lethargic body. After a few minutes of swimming underwater, she resurfaced, feeling alive from the revitalising water which had cleansed her face and body. Gingerly pulling herself back up onto the bank, she sat on the edge with the balls of her feet circling the surface, which caused undulating waves to radiate. Recharged and relaxed, she meticulously wrung her hair before gently combing her fingers through the wet strands. She got to her feet and palmed the excess water off her goose-pimpled body. Heading towards the temple-shaped silhouette, the sky of the breaking dawn was littered with wispy strands of cirrus cloud.

The sound alerted Mei, who warmly welcomed Kate back to his humble abode as she entered through the creaking door.

'Good morning, Kate, fresh eggs for breakfast?' Mei was feeling around the straw-covered bottom of the chicken run, searching for his breakfast as Kate crossed the yard and approached him.

'Good morning to you, Mei. Please, let me help, it's the least I can do,' replied Kate as she walked past him and into the small holding.

'Be my guest, young lady. You sound more at ease today. How did you sleep?'

She carefully retrieved a few eggs, placing them in the basket that Mei had passed to her, and answered his question as she closed the gate. 'Perfectly. I can honestly say I can't remember having ever slept so deeply. Well, not for a long time anyway.'

'Good, good, good. You'll need all of your energy for today. We're going to be busy. Would you like to refresh, or was that swim you just had sufficient?' The two exchanged smiles.

Mei was dressed exactly as he had been when she had arrived the previous afternoon. He went into the small room behind the heavy curtain and pulled back the cloth. He beckoned Kate over, and with the eggs nested in the basket, she followed him through the doorway.

Mei's room was basic. Apart from a small stove and oven-like chamber, a tiny draining board accommodating various cooking utensils, and his bamboo cane bed, it was almost empty except for the dust. Two large carafes filled with water, most probably from the brook, sparkled in the light that poured through a small window above the kitchen area.

'Here, towel yourself down, you'll catch a cold.' He passed her a perfectly folded white towel, which looked identical to hers. Kate pulled the towel to her face and inhaled the scent of the detergent, it smelled like one of her towels, and with her face covered in the soft fabric, she could have been thousands of miles away in her en-suite in Courtfield Mews. This was the only thing in the room that was pure, untouched, and wholly out of place.

'How would you like your eggs? Boiled or poached?' was the question by the eager chef-to-be.

'I'm easy, Mei. However, you have yours, is fine by me.'

He turned to Kate, raising his eyebrows. 'Poached it is!'

After breakfast, Kate washed the utensils and left them to dry on the tiny draining board before strolling into the courtyard.

'Kate, come here and join me. We can start,' instructed Mei as he sat on his arse-grooved bench.

Kate perched on her bench, her knees pulled up to her chest. She arched forward with both arms supporting her chin as they bridged her knees. A white ceramic container, smeared with brown fingerprints around the exterior and lid, was placed between his legs.

'Yesterday, I mentioned that your pregnancy has freed the once-dormant yingling that has either slept within you or within an inanimate object that has been close to you. You need to make a new home for the yingling, somewhere it can reside for the rest of eternity. There are many temples in China and Taiwan full of dolls that are home to the souls of terminated and stillborn children...'

Kate interrupted Mei. 'Dolls? What sort of dolls?'

'Any doll. They make a good home for a foetus ghost until it is ready to move on, move to the spirit world, or return to its host. If you had a doll as a child, it may have lived within the vacant hollow, biding its time.'

Kate mumbled: 'I have a doll, a China doll.' She silently motioned to herself, wondering if the lost spirit had used her toy as a temporary host. 'I have had her since my childhood, she was given to me by my Uncle Tom. She has always been with me.' An uncomfortable silence filled the fragrant air.

The silence was broken by clinking sounds as Mei hunched over the glazed pot and teased off the lid. Kate could see a damp blue rag covered in brown stains inside. Mei removed the cloth and placed it on the lid at his feet. The contents was instantly recognisable to Kate, as she had used the moist orangey-brown substance before.

'I'm guessing you know what this is?' Mei suggested with a flicker of humour.

'Well, it looks like clay.'

'It is clay, but this,' he looked in reverence at the sticky material, 'this is unique clay. For years, scientists have tried everything, even using pollen compositions, to ascertain the clay mines' location and the kilns Qin used to manufacture his army. This is not just any clay, this clay has come from a secret pit... this is the clay used for the Terracotta Army. As you know, this clay will stand the test of time. This will be a good home for your ghost to live in.'

The irony and the appreciation of her journey did not pass Kate by. 'The Terracotta Army, that is where it all started for me. I have come full circle.'

Mei scooped out a lump, about the size of a small grapefruit, with his fingers and instantly, but loosely, modelled a headless human torso. Happy with the consistency and amount, he rolled the clay back into a ball and placed it in Kate's cupped palms.

'Here, you need to make a new dwelling. Fashion a doll, one that your yingling can inhabit for eternity. You need to put all of your love and care into the details. I know you have the talent.'

Mei handed over a small frayed roll containing pottery tools as he got to his feet. Leaving Kate to create her new doll, he scurried across the yard, again feeding the animals en route.

Kate held the heavy lump in her hand as she kneaded the malleable clay between her fingers. Roughly mimicking Mei's actions, she sculpted the doll's head, body, arms with hands, and legs with feet. As she concentrated on the cosmetics of the finer details with a clay scalpel, her heart skipped a beat as a vision of a human foetus appeared in her hands. She could see and feel the clammy pink flesh between her fingers as she stared at an unborn child's partially formed facial features. Kate's mind went into overdrive as she leapt to her feet. The terror of the hallucination and the fear that shrouded her body caused her hands to throw the effigy to the red carpet under her feet. The clay head flattened as the sculpture hit the floor, leaving an impression of the dusty rug across its newly formed face. Terrified and physically shaken, with her eyes shut tight and her hands clasping her head, a bemused Kate tried to grasp what she had just witnessed in the palm of her left hand.

'Pick it up,' bellowed Mei from behind the curtain. 'What are you scared of? It cannot hurt you!'

As best she could, Kate regained self-control and looked towards the heavy-drawn curtain concealing the entrance to Mei's quaint residence. Confused about his ability to see through walls and dumbfounded by the figment of her imagination, she looked around the courtyard to ensure everything around her was as it should be. A tingling shot up her spine. Nervously retaking her seat on the bench, she apprehensively retrieved the clay doll from the floor and picked out the splinters of dirt from its hardening face before carefully repairing the squashed head. As she continued to work the clay, her body spasmed as though someone, or something, had stirred in her soul. After two hours, she'd finished the naked sexless doll, undisturbed from any further visions. When Mei reappeared after his siesta, the figurine was complete.

'Let me look,' he asked, holding out his hands.

Kate moved to one side, displaying the doll on the bench, as Mei looked down at the doll and gently ran his fingers over its form.

'Perfect. We just need to fire it. You go and rest now, Kate, I will wake you when it's time.'

Exhausted from the concentration she had imparted while making the doll, she nodded. 'Okay, if you're certain.' Kate was still dubious about how the seemingly blind man could see so much as he wandered behind his curtain with the drying clay. Kate left the house and meandered to the brook, washing the clay residue off her hands and body before returning to her room, lying down on the bed and drifting off to sleep.

Chapter 24

'Kate, Kate, it's nearly time.'

Kate woke to Mei's voice, full of excitement as he stood in the doorway dressed in all his finery. Kate stretched her body, lengthening her limbs as she lay on the bed. The heat from the late afternoon sun suffocated her as she got off the bed and followed Mei into the courtyard.

The remarkable ceremonial daopao, worn by the Taoist priest, was like no robe she had ever seen. The crimson cloth was tailor-made using the most delicate silk. It was completely covered, front to back, with a sizeable tiger-dragon motif and numerous illustrations of meticulously hand-inked ornate flowers and cranes in liquid gold. The striking flared sleeves, which spread like the delicate wings of a butterfly, were decorated with patterns of concentric circles and finished with black silk cuffs. A bright green sash hung around his neck, draping beneath his white beard and down to his waist. His mitre was pinned in place on his head.

Mei approached an old chest that was placed next to the bench. The flat lid appeared to be made of compressed earth. He looped the carrying strap over his shoulder, picked up the box, and headed towards the temple's entrance.

'Come on then, let's go,' instructed Mei as Kate followed him around the back of the house and across the three rice fields. The dykes provided a perfect pathway to wherever they were going.

The sun was inching itself down as the intense heat dissipated slightly.

However, Kate could still feel its radiance on her tanned and aerated skin.

'What do you see?' Kate inquired, she was surprised by his perceptive knowledge of the surroundings, even though it was evident that the cataracts had all but blinded him.

'I see everything in shades of grey, a two-dimensional image of perceived edges. For example, I can see your body by the outlines and contours of your figure,' Mei explained before continuing. 'The rest of your shape is filled with grey. A soul or a spirit scratches around the physical edges of the three-dimensional shape that it resides in. A neon halo effect, I guess, is the easiest way to describe it. I see halos of everything living, everything that had once lived, and everything manmade. Even steel has atomic energy!'

Shocked by this revelation, Kate queried Mei further. 'You can see me? I was under the impression that you were blind.'

'I told you yesterday I lost my eyesight a few years ago, but I can sense the physical world and see the spirit world. So, I can see, it's just not what you would perceive as sight.'

A blushing Kate could feel her nakedness, as blood filled the cheeks of her face and her body temperature rose.

'I sense your embarrassment,' Mei smiled as he turned to Kate. 'You worry too much. Just relax and keep walking. We are nearly there.'

Knowing she could do nothing about her nudity, the mother-to-be sauntered ahead, following the well-trodden track. After walking, for what she thought was more than a mile but less than two, she stopped and admired the beauty of the surroundings. The medium-sized lake was set against the splendid backdrop of the sun as it set over an extensive range of snow-topped mountains that reached far into the distant, darkening sky. Overhanging bushes and bulrushes ringed the pool as large koi swept beneath a covering of lilies that rested on the surface of the still water. The flowers' exquisite whiteness contrasted against the plant's dark green circular pads. In awe of nature and not wanting to interrupt her enjoyment of the view, Mei confirmed that they had arrived with a shake of his head and a grunt. He walked beyond her vantage point to the water's edge as she duly followed.

'Here, this is the perfect spot.' Mei squatted down, and without wasting time, he unpacked the box. After carefully removing the heavy earthen lid, he pulled out a black silk cloth and placed it on the grass, followed by a blanket, which he spread for the mother-to-be. 'Please be seated,' he instructed Kate.

Kate smiled in acknowledgement as she took her place on the blanket, which was surprisingly soft. She sat with her legs curled under her body, leaning on her left arm. Her right arm draped across her body with her hand resting in her lap as she watched the hunched man continue emptying the contents. Kate could make out a red paper boat, a small lantern candle, a vial of liquid and the terracotta doll. She proffered her open palm towards Mei as he placed the ridged clay doll into her hand. The figurine was still cooling from being fired, and it looked better than she had remembered after the apparition of the human foetus had eclipsed her memory.

With the closed box between them, Mei placed the black silk square across the top as he strictly and methodically configured his makeshift altar, explaining the importance of each ceremonial item to Kate as he went along. The priest placed a large candle at either end of the box lid and snapped his fingers. Kate was astonished to see a small flame materialise in the palm of his right hand.

'Sorry, but I do like my party tricks,' he jested as he lit each candle. 'These represent the sun and the moon.' He placed two small earthenware bowls containing tea and water between the candles and a large oil lamp with a lotus-flower-shaped base. 'The tea and water symbolise the union of yang and yin energies in nature and the body.

The tea is yin, or the dragon's blood, the water is yang, or the tiger's saliva,' he said, pausing to admire the artefact in his hand.

'The Sacred Lotus Lamp is the lamp of wisdom, the light of the Tao, the universal energy that maintains and harmonises everything that exists.' He gently polished the gold lamp to a brilliant shine as it sparkled in the candlelight. 'Kate, this lamp symbolises our immortality. During the ritual, this lamp must never be extinguished, or this will allow dark forces to enter.'

A strange-looking compass was placed in the front corner of the ceremonial table. 'The luopan or geomantic compass is used for foresight. The eight trigrams enable me to make precise readings about the spiritual balance of a given location, and it can also detect the presence of ghosts.'

Small bowls of fruit were placed along the back of the altar. 'One for each of the five elements: wood, fire, earth, metal, and water,' explained Mei.

The last major piece on the almost complete altar was an incense burner placed centrally at the front. 'The three incense sticks represent a human being's life force, consisting of a trinity of diverse energies – generative, vital, and spiritual. When these energies become poisoned, usually through attachment and craving, purification is required for spiritual growth. As the smoke rises and the ashes fall, this will evoke the separation of the yingling as it leaves you.'

The final bowl was placed in front of the incense burner. 'This uncooked rice and fish represents the union of the tea and the water. The yin and the yang, as it absorbs energy from both the sun and soil, the Heaven and the Earth.'

Finally, Mei placed three ancient-looking scrolls on the table. 'The ancient paper scrolls will allow me to open the celestial gateway and block the passage of any evil spirit. The incantations I will chant during the exorcism rite are usually completed behind closed doors, unknown to all. But as you will be unconscious, this will not affect you.'

With the preparation of the altar complete and readying himself for the ritual, Mei took his place on the blanket, kneeling opposite

Kate, continuing where he had left off with their earlier discussion about his vision. 'The halos that I see are smooth if the creature is harmonious or slightly scratchy if the chi of the creature is stressed or agitated. Your halos, the ones my brothers and I see, are going haywire, a chaotic trinity. The halo of your unborn child is surprisingly serene and at peace, considering the battle that rages inside you. But yours and the third, the yingling's, are a dark, tormented, and tangled mess.'

Mei took a deep breath before continuing. 'The yingling, however it got hold of you, is brooding. For some unknown reason, it is jealous of your existence, and if you say you have never had an abortion or a miscarriage, then only the yingling will be able to give you the explanation you crave.'

Mei paused for thought as he scratched at an invisible irritation on his neck. 'Kate, tonight you must find spiritual equilibrium. I will free your mind, and you will, in effect, go into an unconscious, virtually comatose-like state. By giving you the key to open the door, I will allow you to see and feel, through and beyond your subconsciousness, into the hidden depths of your psyche. If the two spirits, yours and the yingling's, are agreeable you should get answers to the ghostly presence within you. Only then, when the foetal spirit of the unborn becomes omniscient, will it leave you and take refuge in the doll.'

'How will I know? I mean… if the spirit leaves me.'

'I will see it leave you, and then you will be left with two: yours and that of your unborn child.'

'What do I need to do?'

Mei instructed Kate. 'Just as the sun sets, you will prepare the meal of rice and fish on a freshly picked lily pad. This will feed the departing yingling's hunger, strengthening it for the final journey. You will then light the lantern and gently place it inside the paper boat before pushing it and the lily pad onto the lake. Only if the spirit is placated by your efforts will it feast on the offerings before following the candle-lit boat across the lake to the realm of the spirits.'

'But what about the doll?' Kate was puzzled.

'The doll will become a refuge for the yingling's soul. Once the soul of the unborn foetus is safely interred, I will ritualistically bless the effigy before burying it. The soul will then split into yin and yang energies. The yin energy, the feelings of sorrow and passion and anger, remain within the doll. The pure spiritual essence of the yingling, the yang, survives and goes on into the realm of the spirits.'

Just at the point when the sun had all but disappeared behind the mountains, and with the lights of the candle and oil lamp flickering brightly in the stillness of the night, Mei spoke the words that filled Kate with mixed emotions. She was excited about exorcising the yingling, though in fear of her journey into the nightmare of her darkest secrets, the mysterious, uncontrollable world of dreams and visions.

'Kate,' was the only word that met his hand gesture as he pointed with his open palm towards the lake, alerting her that it was now time.

Getting up slowly, she apprehensively picked up the small ceramic bowl of sticky rice and filleted fish resting by the altar and walked slowly to the lakeside. Bending down, she could see herself in the blackness of the still pool as the stars danced across its surface, her head resting on the ridge of her knees as the gentle ripples waved back her reflection. With both arms outstretched, she plucked out a lily pad and snapped its stem. Placing the hand-size disc on the bank, she emptied the contents of the pot onto the leaf with the fillet lying alongside the rice. After meticulously rinsing her hands in the water and shaking the droplets from her fingertips she stood, keenly watched by Mei. She returned the pot to its place next to the altar. Using the dancing flame at the top of the right-hand candle, she picked up and lit the lantern before positioning the small light in the centre of the boat.

Kate looked at Mei, ensuring she was doing what was expected, as he nodded his approval. For the first time, she could sense an unease as a concerned-looking Mei stared back at her, seemingly unsure of himself and putting her even more on edge.

The perfume of the incense filled the air, and the tiny trails of smoke from the end of the joss sticks snaked upwards into the night sky. Kate gently raised the boat and measured each movement to where the lily pad was patiently waiting to play its part in the proceedings. Glancing again in Mei's direction, he brusquely pushed both hands at her, indicating her to continue.

A pessimistic feeling in her gut caused her to pause as she tilted her head to one side. Delicately releasing her grasp on the pad and the illuminated watercraft, the flotilla glided across the current-free water with some indiscernible guiding force tugging them into the dark expanse. Uneasily, they watched the items floating away, and with her heart pounding, Kate now knew that the time had come to face the music. Pulling at the robe stuck to his moist chest, Mei looked increasingly edgy as sweat oozed beneath his hat and trickled down his forehead. The priest waited for Kate to return to her seat on the blanket while scrabbling with the small vial of fluid he'd unpacked from the box.

Wasting no time, he thrust the small glass bottle towards Kate.

'Drink this. It's a herbal potion to help relax your tired body. It will harm neither you nor your baby.'

Sharply, almost impatiently, he nodded his head twice in Kate's direction, urging her to drink. Kate was extremely uneasy with the situation but she concluded that she was now in too deep and that pulling out of the ritual was not an option. As prompted, and without a word of argument, Kate pulled the cork from the top of the vial, releasing a sickly smell that was a lot like hashish. She put the glass bottle to her lips and threw her wrist upwards, pouring the strange-tasting liquid into her mouth. She replaced the cork and gave the empty vial back to Mei.

'Kate, lie down and wrap yourself in the blanket. Your dreams will give you your answers.'

With trepidation, she surveyed the darkness of the night sky, fighting the instincts of her drowsy eyes. A psychedelic light show materialised in her mind as the distorted images of her reality merged into a hazy kaleidoscope of chaotic colour. Unable to focus as her head began to spin, a potent urge overpowered her. Powerless to resist the hypnagogic feeling any longer, she gave in to the experience.

Chapter 25

Kate stood at the edge of the pool mesmerised as she gazed across an inlet towards the horizon. An extraordinary coastline had been forged as bubbling, red-hot magma inched forward into a hissing, steaming ocean. The result was a mass of black volcanic cliffs contrasting against the crystal blue sea as it merged with the sky. Streaks of brilliant white clouds and gently folding white waves broke the glorious monotony of the blue background filling the stage.

The midday heat radiating from the golden sun beat down, warming her naked flesh. She was alone, not even her shadow accompanied her. Mozart's 'Laudate Dominum' was being played in heaven, filling the atmosphere. The angelic voice of the soloist, the virtuous choir, and the strings' chords all in perfect harmony. The rugged jaws of an unearthly amphitheatre kept the hostile sea at bay whilst a tongue-like island of solidified lava plugged the entrance to the inlet of the rocky-walled arena. The tongue tenderly broke the oncoming waves into streams of shimmering clear water that meandered across its craterous face and trickled down into the basin.

The angry pulse of the ocean slowly intensified as it gathered momentum. While it prepared to display its natural supremacy, aqueous white swirls crashed into the volcanic fortifications that lined the shore, defending the land from the torrents as surge after surge of waves tried their hardest to enter the ring of rock. The raging water seemed focused on the inlet as it relentlessly targeted the shallow blockage at the mouth of the theatre. Upping the tempo to a brutal finale with evermore vicious attacks, the besieged dam finally succumbed to the rising tide.

A violent flow of icy water flowed into the womb of the lagoon. Kate could feel the power from the sea invigorating her, showering her flesh with its salty liquid. The escaping oxygen from the influx of watery missiles caused clouds to appear in the once transparent pool, disseminating instantly. Mini caves in the rock walls became foaming white waterfalls as each swell receded. But it was quiet, no sound came with the sea.

After the waves had relinquished their claim, Kate remained spellbound as the turquoise hue of the pond enticed her. Timidly, she sat down on the edge, her legs and feet placidly testing the crystal clear water as the sun's rays danced across its surface. Elegantly lowering herself into the ocean pool, which peaked at her soft, rounded breasts, she felt the water engulf her.

The fleeting coldness caused Kate to judder and a silent gasp escaped her parted lips. Now accustomed to the cool water, she pushed herself off the bottom and away from the black lava-rock wall. Effortlessly and gracefully, she glided towards the centre. A sense of peace overwhelmed her as she swam just out of her depth and treading water. Floating crucifix-like on the water with her eyes closed, her sun-kissed skin emerged above the waterline. With Mozart's anthem still resounding around the barren coal theatre, Kate lost herself. The effects of the setting sun on the craggy walls of the amphitheatre cast an audience of shadowy faces on the façade of the enclosure.

As the final act was about to commence, the ghostly spectators murmured with an indiscernible hum. Brushing her body against something soft, something familiar, Kate opened her eyes and turned upright in the pool. Startled but not unnerved, she had been joined by her double. Kate did not feel threatened. Unlike her previous encounter dressed as Satan's whore, she felt comforted.

Looking knowingly into the eyes of the naked apparition opposite, she reached out towards her double. As if feeling skin for the first time, a host of new sensations tickled her senses as she tenderly stroked its face with her right hand. Unhurried and energised, her charged fingers followed the watery contours of the vision. From its face, glancing down the neck, across the chest, Kate's palm turned as her hand passed between its breasts, downwards over the abdomen and towards a soft pubic triangle. The movements of her hand and the sensations running through her fingers were mimicked on her own breathless body as an invisible hand passed over her flesh. In spasms of ecstasy, she climaxed.

Both still treading water, the twin pulled away from Kate and started to swim around her, goading and teasing her. The two laughed and frolicked with each other like sibling children, showing off like they'd never seen another human being before. The warming water washed over their bodies, baptising them together for an eternity.

Without warning, the double grabbed Kate's right hand and forcibly placed it just below her navel. Kate's heart missed a beat as her palm touched her twin's abdomen. Kate's entire life instantaneously flashed before her, back to the moment of her conception. Great vibes of horror accompanied the muffled tones of her screaming mother. Unknown to Sarah, stress within her body communicated an awfulness that greeted her daughter's fledgling soul inside her. The vision lasted no more than a split second as a traumatised and visibly shaken Kate instinctively pulled her hand away, unsure of what she had just experienced or envisaged.

A potent disturbance immersed the women as a single wave smashed into them, filling the pool with saline. Terrified and separated, the double had been hurled to the far side of the cauldron-like pool, opposite the inlet as she seized a black barb that jutted from the harsh volcanic surround. Frantically brandishing an outstretched arm in her direction, Kate could only watch in vain. Whilst the drowning sister grasped at her hand, a second violent wave momentarily sank Kate before sucking her the short distance across the bubbling pool and back towards the mouth of the cove as the water finally withdrew to the ocean. Kate grabbed her own barb immediately adjacent to the inlet before screaming at the top of her voice for the well of water to subside, but to no avail. The music from heaven drowned out her voice. She had no control, no say. She was impotent. As the water fleetingly stilled, the twins looked across the void to each other, both relieved and thankful that the worst was over.

An unseen foe effortlessly entered the arena and without warning, it pulled the ghostly figment from her spur and forcibly dragged her to the pool's centre. Struggling for her life against the unnatural force, the twin was sharply and violently pulled under the all-consuming water. Her grasping hands thrashed around above her head, searching for something, anything, to stop her descent. They failed, and she disappeared into the depths.

Tears streamed down Kate's face as she clutched onto the jut, watching as another wave entered the lagoon. Free from any downward pressure, the double's head suddenly bobbed back above the surface as a pool of red materialised from beneath her, colouring the water. Screaming in agony, her contorted face expressed that something awful, something evil, had just taken place. Kate could only watch on helplessly as a mutilated, dismembered limb floated past her, through the inlet, over the lava tongue, and into the expansive blue ocean beyond.

Defenceless to the entity that carefully and relentlessly pursued her, the double was again jerked under the water like a fish teasing a baited hook. Thrashing around and fighting the invisible enemy, a fresh spurt of red appeared around the twin as she splashed above the waterline. The second leg was extracted from the bloody red pool, taken out on the current of a receding wave. Now unconscious, the twin was still alive but slowly bleeding to death.

The antagonist callously and calculatedly rotated the upper body of Kate's sibling within the heart of the pool. With her head held steady, crowning towards the inlet, an invisible perforator crashed through the once pliable soft spot of her cranium – and punctured her skull. An intense burst of blood and brains gushed out of the opened wound towards the ocean as her skull collapsed. Kate could see the scrunched-up features on her once beautiful twin's bloodied face. Horrifically disfigured, the tattered and lifeless corpse was flushed out of the cove as the ocean ingested the carcass.

Without warning, everything became motionless. The waves subsided, the water level dropped, and a static pond of bloodied saline water remained in the womb of the cove. Still clinging tightly to the rock barb, Kate was alone. Her head was pounding to the tune of her thumping heart. Scratched and bleeding from the rocky crags she lay against, her body shook uncontrollably. Confusion reigned in her soul as she tried to comprehend what she had just witnessed. Gradually, she regained her senses and sanity as she repeatedly inhaled through her nose, filling her lungs with air. As her battle-weary eyes closed, the sky turned black. The last word of Mozart's anthem left the ringing tones of 'Amen' resonating through her mind.

Chapter 26

Kate had returned from China a week earlier than planned, landing at Heathrow late the previous afternoon. She fell asleep replaying the Chinese experience of the past seven days with thoughts of Mei and the ritual tumbling around her head.

The alarm had been set to go off early, and the buzzing broke into Kate's dreamless state as the flashing red numerals displayed 05:30. Considering how over-tired she had felt, she'd slept relatively well. After the events of the last four months, Kate desperately tried to get a grip. She wanted to feel like her old self and desperately wanted her life back.

She turned on the TV as she made a valiant attempt at her neglected daily routine. Dressed, but not to her usual high standards, and loosely throwing the covers over her bed, Kate caught the end of a news item... 'The two men, one in his late fifties and the other in his sixties, were stabbed to death in the early hours of this morning, in what police believe to be an act of random violence. Eyewitness accounts state that a man of Chinese descent, dressed in black, murdered the two men after a brief altercation in back street Chinatown. A man is helping police with their enquiries after he was also stabbed in the thigh whilst trying to apprehend the assailant. Police are interested in hearing from anybody who was in the packed West End, who may have seen the assault or the assailant running from the scene. The police have not yet released any further details of the deceased.'

Kate sighed at the news. After the recent spate of stabbings in the capital, another two innocent lives had been snuffed out and added to the Met's statistics. She turned off the television and the lights, as she left the Mews. Her seven o'clock car was waiting.

'Swindon. This is Swindon,' announced the onboard tannoy as the 07:57 First Great Western train from London Paddington pulled to a halt on platform four. Kate considered staying on the train as it neared her stop, but she'd decided that the myriad of questions posed by the lake vision needed face-to-face addressing with the one person she believed could give her much-needed answers.

Clutching her handbag from the seat next to her, she pulled herself to her feet and reluctantly made her way to the train doors, down two steps and onto the platform. The electronic sign suspended from the terminal roof strut told her the time was 09:16. Unusually and to the amazement of the other passengers disembarking the train, it had arrived on time. Any visible signs of an extreme Saturday evening had been swept away, and an elderly gent, sporting a fluorescent orange safety jacket and donning an old flat cap, was spraying clean the stains of indulgence from the grey Tarmac floor. Hastily, Kate checked she had everything and walked down a flight of steps and out onto the station forecourt to be greeted by the late summer's sun.

A row of highly polished Hackney Carriages were queued up, awaiting their fares. Kate popped her head towards the cab's passenger seat at the front of the line.

'Good morning. Could you take me to Christ Church in Old Town, please?' she asked.

'Yes, of course. Get in,' replied the Eastern European voice that answered.

She got in the cab and looked through the window as the driver pulled away. This was a route Kate had taken many times on her way to the old town part of Swindon, and she reminisced to herself about how the ancient Victorian architecture used to look before the steel and glass buildings had infiltrated the area.

Swindon had once been a thriving railway town with a soul and a sense of community, but now it had become cold and heartless, full of migrants. The driver glanced in his rearview mirror at Kate but said nothing. The short journey to Christ Church took about five minutes on the quiet roads. As the cab crossed the infamous Magic Roundabout and made its way up Drove Road, Kate could see the beautifully restored ornate spire of the old Victorian church towering above Swindon.

Kate had been a regular visitor to Swindon, spending most of the school holidays in her Nan's bungalow during the golden years of her childhood. She had spent months playing at Lawn Woods, jumping the boggy drainage ditches, or flying kites in the fields. During the summer months, she would attend the Sunday Service at Christ Church, and whilst most of the religious meaning went over her head, Sunday School was always fun.

Her mother's parents had both been cremated – first Granddad just before Kate's sixth birthday and her beloved Nan when she was seventeen – and their ashes were interred just behind the church. A stone sculpture of Christ Jesus, a lamb held across one arm and a staff in the other, set within the church's transept, kept watch over his cremated and coffin-housed flock. Kate had hardly ever returned to Swindon since her Nan's passing, except for the occasional visit to see her mother and for weddings, christenings and family funerals of one or two dear friends she had kept in touch with from her childhood days. Whatever the reason, Christ Church always seemed to occupy a central role in any visits Kate made.

The taxi pulled into the winding slip road to the car park. Kate saw her mother walking in the church. It was the 9:30 service, and Kate had arrived with minutes to spare. Kate passed a ten-pound note through the glass hatch between the driver and herself.

'Thanks, keep the change,' she stuttered as she exited the cab, looking toward the old timber doors behind which her mother had just vanished. Kate paced up the gentle slope to the entrance and fleetingly looked up at the imposing spire as limestone gargoyles and the faces of angels looked down. She went through the doors and was greeted by the unmistakable and instantly recognisable voice of a female warden handing out service booklets.

'Kate!' came the excited and warm welcome. 'Wow! It's been a while. It's so good to see you again.'

The voice belonged to the daughter of her mother's lifelong friend, Linda, and although unacknowledged by Kate, the warden, Rachel, was her only real friend. The two childhood friends had little in common away from Swindon. But their tried-and-tested relationship was built on a solid foundation of mutual respect and complete discretion. Ordinarily, she would have been Kate's first stop on any planned visit to her mother's.

Kate's heartstrings had been tugged as she instantly found herself in the unenviable position of being torn between the safety and comfort of her friend's familiarity and her search for answers.

'Hello Rachel, it's good to see you too. Look, we'll catch up later, yes?' Kate replied, and without waiting for a response from the open-mouthed Rachel, she hurriedly turned away, heading toward the left-hand row of pews where her mother always seated herself for Sunday Service. A concerned Rachel started to follow her, but seeing Kate's demeanour, at least for the time being, decided to hold back.

Kate could see her mother sitting on the same pew, head bowed, hands together, and eyes closed while she gathered her thoughts in preparation for the service. Kate quietly sat down and placed her hand on her mother's knee. A startled Sarah opened her eyes and turned towards her. Her irises widened as they tried to take in as much light from the shadows cast around the grey stone walls. The background murmur of the congregation was abruptly broken by the sound of weekly notices being read out.

'Oh, Kate! You gave me quite a shock. What are you doing here?' came the thrilled response to unexpectedly seeing her daughter sitting beside her. Tears of joy filled Kate's mother's eyes as she embraced her only child.

'Hello, Mum,' came Kate's unsure response. 'I really need your help. I need to talk.'

Kate's voice was close to breaking, and Sarah immediately realised that this visit was not a social call, she had never seen Kate looking so distraught. With her late-developing maternal instincts telling her something was wrong, Sarah attempted to usher Kate to stand so they could leave.

'No, no, after the service. I want to stay,' Kate demanded, and with a hint of a forced smile, a worried Sarah nodded in agreement.

The 'house' vicar was a dedicated family man, affectionately known as 'Dave the Rev'. As his joyful tones filled the church, Kate just stared at the stained glass window in the alcove next to her. The service continued, and the Eucharistic Prayer temporarily returned Kate's mind to the dream of the charcoal baby. After an hour and a half, the two women, sitting hand-in-hand, never said a word to each other except to offer 'the peace of the Lord'. Kate felt comforted. The Christian service was a welcome distraction from the bedlam in her life and the turmoil she was feeling.

As they waited to leave the church through the vestibule in the far corner at the back, Kate deliberated over the etchings in the glass doors. Seraphs triumphantly blew their trumpets, praising the glory of God as he looked down from on high, a silent witness to all of mankind's happiness and heartache.

A concerned Rachel hovered with prayer books in hand, looking towards the dishevelled shell of her childhood friend, and after concluding that the usually stunning brunette was distracted beyond belief, she decided to give Kate some space. Whatever was wrong, it was not her business.

After a brief chat with Reverend David, the women departed through the side porch, slow-marching in silence across the church grounds, onto the streets of Old Town and through the woods to the Swindon family home. This was not the time for small talk that was patently clear to both parties.

The rustling leaves blowing in the gentle breeze, for some unknown reason troubled Sarah as she became filled with dreaded anticipation. She knew what was coming. She had been ignoring it. It was buried deep inside her subconscious, only two others and God himself had ever known the truth.

Apprehensively, they walked up the gravel drive to the dark green front door. The crunching stones underfoot sounded like a battalion of soldiers on a drill square, adding to the tension that had been building. A culmination of a sad and desperate predicament was drawing closer. Kate noted that the willow tree in the centre of the garden had grown, and the shrubs and ferns in the rockery had matured. Apart from that, nothing else had changed at the idyllic picture-postcard bungalow since Nan had passed away. A biting gust blew at their backs, forcing them towards the door. It was as if God himself could wait no longer for the truth to finally be revealed to Kate.

Chapter 27

Walking a couple of paces in front of her daughter, Sarah was all fingers and thumbs getting the key into the lock before pushing open the door. Without a word, she hung her coat and headed to the kitchen, flicking the switch on the kettle.

Lost in thought, a vacant-looking Kate stood on the threshold, motionless, staring at her mother's back before entering the lounge. She took a seat next to the window as she surveyed the front room, remembering how it used to look when her Nan was alive. Whilst most of the ornate mahogany furniture was exactly where it had always been, the white doilies that covered the sideboards, protecting the polished surfaces from the host of photos, had gone. The glass-fronted trinket cabinet used to be crammed with holiday souvenirs and tat, but Sarah had consigned the family memories to the local charity shop years before.

After a few minutes of crashing cupboard doors and rattling cutlery drawers breaking the silence, Sarah steadily walked into the room with two cups of tea. She placed a bone china cup on the side table next to Kate and, as if treading on eggshells, she tentatively walked towards the chair across the room, next to the fireplace. Placing her cup on the mantelpiece, Sarah fastidiously ran her hands down her dress before sitting hunched on the edge of her seat – Nan's old chair – teasing a handkerchief between her sinewy fingers. The print of the floral dress clashed with the chair's upholstery.

As Kate looked intently at her mother, she could only see the cold and heartless woman that blighted her childhood. The room's ambient light made Sarah's face look haggard and so old, almost like an imitation of her loving Nan.

Pale and tense, Sarah stared at her daughter. 'Right, Kate, what's wrong?'

After all she had witnessed and experienced, Kate did not hesitate with her response. 'I'm pregnant, Mum... it was a one-night stand. I don't know who the father is and honestly, it doesn't really matter... as I've decided to keep the baby.'

The pointedness of the statement startled her intrigued mother. As they walked back to the house, Sarah had suspected that Kate was expecting by the slight weight gain around her daughter's lower abdomen, visible under her jacket. Sarah looked at her daughter but didn't respond. She wanted Kate to open up, and her intuition guessed this short outburst was just the start.

Just wanting it all out in the open, Kate continued as she spoke without taking time to breathe.

'I'm nearly five months pregnant... I've been having a terrible time with it... I have been having some shockingly vivid nightmares, insidious ones... I met a man in China, a wise old man, a caring man... he informed me that I was carrying a yingling with me and that I always have...' Kate wiped the tears from her eyes with the palm of her hand.

Sarah pondered, lost in what she was hearing, trying to regain control of the situation. 'Calm down, Kate, one issue at a time.'

'Don't you dare calm down, Kate me. I had a yingling living inside me!'

Sarah was perplexed. 'What's a yingling, Kate?'

'The lingering soul of a dead foetus, Mum,' Kate yelled, 'a soul that has lived in me forever.'

As the remaining colour drained from Sarah's gaunt face, she snapped back at her daughter. 'You don't know what you are talking about, my girl. Just leave it.'

'NO! I need answers. Tell me about this soul. Whose soul is it? Did I have a sister? I need to know. I've dreamt about her mum, and please, don't dismiss her. She told me that you know. Give me some answers!'

The bloody-minded Kate was not in the mood to be fobbed off. All she wanted was honesty from her mother. She wanted a resolution to all the issues that had taken root in her soul over the last four months. She wanted closure.

Sarah knew. She knew damn well that after more than thirty years, her past had finally caught up with her, and with a vengeance. Somebody, or something, had given Kate an inclination of an untold secret, and now was the time to tell the truth, no matter how painful the recriminations might be or how many lives would be forever ruined.

'Well, go on,' Kate directed at her stony-faced mother with a sharp nod. 'Go on... tell me. Don't you think I have a right to know? I am going fucking mad! I need some answers, Mum, please,' Kate pleaded. Pushing her left hand through the bedraggled mess of her hair, she let out a long, dejected sigh.

Sarah twisted the handkerchief, her expression changing to one of deference. She had misgivings about whether she was ready to pay the price for her honesty.

'Okay, Kate, okay,' she mumbled reluctantly. A constant stream of tears now flowed from Sarah's eyes as she looked down at the green and cream paisley carpet surrounding her, the shapes in the pattern seemed to move under her feet, causing her to feel nauseous. She licked her lips to moisten them as she composed herself.

'I was twenty-five years old, and your father and I had argued that day. I can't remember what it was about, and it's not that important now,' she paused before continuing. 'It never was that important.'

Sarah's choking tone and her stark expression were an indication of a dreadful horror that she was about to reveal.. For more than thirty years, the bitterness of the moment and the aftermath had been chained up, and locked away, but was now ready to be unleashed.

'Kate, you need to understand something about your father and me. Times were very different before you came along. We were very different, more open, more honest. Kate, we used to have an open marriage,' she confessed. 'And it worked well,' she added as if to justify the statement.

'What do you mean, an open marriage? You used to sleep with other men?'

Ashamed of her situation, a humiliated Sarah ruefully nodded as she murmured, 'and women.'

'No, never. My father would never condone any such behaviour. You're lying!' Kate could not believe what she was hearing or where the conversation was going.

'Do you want to know or not?' Sarah scowled at Kate as she condescendingly raised her grey thinning eyebrows.

'We had planned to attend a party that evening, but your father had already made his mind up, he wasn't going, and nor was I, he said. That upset me!' Sarah looked heavenwards to the stippled ceiling, her eyes begging for succour, and a sanctuary from the nightmare she had been reliving repeatedly. While trying her hardest to control the situation and planning her sentences carefully, she was now ready to tell the whole story.

'Well, I ended up going on my own. When I arrived, the party was in full swing. It was loud, people were already drunk and stoned, and some were even tripping, but everyone was having a great time. I knew a few people who had planned to be there, so I never fretted about going alone or being alone,' with her eyes shut, she solemnly pressed on. 'I remember I was in the kitchen when Tom walked in with a few of his mates. I could see he'd already had a few and was up for a good night. He walked over to me. I don't think he could see anybody else in the kitchen. He seemed completely focused on me.'

'Anyway, he walked up and kissed me like always and enquired about his little brother. I told him that your father had decided not to come. Tom didn't push me for any more information. I don't know, I guess he could see, or maybe sense, that I was upset.' The pitch in Sarah's voice changed markedly.

'We went outside for some fresh air. It was a moonlit night, and I sat on an old wooden swing, Tom stood with me leaning against its frame. He pulled a joint from his pocket and lit it...'

Kate was aghast by her mother's revelation so far. She wondered where this admission was going.

'I could feel his eyes all over me, and I enjoyed it, I enjoyed the attention he was giving me. I'd only ever seen Tom with younger girls, and the fact he was undressing me with his eyes excited me, and I hadn't felt that wanted for a while.'

Sarah hesitated expecting Kate to butt in. 'Just spit it out!'

'Your father had been away on business for weeks, and whenever he came home, all he wanted to do was work. He never looked at me like he wanted me, just his bloody paperwork. I was only good for a quick fumble. Well, I needed him, but he'd changed. I still had needs, urges... desires.'

Kate stared at Sarah with her piercing hazel eyes that were full of anger. Kate was close to hyperventilating and incandescent with rage. As she ground her teeth, her jaw was clamped shut so tightly she feared she may crack a tooth. As every unbelievable word uttered by her mother increased her angst, and with her hands now tightly gripping the arms of the chair, Kate's s taut-white knuckles caused Sarah's apprehension to peak.

'You flirted with Uncle Tom?" Kate spluttered.

'No, I was just... well, no. I wasn't.'

'Either you were, or you weren't?'

'No, I wasn't.'

She slowly exhaled, contemplating her next words before Kate bellowed, 'Tell me!'

Sarah raised her head to her daughter. 'Don't you dare use that tone with me, my girl. Just who do you think you are talking to?'

'You want to know, do you, do you?' Sarah's voice was now full of fury. 'Well, I'll fu... fucking tell you.'

Kate had never heard a profanity escape her mothers lips not once, not ever. Sarah was tugging at the handkerchief in her hands as years of hiding the truth finally spilled out.

'I smoked the joint with Tom and started to relax. I could feel his eyes looking at my thighs as I sat on the swing. I teased him... I opened my legs. I never wore knickers in those days... nobody did.'

Sarah didn't hesitate. 'Tom stopped and stood before me, looking down at my skirt. I followed his eyes and realised it had risen almost to my waist. I could see he was aroused, and he wanted me.' Sarah returned her daughter's menacing stare before sniping: 'Don't look at me like that, I had a life before you were even thought of.'

Kate was at boiling point. Sarah had hidden this alter ego from her for a lifetime. She knew that her mother had been a rebellious teen, but she never dreamt that she slept around.

'We went back into the house, my body was buzzing, I felt slutty, but I didn't care. Not for me, not for your dad, not for nothing. We ran upstairs and into one of the bedrooms before we jumped on each other. Tom had his hand up my skirt as I undid his fly... well, we started petting... heavily. I remember music pounding through the house. We were kissing passionately as he went to go down on me...' with the tears streaming down her face, Sarah remembered that fateful encounter. '...Then I wanted to stop.'

Kate, unmoved and unsympathetic, continued staring angrily at her mother.

'Even drunk and stoned, I realised it was wrong. We hadn't gone too far, we hadn't... no harm had been done, so I tried to persuade Tom to stop. But it wouldn't. Maybe I wasn't forceful enough, I don't know. I'll never know. He rolled me over onto my front, pushed my head into the bed and,' struggling with the memory Sarah found it difficult to say, but then just blurted it out, 'he...he... penetrated me, he fucking forced it into me. I was screaming at him to stop, but he didn't. He was too strong. I felt him cumming in me again and again. When he'd finished, I was sobbing and inconsolable, screaming at him, 'what have you done? What have we done?' He never said a word. He just got to his feet, sorted himself out and left me crying as I lay there hating myself.'

For a split second, traumatised by reliving her wretched past, she was in a trance. 'Strange... I can still remember the time on the clock. It was twenty-eight minutes past four.'

Instantly snapping out of her daze without time to breathe, Sarah continued. She could see the hurt deep within Kate's soulless eyes, and whilst she didn't want to make the situation any worse she had to carry on knowing her next words would answer Kate's questions.

'Well, I missed a few periods. I knew I was pregnant. From the dates your father was working away... the child was Tom's. Your father never knew about the events at the party, it was never discussed. There was no need. We were both at fault, Tom and I, and it is a regret we both learned to live with. Your father loved us both, and we had... between us... betrayed that love. Tom and I came to terms with that night. We adjusted and carried on as if nothing had happened. Your father was away and unaware of the pregnancy, so I went to a clinic for a termination. Yes, Kate, an abortion.'

Sarah continued. 'The doctor scraped your sibling out of me like we were both pieces of meat. So, I thought it was all over. Anyway, he missed you... I was carrying twins, and somehow...,' Sarah stuttered, 'and somehow... he fucking missed you. His botched attempt cost your father and me dearly. It put paid to any chance of us having a child of our own. Our child.'

Kate sat there, her head in her hands, her body rocking violently to and fro as she tried to erase the words from her memory. Anguish ran through, straight to her heart as her anger turned to despondency. While her natural instinct was to cause pain and suffering to her mother, that was not Kate's style. She understood no amount mental torture against another human being would change the past.

Beyond angry, Kate raged. 'You deceitful bitch. Do you hate me? You're a lying whore, and you disgust me. You're a fucking liar. Your life is a sham.'

Unable to look at her daughter, Sarah was now on her feet, her hands clenched and placed next to a large crucifix that stood prominently at the centre of the old wooden mantelpiece.

'Why are you telling me this, you bitch?' uttered the devastated Kate.

'Because it's true,' came the resigned response from Sarah. 'You are an accident, Kate. Tom is your father, and you should never have been born. At the time, I never wanted you, and I have had to live a lie for your entire life. It changed me, and ultimately, you cost me Anthony. Every time I look at your face, the memories of that dreadful night haunt all over again. YOU RUINED MY LIFE.'

Kate choked back sobs through her gritted teeth, trying to contain both her revulsion and sadness. 'What about me? Did my father know I wasn't his child? Did he know he was bringing up his brother's daughter... no, his niece?'

'He didn't, until he was diagnosed with cancer, then it all came out. Your father was infertile. He always had been, but nobody had ever known. That's what finally killed your father. I told him what I've just told you and he was livid, beyond rage. Your father had always thought Tom had left England because of their acrimonious disagreement over the inheritance. Then, after he found out about you, he thought it was about 'our night' together,' Sarah took a deep breath.

'But the real reason that Tom had stayed away was because I had threatened to kill him if he ever came near any of us again.'

Sarah paused then quickly blurted: 'I caught Tom sexually assaulting you just after your sixth birthday. That's when your dizzy spells started. Your father found out and was killed driving to see Tom. Even Natalie didn't know, she knew of the cancer but of nothing else. Anthony wasn't driving to see us as she thought, he was driving to Paris to see his brother…'

'Stop…stop…stop! What do you mean, what sexual assault?' Kate bawled at her frail, pathetic-looking mother. Sarah's spirit was shattered.

'Your father was called away unexpectedly one night. Tom was staying over… I caught Tom in your room… he was….'

Kate interrupted, she had heard enough and couldn't handle any more.

'Did Tom know? You disgusting whore,' Kate whispered, knowing full well that the answer wouldn't make the slightest difference to the hatred she was feeling inside.

'Tom never knew about any of his kids. Well, that is, except for your cousin, and he lives down south somewhere.'

'That's not what I meant, and you know it! Did Tom know I was his daughter?' The loathing in Kate's voice startled Sarah.

'No, Kate, we are the only people who know that Tom is your father,' came Sarah's last words. Dejected and forlorn she crumpled back into the family chair.

Kate had heard enough. She closed her eyes and succumbed to the safety of the darkness that had enveloped her childhood.

Chapter 28

Transfixed in a zombie-like state, Kate turned her head and vacantly gazed back out of the window, down the gravel drive, as her eyes retraced her earlier footsteps. Unable to bring herself to look at her mother, the shell-shocked daughter recalled the series of ill-fated events that had driven her to this desperate point in her life. Her rage, her passion, her angst, all ceased. Kate was in absentia.

The sun was hiding behind the clouds that filled the grey-blue sky, and even though the wind was blowing, only the tick-tock of the Grandfather's grandfather clock could be heard. Sarah was still and lacking any kind of emotion, knowing the irreparable damage she had caused. Even though the two women were only yards apart, it felt like a million miles. Kate's thoughts returned to the room and she caught her mother's eye briefly before looking down at the fraying carpet. She got to her feet and left, turning right out of the front room, along the short hallway and into the tiny kitchen.

A teaspoon and two teabags rested on a saucer beside the cooling kettle. Kate was unsure what she was doing or where she was going, but she needed space. She needed to breathe as it was as if the claustrophobic confines of the bungalow were suffocating her. She snatched at the backdoor key, but the lock stuck fast, stirring an imminent panic attack. Summoning all her strength, she twisted the steel key both ways before the obstinate bolt eventually clicked open. She rotated the handle and the door flew open, allowing a draft inside. Kate tripped into the back garden, gasping the air into her lungs, her chest expanding. Bending over with her arms braced around her knees and her unkempt hair hanging down, hiding her face, she stayed motionless, allowing the blood to rush back into her thumping head.

Her train of thought careered around her consciousness, and the sound of her heart pounded like a series of sonic booms. Little by little, the haziness from the tale of misery, deception and self-pity she had just heard slowly cleared. As she refocused her mind, she became overwhelmed. Kate slowly and methodically undressed. With her clothing folded and neatly piled on the grass at her feet, she quickly scanned the garden, searching as her eyes locked onto the garden shed.

The algae and moss tickled her soles as she walked across the dozen discoloured flagstones to the unstable wooden shed in the corner of the garden, partially concealed behind the overgrowth of trees encircling the lawned area. The stained timber had faded and bowed. Eerily, the branches grated at the tattered and torn roofing felt. Kate flipped the latch and pushed the door inwards as the squealing hinges greeted her arrival.

She looked inside as the musty air filled her nostrils. Rusty garden implements and toolboxes littered the floor as folded deckchairs leant against the side of the shed. Khaki paint flaked off a First World War helmet that hung by its chinstrap off a bent nail on the far side of the shed, and a sizeable wispy-white spider web criss-crossed the corner. A collection of wings were fixed, unable to free themselves from the silken trap. Kate empathised with the flies, but at least she was about to be delivered from her encumbrance.

The floorboards groaned under her weight as she stepped inside. Picking through the worthless junk whilst ensuring not to catch herself on any objects at her bare feet, Kate moved towards what it was she was searching for. She hurriedly lifted the lid of an old wooden trunk that her Grandfather had always kept locked shut with a solid brass padlock when she was a child to stop her inquisitive fingers. The creaking lid startled her as it slammed upright against the side of the shed. There was a sudden, loud smashing noise as the glazed window directly above the cabinet shattered in its frame from the impact of the lid opening. Only the chicken wire lining stopped her from being peppered by the flying shards.

Kate reached into the trunk, carefully moved aside a corroded saw and spotted what she was searching for. The handle felt cold in her hand as she clasped tightly and prised the tool from its resting place. The sharp end was covered with an oily hessian cloth torn from an old coal sack. Kate unfurled the sacking to reveal a sharp gleaming blade. She discarded the rag back into the trunk and slammed the lid shut. Holding the axe head in her hand, she admired the simplicity of the contours and the refinement of the cold steel as she teased the fingers of her other hand over its surface. Kate read the embellishment on the 20-ounce beauty, 'Drop-Forged & Hardened Head. Hickory Wooden Handle. Precision Ground Edge'. This was the first time she had ever held an axe, and she now understood why she had never been allowed to touch the tool as a child. Kate felt a power surge through the handle as her grip tightened, sparking something deep inside her.

The sky had lost any blueness, and the wind had picked up as she stepped out of the shed. She slowly marched through the kitchen with the axe in her right hand and hanging by her side.

Determined to complete her mission, Kate returned to the lounge and stopped just inside the doorway. Her mother was slouched in the chair, her brow furrowed as she looked nervously up at Kate. Sarah was oblivious to the axe, she could only see her naked daughter. Fully aware of Kate's unstable disposition and au fait with how earth-shattering the news would have been, Sarah spoke in an almost caring way to her only child.

'Kate, why have you taken off your clothes? Put your clothes back on, please, darling, you'll catch your death.'

'It's funny you should say that. That's exactly what I have in mind,' the cursed mother-to-be said, wiggling the steel beast that dangled by her side, stressing to Sarah that she was deadly serious.

As she waited menacingly in the doorway, the atmosphere in the room changed. With the shining blade of the hand axe catching the failing afternoon daylight, the apprehensive Sarah was overcome with an instinct of self-preservation. While her life flashed before her eyes, she assessed her options. She didn't move from the chair because she didn't want to do anything to provoke Kate. Forcing each sound through her choked vocal cords, desperately trying to stop the maddening scene from deteriorating any further, Sarah calmly and succinctly questioned her daughter's actions.

'What are you doing with the axe, Kate?'

'I am not Kate, mother! You know who I am.'

'Of course, you're Kate; I know my only child.'

'Oh, of course. I apologise. In which case I must be Kate, and you must be in denial. Either way, it's time.'

'Kate, please, put the axe down. You're scaring me. I understand how you're feeling, but this is not the answer. Let me call you a doctor, and we'll get you some help.'

Kate's unblinking stare and dark expression alarmed Sarah as she conceded that the tactful approach wasn't getting her anywhere before bawling, 'Have you gone completely mad?'

'Me... mad...' she laughed manically. 'I don't need a doctor. Nothing is wrong with me, but you must confess your sins in penitence and faith. You need to ask for forgiveness, you evil bitch, get down on your knees and pray to your God...' Kate waved the axe in Sarah's direction and shouted, '...just fucking do it!'

Astonished by the vitriol in Kate's voice, the trembling Sarah pushed herself up from the chair, taking a subservient position on her knees as instructed, her back hunching as she cowered in submission.

'Please stop, Kate, please. We can sort this out. I'm begging you, please.'

Sarah looked up at her daughter through the tears streaming from her reddening eyes. She had seen that body, that face, a thousand times before, but she didn't recognise the evil within.

Sarah pleaded again, 'Kate, I have paid my dues, the Lord has forgiven me.'

Kate gradually raised her right arm until the axe head touched the ceiling above, the blade pointing down ominously above her head. Sarah cowered like a frightened animal, her body trembling and her heart racing as she recited the Lord's Prayer under her breath.

'Please, put the axe down. We can sort this out.' Sarah looked beseechingly past Kate's nakedness, past the wickedness in her eyes, up the length of her arm and the wooden handle, to the glinting steel that shone like a star.

'Pray!' Kate screamed, demented. 'And not to the deity you deceitfully worship every day but pray to your true God, the one you disavowed years ago. The God of sex, horror and injustice,' she commanded.

Sarah bowed her head, hoping for some merciful intervention, but alas, Kate was possessed and her arm crashed downwards forced by the weight of the axe head.

'No!' was Sarah's last cry as the axe fell, fuelled by Kate's hatred and contempt.

Like a slaughterhouse worker, Kate unleashed the first blow with brutal efficiency as the blade crashed down on her mother's feeble frame, through her dress, and into her sagging flesh. As the axe hit, echoes from broken bone met the squishing noise of a severed artery as the weighty head wedged itself into Sarah's neck. Kate pulled back the axe, freeing the blade as a jet of crimson spewed from the wound. Spraying blood covered a cup of cooling tea and the silver Crucifix that stood proud on the mantelpiece above the victim. Kate lifted the weapon above her head.

Every cleave that hit down became more accurate than the last, with blow after heavy blow raining down on Sarah's mutilated frame, and each gouge more satisfying to the insatiable executioner. Kate wanted her mother to feel the pain she felt as she revelled in the retribution she was performing. Deliberately avoiding her mother's head, she dementedly hacked at the powerless limbs as chunks of bloody flesh were strewn over the soaked carpet. Sarah was barely alive as her consciousness agonised over the excruciating torture she was still unwillingly accepting. The massive trauma that had been inflicted caused erratic convulsions to shoot through her body as her amputated limbs twitched in the sticky red mess.

The exhilarated daughter let go of the smeared hatchet, throwing it to the floor, barely missing her right foot. Content that Sarah had suffered, Kate prepared to serve the pièce de résistance. She grabbed at the base of the solid silver crucifix, dislodging the cup that, like her sanity, teetered on the edge. The final insult, or act of justice, was now hers to bestow. With a lifetime of wrath unleashed and recognising this would be the last time she would speak with her mother, the nefarious twin's portentous words became Sarah's last rites.

'You know who I am. You can't deny me this moment, and just like the Good Book states, 'an eye for an eye'. It's time for your execution, Mother Sarah. It's time to put an end to your miserable existence. You are now the disposable one!'

With the words still ringing in the women's ears, and at the exact moment the cup hit the hearth, a silver Christ descended at speed as his outstretched and nailed right arm smashed into Sarah's skull. With the rigid cross embedded in her mother's head, Kate stopped.

Confident she had mastered, even perfected, the act of matricide, Kate stood over the mangled and hacked body parts of her deceased mother, marvelling at her handy work.

Sarah's mangled face looked as it had for thirty-three years: cold and lifeless. Jubilant she had succeeded, but tired from the physical exertion, Kate collapsed to her knees and looked intently into the glazed open eyes, hoping to see the essence of her mother departing for an eternity of brimstone and fire in hell. With a closing act of vengeful defilement, Kate gripped either side of her mother's drooping head and raised it to her face. She forced her thumbs into the eye sockets, kinked them and plucked out the windows to her soul.

As her body fell, a misty red cloud blew from her lungs, covering Kate's face. She was impassive as she got to her feet and stood over the mess in a half-conscious state, admiring her work.

It was sometime later when she turned to the door and left the room, taking with her the blood and brains of her mother that cloaked her torso.

Chapter 29

An acknowledged and highly-regarded expert in his field, the handsome grey-haired Clinical Professor of Psychotherapy was also an expert Criminal Psychologist. Harry Ford sat in his leather chair, leaning over his desk. Gently gripping the pencil in his right hand, he lightly stabbed at the coloured dossier beneath with the sharpened point. Pulling at his closely shaved chin with long, bony fingers, the desktop that supported his left elbow was strewn with papers containing a collection of pictures with the faces of shattered lives. With the pencil leaving an irregular pattern of graphite dots on the front of Kate's case file, he stared into oblivion. He had scrutinised and observed his patient for eight weeks, yet he still couldn't put his finger on the missing piece.

His unironed white shirt set off a gravy-stained burgundy tie and the shabby tweed jacket swamping his frame. Threads of frayed wool peeping through the worn leather patches on either elbow testified to the time he spent crouched over his desk. His clean, sweptback hair was loosely tied in a ponytail that covered the grubby collar of his jacket. He was a riddle himself. His body and mind were clean and ultra-smart, but his desk, like his clothing, was a confusing, untidy mess.

The caring and compassionate bachelor, fast approaching 60, had only one love in life, and that was to help his patients. His retirement date had already been agreed upon. However, a change of heart, brought on by a recent bizarre case that had landed on his desk, caused him to rethink and postpone the inevitable. In more than thirty years of studying the complexity of the human mind, he had never examined a case so baffling. Yes, he had seen so many troubled souls, from the vilest rapists to the most heinous serial killers. But, Kate Summertown was a riddle, and it was based on his initial diagnosis and recommendation to the courts that the judge sectioned her under the Mental Health Act.

She wore a white forensic suit when he first met her in the secure suite at Wiltshire Constabulary's Swindon HQ. She had been found late the previous evening and, after being checked by the Force Medical Examiner, was supervised until his arrival. Her unreadable expression reminded him of The Mona Lisa the instant he set eyes on the murderer. Devoid of the slightest bit of emotion, except for an enigmatic smile, she was lost in an otherworldly state. Every inch of her visible body – upper chest, neck, face and hands – was caked in dried blood, and her hair was thick and matted with it. Sat upright in a reserved posture, her cuffed hands overlapped as they rested on the arm of the chair. Her eyes were fixed on the two-way mirror as she was staring at any onlookers with an alluring gaze. For some reason, he felt beguiled by this perplexing woman.

From the moment of her arrest, and while he undertook a clinical assessment of the expectant Kate that was held in C-Wing, her mind seemed locked in an inaccessible chasm, impenetrable by sight or sound. During her daily medical examinations, there was no visible reaction to even the brightest light that shone into her soulless eyes. Professor Ford, the most senior of three forensic psychiatrists who reported to the courts, suggested that an "indescribable surge of emotional energy had exploded in her head" and was the reason for the profound, murderous assault. The human equivalent of an electromagnetic pulse causing her brain to short circuit.

His patient, with the captivating yet unmoving smile, just stared at the walls of her cell. She willingly ate, but the only word that passed her lips was the incessant droning of 'yinnnnglinnnng'. Although she showed no signs of the powerful rage that had caused her to murder her mother or the slightest threat to herself, her unborn baby or the staff of the secure unit, Professor Ford had decided that Kate should be confined and restrained for safety as a precaution. Due to the effects of the approved drugs commonly used on patients with her still undiagnosed but presumed mental condition, and taking into account her physical condition, the pregnancy, she was prescribed an experimental line of homoeopathic sedatives.

A customary part of Professor Ford's job was to profile his accused patient, and from the outset, Kate's case didn't make any sense, especially the indescribable viciousness of the seemingly unprovoked assault by the seemingly contented daughter; he was at a complete loss as to why her life had imploded like it had and over such a short period of time. The Professor's clinical diagnosis and assessment would be split into interconnected elements as he tried to pick apart then reconstruct her life.

Commencing his investigation into her background and the events leading up to the murder, he accepted that this would be slightly more difficult than usual due to his patient's lack of direct input. Most of the puzzle pieces were there, they just had to be dissected and examined. Professor Ford approached each subject he was studying with an open mind as he began formulating his diagnosis by investigating recognisable parallels, which were most common in patients with Kate's suspected condition. As was customary, his first port of call was always the crime scene.

Having been given open access to the Wiltshire Constabulary's crime reports, the Professor read through all the statements, reviewed the video footage, studied stills and visited the crime scene. He listened to the testimony of the two officers dispatched to the dwelling of Mrs Sarah Denise Summertown after an anonymous caller using a burner phone had contacted the emergency services. Due to the lack of information provided to the operator and a delay in officers being sent to the scene, it was more than an hour before the first responders eventually arrived at the bungalow.

At 7.45pm on Sunday, 17th August, 2008, two policemen – a sergeant and a constable – arrived at the suspected crime scene. The late summer sky was turning to dusk, so aided by torchlight, they peered through the window into the darkness of the front room to assess the situation. The senior officer decided to force entry, suspecting the soaked remnants at the room's far end to be that of a large animal and the trail of footprints to be those of the assailant.

The house was silent, with no visible signs of a break-in, except for the one committed by the officers. Hitting the light switch as they tentatively entered the front room, the gruesome crime scene that greeted them was incomparable to anything the officers could have imagined in their worst nightmare.

Just one look, long enough for his mind to mentally reassemble the mess and register the horror, caused the constable, new to the job, to turn and run back outside. No amount of police training could have prepared him for the sickening sight as he manically emptied the contents of his evening meal all over the welcome mat. The bloodbath could be compared with that of an abattoir. The body of the innocent lawyer, who was a highly respected and reverent member of the community, had been dissected and hacked apart piece-by-piece using a hand axe, which had been discarded on the living room floor next to the body. A ruby-stained, silver crucifix was left embedded in the skull of the victim, and the broken half of a cracked china teacup was implanted in her right temple as a result of her head falling onto the already broken cup. The blood-sodden carpet had assisted the sergeant's discovery of the suspect as he followed the red footprints of bare feet to the third bedroom.

Naked, covered in blood and in a deep sleep on a double bed was Mrs Summertown's only child, Kate. Clenched in each hand was some kind of jelly-like pulpy mush, which later transpired was the crushed eyeballs of the deceased. Taking a few moments to assess the situation and joined by his colleague, the sergeant composed himself before deciding to handcuff the suspect, causing her to wake. Unmoving and just seeing straight through the officers, they threw a cover over her body, leaving her lying on the bed. As they waited for backup and a forensic team, they watched on in total bewilderment, struggling to comprehend the events of the late-summer Sunday afternoon. Kate's clothes had been found neatly folded and piled up on the back lawn. The only utterance from the pregnant suspect was a droning of the word 'yinggggglingggg'.

As would be expected, the national press had a field day sensationalising the gory details of the murder of an old widow alone in her home. The police issued a statement within 36 hours of the attack stating that a suspect was in custody and no other person was being sought in connection with the crime.

Professor Ford also interviewed witnesses from the Christ Church congregation. Rachel recollected the brief encounter she'd had with Kate as she entered the church looking 'somewhat lost, pensive and definitely not her usual self'. Rachel stated that she had concerns for Kate but admitted she had been unable to catch up with her friend due to being needed for 'tea and biscuits' immediately after the service. The Reverend, who'd briefly spoken to Kate, agreed that although she was 'visibly not at her best' and 'evidently upset', 'she certainly wasn't angry or homicidal'.

The second part was Kate's medical history. Her only immediate living relative, Thomas Summertown, had come forward as soon as he had heard about the tragic events. Though he'd had limited contact with his niece, he was an upstanding member of society, and the court appointed him 'next of kin'.

Following a series of conversations with Tom and after checking her medical history, Professor Ford understood that his patient had, in the past, suffered a series of brain seizures resulting in 'temporary blackouts' and behavioural problems, which had often culminated in 'bouts of violence with her own reflection' as a child. These episodes stopped at the time of her first menstrual cycle. There was no family history of mental illness on her father's side, which was confirmed by Tom, and no recorded problems on her mother's.

While her distressed Uncle was happy to assist the police in any way possible, the Professor had decided to keep Tom away from Kate. Other than this 'blip', her medical history was exemplary. Except for a few minor infections over the years, she had always been fit and healthy. Since she had never had any other stress-related psychological issues, he was unable to correlate her recent violent behaviour with that of her childhood. However, Professor Ford refused to dismiss the episodes out of hand due to the growing awareness of antenatal depression that he understood could affect up to 20% of women. The symptoms Kate had shown were, at the very least, similar, but his patient's actions were more extreme than any other reported case. He acknowledged that some women were susceptible to the excessive levels of hormonal changes and that it could be brought on by genetic or environmental factors, even by an adverse childhood upbringing or trauma. But as none of the criteria had been mentioned, logged or recorded, his professional opinion was that he would have to assess this after the birth of the child. Chemical analysis of her brain and possible 'mirror treatment' would have to wait until after she had given birth, as he did not want to unsettle Kate and risk another episode or jeopardise the unborn child's life.

The third part of his investigation was concentrated on Kate's lifestyle in the months leading up to the murder. The senior management of APGH described how the career-driven Kate had suddenly upped and left, taking six months off, which had come as a massive shock to all of her associates. The opinion among her peers was that, after winning a multi-million dollar account with a reputable pharmaceutical company, she had developed a 'god complex' with delusions of grandeur until she'd ultimately 'lost the plot'. The only person who felt for her predicament was Isabella, her sympathetic assistant, who'd pointed out that, as far as she was concerned, Kate was perfectly stable and no different than usual. She forcefully informed the psychologist that in the weeks after Kate had left APGH, she had stayed in telephone contact with her. But much to her regret, their lives had drifted apart, and the conversations had ceased after about three months as Kate had become increasingly more challenging to get hold of. Professor Ford had formulated a mental image of a dedicated executive with everything to live for. Yet, just twenty-four weeks later, he was overseeing the treatment of a psychotic murderer.

The fourth part of his investigation entailed a visit to the Mews. Here he ascertained through discussions with her still-flabbergasted neighbours that Kate had become a recluse in the months preceding the visit to Swindon. Her house was in a shambles and showed weeks of neglect, which contradicted everything he had been told about her high standards of cleanliness, her love of her own reflection and her personal hygiene. He studied her phone bills, building up a database of contacts, most of which delivered barely edible fast food, which went against the healthy-eating lifestyle she upheld. The dozens of empty wine bottles that filled her bottle bin were a giveaway of her excessive drinking, and he assumed that this was an attempt to self-medicate.

His fifth and final part of gathering information involved observing Kate's physical state since arriving at the institution. Her symptoms were classic. She showed a complete lack of emotional interaction, and had neglected any form of self-care, except for that of her unborn child. Her vacant, expressionless face and her deadpan eyes matched her flat voice. After he heard Kate constantly repeating 'ying-ling' he attempted to find out its meaning. Having made no progress on the two different parts of the word, he searched in various dictionaries and web engines, trying to fathom its meaning and a link to Kate. The definitions ranged from aircraft companies to 'America's oldest brewery', none of which made the slightest sense. He felt defeated after exhausting his searches for the meaningless word and his patient's condition. By a quirk of fate and with more luck than judgement, he stumbled across a website that stopped him in his tracks. The intrigued Professor found himself reviewing an article about the souls of aborted foeti. The particular article and subsequent sites he discovered related to the guilt and anxiety that women suffer after a termination. While he had no proof, or even any suggestion, that Kate had previously undergone an abortion, it could well be a contributing factor in her diagnosis, especially if it was linked to her antenatal depression. If her delusion was a manifestation of the belief she had been possessed by the evil spirit of a dead foetus, then that would confirm her condition irrefutably.

One mysterious factor was the identity of her unborn child's father. There was no mention of the pregnancy on her medical records. In fact, her GP was shocked to discover that she was pregnant. He had prescribed the pill to Kate for most of her adult life and, as far as he was concerned she had always made sure that she took precautions to prevent catching any infections, and to be extra careful to ensure no unwanted pregnancy would befall her. In all of the Professor's conversations, never once was a male partner mentioned, not even by Isabella, and if anybody at work were to know, then it most certainly would have been her. With no plausible explanation for the father's identity, the missing piece of the puzzle would have to remain unresolved.

Unable to interview the two people who would have been best placed to help him – her mother and her old employer, Sir David Appleway – he had gleaned various unconnected clues from his conversations with the Met police. Unbeknown to Kate, Sir David and his friend, the Chinese Ambassador, were both stabbed to death following an unprovoked assault in London's Chinatown during the early hours of the same morning Kate murdered her mother. He had deduced that Kate would have been unaware of this as her mobile records indicated she had had no calls, and the names of the two deceased men hadn't been officially released until a press conference on the Monday morning.

It also transpired that two officers, who had attended the Mews to find information to contact family members, had walked in on a burglary in progress at Kate's house in the early hours of the Monday morning. Except for a missing laptop, nothing else seemed to be out of the ordinary. No arrest was made as the offender escaped after hitting both officers at the back of the head and leaving them in an unconscious state.

Detectives who attended the scene of the double crime also ascertained by her passport – which was found on a kitchen worktop – and the luggage labels on the handles of her charcoal grey suitcase just inside her front door, that she had returned from China the day before she had murdered her mother.

The Met were vaguely interested in the Chinese connection, but due to the lack of information, Kate's unresponsive state, and a pressure placed on the Met's Commissioner, they felt unable to waste any more man-hours until new evidence came to light. The murder of the Ambassador had caused some political ructions for both the Home Office as well as the Foreign Office and within a fortnight of his death, the PRC's 'spooks' had carried out their own inquiry into the death of the Ambassador and confirmed that they were not responsible for Kate's situation or that of the Ambassador's unfortunate demise. After following the trail, the Professor found the Met's halt on the investigation bizarre, believing it to be just another political whitewash.

The Professor had almost built a complete picture of Kate's background and her downward spiral to her breakdown, as best he could, and he was amazed that nobody had seen the signs.

After two months of painstaking research and combining all he knew about his patient, if she was initially pigeonholed as a high flyer with the world at her feet, then the only considered diagnosis he could now find for Kate was 'paranoid schizophrenic'.

It was obvious that her future was not going to be resolved until they could at least make some headway into her psychosis, and that would be well after the scheduled childbirth provisionally booked for Monday, 19th January, 2009, roughly a week before her estimated due date. After being agreed upon by all relevant parties, it was decided that the best course of action for the expectant mother would be confining Kate to her bed as they continued treatment that had stabilised her.

Chapter 30

Kate was looking and feeling beautiful. Her hair was shining from the natural light that was illuminating her surroundings as the blistering summer sun, once more, infused her body. The sky looked airbrushed with wispy tendrils of white cloud grasping at the vibrant blue. The sadness that had been suffocating her for the last eight months, had vanished.

Her incarceration had taken its toll, but she was beginning to feel like her old self. Kate smiled at her perfect reflection. The surreal backdrop to the mahogany framed, full-length mirror was the green field she was daydreaming about. She recognised the grassy plain. On her left stood the tree that had once taken centre-stage in her parent's tent at the festival. The tree bark looked as grey as the memory of her father's ashes that her mother had scattered from the urn at the base of a trunk many years ago. The lush grass gently and tenderly caressed her feet and ankles. It felt as if Christ was washing her feet, cleansing her soul.

Putting the nightmares behind her and content that the misery and disorder were over, Kate looked down at the bundle of joy that rested in a crib beside her. Elegantly dressed in a handmade, gold frilly dress made of the softest silk, the smiling newborn baby had the face of an angel, with bright blue eyes and auburn hair. The chubby legs that kicked from beneath the silken gown while the unrestrained tiny pink arms grabbed at the air. Finally, after all the horror and hurt, Kate could look forward to a future with her daughter. She had never felt so fulfilled.

A judder went up Kate's spine as if someone had walked over her grave. She became aware of ominous black clouds rolling towards her from a distance, erasing the blueness. The atmosphere began to choke as a sinister darkness formed, infiltrating the mirror's image. Kate looked around in a panic, unsure of what was happening. She anxiously watched in the mirror, loathed to look directly at the foreboding sky behind her as a conceited grin appeared across her reflection.

'Hello Kate,' came the words as her reflection spoke. 'I must congratulate you. For you have helped me escape my internment.'

Kate was perplexed. This was her reality, so why was she still here?

'You are not real, you have gone. You left me by the lake,' Kate spoke firmly..

'Don't be so candid, you just don't get it, do you?' Sniped her sibling with the utmost contempt.

Kate was filled with angst as, once again, she found her reality becoming entwined with her dreams through the manifestation of her twin sister. The hands of the reflection reached forward and grabbed the mahogany surround as its fingers appeared outside the mirror. A startled Kate jumped back. The reflection continued unabated as she slowly but forcefully pulled her body towards the mirror. Her head followed her fingers through the glass, quickly joined by the rest of her torso. As the reflection stepped out of the dark wood surround, the twin left behind a lifetime trapped within her sister's body and out into the real world.

Standing directly before Kate, she leaned down, hovering over the crib. She was fixed eye-to-eye with the young baby, her head slightly rocking. Before the reality of what was happening had fully registered with the bewildered mother, the apparition's flawless face was nose-to-nose with her own as she continued her verbal onslaught against the disbelieving Kate.

'I find it incredulous that you trusted that crazy soothsayer and his prophetic verses,' said Kate's twin. 'You thought, and now, of all times, I would leave you when all I've ever wanted is a body I can call my own. After all we've been through together. Finally, after a lifetime of shadowing you, I can live my own life.'

The beguiling twin stopped and stared at her forlorn sister. Observing itself in Kate's mirror for the first time, she took immense pleasure in her newfound freedom as she felt the bliss of her escape.

'For someone so intelligent, you really are a wretched excuse. The doctor should have scrapped you off the inside of our mother, and, just maybe, she would still be alive!'

Kate was clasping her head, her fingertips embedded into her long silky hair, her eyes shut tight, trying their hardest to block out the vision. Tiny rivulets of blood trickled down her forehead as her manicured nails punctured the skin covering her skull. Kate fronted up to the vision as its breath burnt her face.

'Please take whatever you want, leave me alone… leave us alone!' Kate pleaded, dismissing the spectre. 'This is a dream!'

'No, Kate, this is not a dream but your new reality. You are going to spend eternity ensnared in your soulless body, trapped in the confines of a cell, as I have been cloaked in the cell of your ageing body,' it paused and inhaled, filling its lungs with air. 'I am now free. Free of you and living my life in the body I have always coveted, the body of your baby. She was my catalyst, and this is your eternity.'

'No… NO!' Kate's heart was pounding louder than ever, and the beating resonated through the soul of the spectre.

'You hear that, the sound of the drum is calling, Kate. It will soon be my time.'

As Kate realised, the vision cackled as it delighted in the torment of her naïve sister. 'You never knew, did you?'

'Knew what?' Kate refocused, inwardly praying that she would soon wake from this terrifyingly real scenario where she found herself centre-stage.

'Ahhh!' came the sigh, 'You never knew. That pitiful fool, Mei, never told you!' sniggered the perverse sister.

'Told me what?' demanded Kate.

'He was frantic as the flame on his precious lamp blew out. The crazy old man had no stomach for the fight. He failed you, dear sister, his efforts were futile, and he knew I was free. He watched on powerless as I unshackled myself from your binds. His foolish incantations were useless against a will as determined as mine. He could not beat me, Kate.'

Blood and tears mingled on Kate's cheeks as she stood there, helpless against the revelation.

'This is not real, this is not real, this is not real,' Kate repeated, trying to exorcise the macabre visions forever.

'Yes, sister, a yingling did leave you, but the soul that departed was not mine, it was the soul of your unborn daughter. I dragged her out and tossed her aside, a stillborn soul that would never know any different.'

'JUST FUCK OFF... GET OUT OF MY HEAD!' Kate screamed in her dream, hoping the sadness in her heart would wake her unconscious state.

'I've wanted to unleash my vengeance on the mirror image of your face for more than twenty years, ever since your adolescent body learnt how to repress me. You forced me to the darkest recess of your mind, and you, dear sister, you've taken great pleasure in teasing me with the occasional taste of freedom whenever you wanted to get dirty, whenever you felt the urge for immoral gratification.'

The twin spat out her evil words: 'Like a drug, you allowed me to come to the fore. The emotional energy of your sex drive allowed me a fleeting escape, and you took great satisfaction from my yearnings. Deep down, you've always known that your sexual impulse was the only way you let me control your weak mind, that's until you willingly acquiesced, allowing me to exact my retribution on the bitch that had caused your pain and had me slain. Yes, Kate, you opened up to me, you allowed me to kill our mother. You wanted her dead!'

The twin was relishing the irony of the situation as she continued her verbal onslaught.

'Now, Kate, it's my turn to live, you have had your shot at life. I am leaving you. You will be quiet inside. We will be free of each other for the first time since our mother's visit to the doctor. You can look in a mirror now and see nothing but yourself. The only way I will haunt you now is in the memories that are forever etched in your consciousness and the knowledge that you are confined for the cruel murder of your vulnerable mother... How poetic!'

The twin's focus changed as she looked intently toward the baby. Kate tried to move to protect her precious bundle against the unpredictable actions of her evil sibling, but the twin simply glared at Kate, causing her to stop dead in her tracks.

'Today is our birthday, dear sister, and this is my special gift to you. It's time for me to break these bonds that have entwined us for more than thirty-five years. I have finished with your once-perfect body, you can have it back, as I now have my own. I'll always think of it as your birthday gift to me. Kate, your beloved child is mine, and I am now her.'

Saying that the twin picked up the child by both its hands, dangling the innocent creature above its crib at arm's length.

'Let me show you how I ripped the soul out of your bastard and tossed it aside!'

The apparition violently twisted and rotated her hands, causing the tiny limbs to dislocate and the baby to squeal in agony as the startled mother desperately tried to cling on to her own reality by her fingertips. In a single action, the twin violently spun around on her spot, swinging the mangled infant in the direction of the mirror. Releasing her grip on its swelling arms, the twin launched the howling baby full force into the mirror. On impact, the glass smashed to smithereens, spraying shards all over the identical twins, heavily lacerating Kate's lower abdomen. Kate was transfixed and could only look on in horror as tears and rage filled her terror-struck eyes as she witnessed the callous act of retribution. The moment the abused newborn passed through the mirror's wooden frame, Kate's reality slipped into a permanent state of nothingness.

Kate woke, groggy and confused, lying on a table. She was supine, legs flat, with green paper over her upper torso. An array of bright lights shone down on her face from the sterility of what she gathered to be an operating theatre. The masked faces of staff, wearing green surgical covers and latex gloves, surrounded her. The clattering of surgical instruments fused with the sounds of the theatre nurses giving instructions filled the air. Kate raised her head as she came to her senses only to witness the surgeon and midwife pulling the newborn through an opening in her abdomen. The surgeon held up the baby as if he was presenting it to the world, Kate could see her daughter's flesh, covered in the slippery stains of birth. The child kicked and screamed as the twisted umbilical cord was clamped and severed. Kate was not ignorant, she knew her sister was free as soon as the cord was cut. Kate let rip a hysterical shriek of anguish. With her heart broken, her world shattered, the only thing left was her gashed and bloodied torso. An unimaginable blackness overwhelmed her as a feeling of complete emptiness entered her open womb and pervaded every corner of her soulless frame. She was utterly vacant except for the recollections of revulsion that remained entrenched in her mind

The child was born on the 17th of January, 2009 at 04:28.

Chapter 31

It was a fait accompli, the deal had been done. Kate could look after her daughter with a proviso: only under constant supervision until the newborn was three months old.

For her own inner peace, these details were kept confidential from Kate.

Overseen by two concerned yet excited nurses, Kate was wheeled back to her white cell to be monitored until she came around from the surgery. Inadvertently, and to the horror of the anaesthetist, she had briefly regained consciousness during the C-section but had passed out again just after the birth. The waves racing around her sedated mind forced Kate's constrained body to start jerking as she lay in silence, searing the ceiling with her stare for a few seconds before the memory of her vision erupted into an inferno of revulsion and rage. Throwing every ounce of strength into her shackled limbs, the hate-filled Kate tried to free herself from the padded leather cuffs that calloused the skin on her wrists and ankles.

'Where's my fucking baby?' she screeched through her tight vocal cords as her rant developed into a full-blooded, angst-ridden scream. 'Where is she? I'll rip the fucking bitch's face off... WHERE'S THE FUCKING BABY!'

She terrified the two startled nurses, who were engrossed in a quiet conversation, as the venomous diatribe and the mental wrath of the possessed patient caused the bed to shake like thunder. In an absolute frenzy, she cut short her furious outburst and, like a caged beast, focused on trying to chew at her arm. The veins in her head and neck were bulging from the increased blood pressure as her face contorted with evil. Thrashing around in a white surgical gown, the straps holding her down creaked under the strain.

'You cunts. Where's that fucking bitch! I'll kill her.' She showed no signs of discomfort or even the slightest recognition of physical pain as the newly stitched seam in her lower abdomen split. Bright red scarlet oozed from the incision, seeping into the white cotton that shrouded her body as the stain intensified with her anger. For months, the docile mother-to-be had shown no hint of aggression, yet within hours of childbirth, she had become frenzied and wild.

Whatever had caused her rage on the late August afternoon, the scorned murderer was now back. One of the two nurses jumped up and struck the panic alarm inside the door, sparking a whirring siren to drown out Kate's tirade. Two brawny ward-minders entered the room, armed with a stun gun and hypodermic needle, and immediately carried out their procedure in such circumstances. With a syringe full of tranquilliser, the crazed Kate instantaneously passed out.

Professor Ford was confused. Why, after showing nothing but calm and care for the unborn while pregnant, would she so violently flip immediately after its birth? His mind was as befuddled as Kate's. There was no rationalisation, no explanation. The treatment plan was thrown in the bin, as was the decision to allow Kate to look after the child. Plan B would now be enforced three months earlier than he had initially envisaged.

'Good afternoon. Is Mr Thomas Summertown available, please?'

'May I ask who's calling?' replied a well-spoken younger man.

'I'm sorry, it's a delicate matter. May I speak to Mr Summertown, please?'

'Yes, of course. Just wait a sec, I'll put him on.'

The muffled sounds of a third-party instruction echoed through the hallway. 'Dad, it's for you. I think it's the Professor.'

'I'll take it in the lounge.' The handset was put down. Though he was making the best of a lazy weekend afternoon, Tom had been apprehensive and anxious for the last week and wasn't sure what news to expect.

'Good afternoon, Tom speaking.'

'Good afternoon, Tom, it's Harry Ford. I'm sorry to disturb you on a Saturday. I know you've been expecting a call, but probably not this one,' a temporary silence led Tom to believe the worst.

'I'll keep it brief, but I thought it best to update you on the situation. Late last night, a decision was made to bring forward the scheduled procedure due to the baby's stress levels increasing, so an emergency caesarean was carried out and was successfully completed earlier this morning. Kate gave birth to a healthy seven-pound, four-ounce baby daughter.'

A relieved sigh met Professor Ford's news 'Oh, that is good news, and Kate, is she okay?'

'Well, she was, but after coming around from the operation, she had an episode. At this moment in time, we are unsure if it was the anaesthetic itself or some other contributing factor which caused the relapse. She has been sedated, and we did have to re-stitch her incision.'

'For crying out loud!' exclaimed the concerned Uncle as he collected his thoughts.

'That poor girl. What has she done to deserve this?' Tom suddenly realised. 'It's her thirty-fifth Birthday today. What a heartbreaking situation... and the child, such a precious gift!'

'I know. Tom, we've taken the decision to keep Kate sedated, at least for the time being, until we can start reducing her medication and then look to address the underlying cause of her psychosis.'

'Well, that's not so good.' The guilt from a sordid hidden secret flashed through his mind.

'I just wanted to confirm our previous discussions. Are you still happy with the arrangements? I'm guessing that was your son, Michael, who answered?' posed the quiet-speaking professor.

'It was indeed, and yes, we are all committed to doing whatever we can to help Kate and her newborn daughter.' Tom emphasised. 'When would you like to see us?'

'Let's say, Friday, the 23rd at 10 o'clock. That will give us time to sort out the relevant paperwork. I'll keep you posted if the situation changes in any way.'

'Well, thank you for bringing us up-to-date, Professor. We look forward to seeing you again then.'

Tom placed the receiver down and looked across the room as sexual thoughts of the night he was caught out, flooded back, racking his conscience with shame.

Tom had moved back to the south of England from Paris just after his twin brother's death. He had sold the thriving antiques business he had purchased with his inheritance from his father's death. The shock of watching Sarah pour Anthony's ashen body from the urn in the field at Woburn had shaken him to the bones.

He had stopped smoking, a vice that had always been with him since his teens, curbed his excessive drinking, choosing to have a glass of red over a half-bottle of malt, and changed his diet. For the last ten years, Tom's healthy lifestyle has seen his youthful glow reappear, and he felt better, and certainly fitter, than he had for more years than he cared to remember.

His farm was set in acres of English countryside on the West Sussex coast. The long sweeping drive, past the weathered planters and the pond, stopped at the six-bedroomed, red brick house annexed into two adjoining abodes linked by two internal doors. The paddocks housed two thoroughbred racehorses, which was another of his vices.

The grounds were well-kept, and the house was too big for a man his age. He made the decision to buy the farm after he had reunited with his long-lost son, the result of his first loving relationship in the early 80s. His son and daughter-in-law, the picture-perfect couple in their late twenties, had shared their lives with Tom for seven years.

Chapter 32

The metallic blue Lexus slowly pulled over and parked in the Borough of Kensington and Chelsea, London. It was late January, and the bitterness of the Northerly wind brought a freezing sting to the air.

The three occupants left the car, swiftly strolling across the street and briefly taking in the pretty old Victorian cul-de-sac. With his body shivering and pinching the teeth of a key into the pad of his right thumb, Tom stared up at the house, remembering how it used to look the last time he had been there in the early 80s.

Having been named 'next of kin', Tom had taken temporary control of his niece's estate and arranged for a local property company to clean and manage the Mews until a decision was made about its future. Due to his opinion that Kate's home remain untouched, neither his son nor daughter-in-law had visited the house. This seemed somewhat bizarre and contradictory to them both, as Tom had had no problems with the three of them visiting Swindon to pack and store Sarah's belongings after the Police had released the 'Slaughterhouse', which had become the local term of endearment for the bungalow.

They crossed the cobbled courtyard in Courtfield Mews, and he pushed the gleaming new key into the lock and turned it.

The opening door bulldozed a large pile of bills and junk mail, trapping it against the hallway wall. Ignoring the post, Tom darted into the lounge. The young married couple stood nervously in the doorway, reluctant to enter uninvited. They waited momentarily then they walked over the threshold, closing the door behind them. Wrapped up in coat and scarf, the blonde crouched down and started gathering up the post addressed to Kate, wondering to herself what use car insurance might be to an axe-wielding maniac.

The musty house seemed eerily quiet. The handsome son instinctively placed his gloved hand on the radiator as mild warmth filtered through the leather. 'I'm guessing the heating is on just to stop the pipes from freezing,' he mumbled to himself as the anticipation of the forthcoming day dawned on him. He was still unsure what his father was looking for, but he had never seen him so animated, racing around, looking as if he was trying to beat the clock.

'What are you looking for, Dad?' asked the inquisitive son.

Tom was anxious to get going, he felt the house walls closing in on him as if the bricks and mortar were aware of his presence. Taking no time to stop and chat, he headed straight to the front room. While searching, he continued the conversation, rummaging through the wall unit and sideboard cupboards.

'It's a china doll. I hope that Kate still has it. I don't believe she would have thrown it away.'

'What do you want with a china doll?' Micheal nervously quipped as his wife stepped forward into the sterility of the front room and began browsing around.

Tom scuttled past his son and was bounding up the stairs when he stopped. After momentarily composing himself, he looked down on the confused face that had followed him into the hallway.

'I bought it for Kate donkey's years ago. I found it in the antique shop in Paris before I bought it too. I love the doll. She's perfect, and we'll name the baby after her.'

The bewildered son chuckled. 'Name the baby after a doll! Seriously?'

Tom was irked by the throwaway remark from his belligerent son. 'It will all make sense to you both soon enough.' He huffed, clambering the remaining stairs and disappearing out of sight.

Joining his wife by a bookshelf, they both looked attentively at a portrait of his cousin. She was a stunner, and the woman's female intuition told her that the enigmatic Kate never took no for an answer. Even in the photo, she exuded confidence, and the alluring eyes that stared out from the image mesmerised her.

'Do you know that face?' the perplexed woman asked. 'I'm sure I know her from somewhere!'

Having seen fuzzy mugshots of Kate on TV immediately after her arrest, this was the first time they had seen a sharp picture of the brunette. Transfixed on her lower jaw and captivating smile, they pondered the possibility they may have seen her somewhere before until the pair's concentration was interrupted by an unrestrained excitement.

'Found it!' A shout emanated from the staircase. Almost falling over himself as he stumbled the last couple of steps, he rushed across the room and joined them by the bookshelf. Tom was holding Kate's elegantly dressed, porcelain doll in his hand as he lovingly ran the pad of his thumb across the name embroidered in a fine braid on the hem.

'It was in her bedroom. I knew she would treasure it. It's as perfect as the day I first laid eyes on her!'

'You want us to call our child Sarah?' pressed Sophia.

Tom looked down at the doll without answering. The sentiment jarred his vocals as he set out his reasoning, ensuring no misunderstanding about what would happen.

'Sarah was a good woman... the best. I brought this doll for Kate so she would always feel close to her mother. I had the name embroidered on the dress. We will call my great niece, Sarah. There is no discussion to be had.'

The two had been firmly put in their place as they nodded their acceptance. A tear fell from Tom's weary eye onto the frilly golden silk dress. Taking immense comfort from the china in his hand, he continued, not wanting to be curtailed or lose the thread of his argument.

'Look, you two... fate has been kind to us all. We have a newborn that needs loving and nurturing. It's something that I missed out on. I know it's something you two have always dreamed of,' he inhaled, holding back his true feelings of contempt for himself. 'We are in no position to put Kate back together, if only we could. But that's for the Professor and his team to take charge of, and we'll support them where we can, but we can ensure baby Sarah has a bright and carefree life.'

Looking into the faces of his son and beautiful but infertile daughter-in-law as they glanced down at the doll, he finished his emotional monologue.

'You'll be a perfect mother to Sarah, and you, my son, will be a wonderful father. We have been gifted a child. Professor Ford and the adoption team are expecting us, so let's collect her and take her home.'

Keeping the framed print as a keepsake for the newborn, Tom, Michael and Sophia left the house, slamming the door shut on Kate's life.

Epilogue

'Hey, George, I don't suppose you can spare me a minute to check out this DNA result for the Summertown child?' Elizabeth, his qualified but relatively inexperienced lab technician, asked looking puzzled.

'Of course. What seems to be the problem?'

'I don't really know, but this result looks very much like one of the 'extreme' examples we theorised about in uni, you know, incest and inbreeding.'

'Let me look', he confidently brushed past his assistant looking at the results. 'Shit, can that be right? The genetic markers indicate a high degree of consanguinity between the child and the assumed parents.'

'Consanguinity? You mean they might be closely related?' The shocked technician was surprised that she had been correct about her appraisal of the data.

'Exactly. The allele matches are more consistent with siblings than typical parent-child relationships. Are these correct?'

'Yes, I've double-checked the samples, and they're consistent.'

'This reading is rare in the UK. Could it be an error in the testing process?' George questioned.

'Unlikely. I ran the test twice on different machines, and the results are identical.'

George was stumped. 'Wow. I'm shocked. I really don't know what to say,' he said, drumming on the table with his fingers.

'We might be looking at parents who are, well... if I'm allowed to speculate, closely related, siblings. It's a sensitive matter, and we'll need to get all our ducks in a row before putting any accusations out there. Schedule a meeting with the Boss. Let's discuss the best course of action before we open a can of worms and ruin any lives...'

deaddavesfuneral.com